SPECIAL MESSA[GE]

THE ULVERSCR[OFT FOUNDATION]
(registered UK cha[rity)

was established in 1972 to provide funds for research, diagnosis and treatment of eye diseases.
Examples of major projects funded by
the Ulverscroft Foundation are:-

- The Children's Eye Unit at Moorfields Eye Hospital, London
- The Ulverscroft Children's Eye Unit at Great Ormond Street Hospital for Sick Children
- Funding research into eye diseases and treatment at the Department of Ophthalmology, University of Leicester
- The Ulverscroft Vision Research Group, Institute of Child Health
- Twin operating theatres at the Western Ophthalmic Hospital, London
- The Chair of Ophthalmology at the Royal Australian College of Ophthalmologists

You can help further the work of the Foundation by making a donation or leaving a legacy.
Every contribution is gratefully received. If you would like to help support the Foundation or require further information, please contact:

THE ULVERSCROFT FOUNDATION
The Green, Bradgate Road, Anstey
Leicester LE7 7FU, England
Tel: (0116) 236 4325

website: www.foundation.ulverscroft.com

John Simes is an experienced teacher of English in state secondary schools, and has served as Principal in two of the UK's largest comprehensives. The founder of Collingwood Learning, which advises on school improvement, he also established Collingwood Publishing and Media Ltd. He now writes fiction and supports programmes in the UK and Africa to set up new schools. John lives with his family in south Devon where he grapples with his addictions to cricket, poetry and the stunning local landscape.

THE DREAM FACTORY: GHOSTS

'As a child I learned to dream . . . It scared me. It terrified me. Still does.' For sixteen-year-old Peter, a.k.a. Pi, his life explodes when his parents — scientists who created a revolutionary new type of artificial intelligence — are brutally abducted by a sinister establishment, The Organisation, desperate to acquire the technology. He flees to the Dream Factory, an old stone hut rebuilt by his father on the remote Eastcombe Beach — and a place people are able to visit through their dreams . . . Can the combined resources of Pi, the brilliant Navinda, and the new local vicar — a literal doubting Thomas — take on the might of The Organisation?

JOHN SIMES

THE DREAM FACTORY: GHOSTS

Complete and Unabridged

ULVERSCROFT
Leicester

First published in Great Britain in 2014

First Large Print Edition
published 2015

A catalogue record for this book is available
from the British Library.

ISBN 978–1–4448–2402–5

Published by
F. A. Thorpe (Publishing)
Anstey, Leicestershire

Set by Words & Graphics Ltd.
Anstey, Leicestershire
Printed and bound in Great Britain by
T. J. International Ltd., Padstow, Cornwall

For *Jo*

Contents

Acknowledgments.........................xi
1. Learning to Dream.......................1
2. A Pesky Youth 3
3. Ghosts.................................11
4. Doris Arrives...........................19
5. Enigma Cottage 37
6. Funny Olde Englishe 48
7. The Whodhavethoughtit 51
8. The Dream Factory 64
9. *Le Manoir*..............................72
10. Just the Car for a Killer.................79
11. Death of a Hawk Moth 94
12. Some Old Fruitcake from Dingwell ..101
13. Miss Cloke's Reconnaissance.........115
14. The Storm 142
15. Miss B 161
16. A Game of Chess.....................172
17. The Masque 200
18. The Old School.......................206
19. Operation Pandora 210
20. Behold — the Birth of a
      Death Star 227
21. A Broken Doll 244
22. Greymoor 254
23. The Old Rectory 264

24. There Is No Such Thing as Time 282
25. There Are No Strangers Here.........292
26. The Fear 308
    The Author 321

Acknowledgments

Firstly, thanks to the brilliant reading team (which included some former students): Jo Simes, Rachel Smithers, Nicola Elliott, Emma Plant, Pat Holness, Sandy Hammond, Chris Simes, Nick Johns, Kate Morley, Lizzie Wainwright, Jane Plant, Felicity Dunworth, Richard Simes, Becky Wynter, and Peter Cook. Rachel suggested I read Primo Levi's 'The Periodic Table' — it turned out to be inspirational for this book. Very special thanks to another former student, Sandie Beaney, and also to Jan Hailwood for their forensic editing and support. I was privileged to have the benefit of James Stevenson's experience, guidance and encouragement. Television astrologist and author, Michele Knight, generously showed me her beautiful house — the setting for some of this book — a great kindness and an inspirational person to meet. I am also profoundly grateful to Chris Dixon — www.chrisdix-onphotography.com — for the superb cover concept and photos. I should also acknowledge the legendary 'Tigger', and other local feral felines. Special thanks also to Sara and Mike Atkinson for listening to a reading of this book and allowing me to work in the most blissful of creative spaces — the 'naya'. *Maravilloso!* Thanks also to Conor Heneghan (*le chef merveilleux!*) and Tracey, guardians of the fabulous 'Journeys End', (The Whodhavethoughtit); to Dave Mannell for allowing us to photograph beautiful Westcombe beach. Warmest thanks also to David Pratt, Sandra Pollard and Stuart Owen for their artwork. Gratitude also to Mark Duffield https://soundcloud.com/ markduffieldcollaboration for the magical interpretations of the 'The Masque' songs, and to another dear friend, Roger Plant. I had the good fortune to work with a superb editor — Angela at CreateSpace, and their talented design team. I owe a considerable debt of gratitude to Richard Simes for patiently guiding his uncertain father through the uncharted waters of websites, Facebook pages, etc. Finally, I extend my deepest gratitude to the brilliant young people who received the dubious benefit of my teaching; so often you amazed me. Now, go and change the world . . . before lunchtime.

Finally, this book would not have been created without the love and support of my wonderful wife, Jo, who convinced me that this journey into The Dream Factory was worth making.

'If the price of finding oneself in the world is that of losing the world in oneself, then the price is more than anyone can afford.'
— Robert Witkin, *The Intelligence of Feeling*

1

Learning to Dream

As a child I learned to dream. I am going to tell you about this dream. It started when I was really young. It started the first time I heard angry voices — screaming and shouting. It scared me. It terrified me. Still does.

I was seven years old. Mum and Dad fought and swore and smashed things. My mother grabbed the poker and smashed it into the kitchen door. Then she did it again and again. I stood in the cold hall in my pyjamas. I watched my father slap my mother's face, and she collapsed like a ragdoll into the curtains. Then she rose up magically, like a frenzied harpy, seized the poker, and banged my father's head. He cried in pain and bled, the sudden gash leaking gore.

I ran in terror to my bed. Wrapped the sheets about my head and prayed, prayed to dream but could not. The shouting stopped. Silence crept out of the walls and watched. I ran back, and they were exhausted on their knees. Mum got a cloth and dabbed my father's head as he quietly wept. They saw me. Their eyes of guilt and pain had no power to make me fear them.

'I want you to promise,' I said, and sniffed back my sobs and drew myself as tall as I could. 'I want you to promise . . .' I heaved a breath. ' . . . that you will not fight again. You will not shout again.'

Their hands and arms reached out to pull me in, and I held them as they held me in the crucible of their violent love. Blood dripped onto my sleeve.

Back in my bedroom, my friend Savaric, the ghost, stood in my room, a shape in the gloom, to watch over me. I had learned to dream, and dream intensely. Dreamed so hard that I could forget where I was. Still do.

Let me show you.

2

A Pesky Youth

Picture a cliff faced with flat rocks of silver, pink, and soft purple. Below, the sea unrolls and plashes on the shingle, shrinking back with a sigh. There is a beach beneath the cliff with spiny rocks, like a dinosaur's back, that stick out of the sea in curvy lines, and the waves play round these in splishes and green-sea surges.

A stream spreads silver onto the beach from the land, creating a wide channel between miniature cliffs of brown sand and shingle, before it washes across the sand to the sea. The stream tumbles and bounds down from a grassy valley, strewn with soft woodlands and drowsy bluebell beds. By the stream, close to remote Eastcombe Beach, is the Dream Factory, wood and stone, with a single puffing chimney. It is no bigger than your bedroom, but inside the space opens out like a universe. When you go there in your head, no one can follow you. It buzzes and whizzes with dreams and ideas. Pi — Peter Young — lives there. Right now he has to.

Pi? Well, one of his exasperated teachers had called him a 'pesky youth.' 'I will call you PY,' he'd told a perplexed class of sixteen-year-old mathematicians. Mr. Root — beetroot-faced and furious in his dusty sport jacket — pointed to Peter. 'PY. This boy is *pesky*, a *nuisance*; cannot wear his school uniform properly; wears it like a sack; and he is a *youth*, a *young* person who thinks he knows everything but will learn *nothing* for himself.' Mr. Root ran out of puff and ideas, as the class blinked at him and Pi, trying to see some resemblance between the boy they knew as Peter Young and a steak and kidney pie.

Peter had let the insults wash over him like spring rain. PY? OK, let it be PY; it was better than his real name. 'Call me PY,' he said to the stout boy next to him.

'Pie?' said the boy, joining the ranks of the bewildered. 'Certainly. You can call me 'Doughnut.''

Peter thought. He loved numbers, figures, probabilities, theories, ideas. He also liked the theory of Pi, which was used to calculate the circumference of a circle. 'Pi' had a sense of mystery and power to it. 'Pi,' he said. 'I want to be known as Pi. P! I! Call me 'Pi.''

Mr. Root spoke to another, less baffling child and, in doing so, neatly spat on his work. Mr. Root had put the sleeve of his dusty jacket to good use.

It was near the end of term, and Pi was once again enduring Mr. Root's maths class. He sighed and flipped open his exercise book. Pi finished his homework in a trice, with a flick of his pen. The words and figures appeared like magic script on the pages of his book, strange hieroglyphics, mysterious symbols.

He shifted his gaze to the computer screen above his desk. He saw his own reflection: the spiky hair, curious restless eyes, unbuttoned collar, and school tie bundled in an untidy knot. He smiled at himself. True — he did wear his uniform like a sack. Pi liked the image.

An artificial face smiled calmly from the screen — the image of Bogle, neither female nor male, quietly smiling, waiting for Pi to ask a question. Pi looked hard at the face. He did not trust it.

'Where do you want to go today?' said Bogle.

'To a place you cannot go,' said Pi.

'Cool!' said Bogle.

Pi closed his eyes. *Go to the Dream Factory now, in your head,* he thought. Best not. Maths was the last lesson, and he would go to the Dream Factory straight from the bus. No point in going home. Mum and Dad had been taken. He had been sleeping in the cellar when the men came. Shouting. A fierce struggle in the hall. He had pulled on his jeans and boots and seized his green jacket. Mum had screamed, 'Run, Peter! Run!' And he had — crashed through the wooden door, up the steps, into the moonlit garden. He had turned to see men in black jackets and balaclavas bundling Mum and Dad into the back of a van. Now he shuddered at the memory and rocked back and forth on his stool, his fists clenched on his desk. *I will not cry*, he said to himself. *I will not cry*.

Pi shifted his eyes to the clock. Almost time. He had tried to enter his house yesterday, but his key would not work. There was a strange car in the drive, and a dog barked. He had run back down Dingwell Lane, past the church, and down to Eastcombe Beach and the Dream Factory. What would he do tonight?

Bogle spoke again. 'Time to go home soon. Are you going home, Peter?'

Pi stared at the face, with its carefully sculpted smile. He wanted to put his fist through it. What business did it have asking him that? Home was the last place he would go. 'Yes, of course. Where else?'

'Where else indeed?' said Bogle. 'That's cool.'

Pi slid the mouse to 'Shut down,' and Bogle disappeared, abruptly swallowed up by darkness. A bell rang, and Pi slid his books into the old briefcase Dad had given him. The loss of his parents hung like a yoke about his shoulders.

Children flooded into the corridors, eager to burst through the doors and out to the buses or to meet friends or their mother or father at the gate. Pi decided to let the wave of sound surge away from him as he sat motionless on the wooden stool in the maths laboratory. He jerked the cord on the venetian blinds and saw the myriad coloured coats and bright faces jostling in the bus queues, and teachers, luminous in Day-Glo jackets, keeping the lines straight. Pi's burden was one he could not share because he did not trust Bogle. That question — 'Are you going home, Peter?' — came back to him. Why ask him that? And if he could not trust Bogle — who could access all the information about him — he could not trust the school.

'Are you all right, lad?' Mr. Root stood in his crumpled tweed trousers and jacket, an array of Biros protruding from the breast pocket. Tufts of grey hair shot out from behind his ears, and one from the top of his crown. 'Is there a problem?' Mr. Root's doorknob eyes enquired.

'Must catch my bus, sir.' Pi slid off the stool and grabbed his green jacket.

As he barged through the door, he heard Mr. Root's parting shot, 'Just do your tie up, lad!'

The bus ground its way through the country lanes. Pi sat with his forehead against the windowpane; hedges, telegraph poles, and cottages slid by. A thunderstorm was stalking the bus. As the light faded, he felt a terrible emptiness overpower him. He fought it by thinking of Navinda. He had met her at the Old Bailey Café in London on a school trip last week. He felt himself being drawn into her dark eyes. He had scribbled his Splot e-address on a till receipt and passed it to her, too terrified to speak. She had smiled.

'Are you going to speak to me, or is this all I get?' Navinda had held up the till receipt. 'What a miserable offering. You have been staring at me all day.'

Pi had stuttered an apology. They had talked. He told her about the Dream Factory, and she gazed at this restless, troubled soul who was struggling to explain himself. The green jacket, the tousled hair . . . and why had he really bothered with a school tie? Navinda leant forward and placed her slim forefinger across his lips.

'I know it. I have been there,' she said. Pi

stared, open-mouthed. 'I must go now. We will talk — possibly.' She had turned and smiled as she pushed open the door, leaving Pi to the contents of his plastic cup.

Navinda had kept her word. Om pulsed in Pi's pocket, and the Splot appeared. 'When you are in the Dream Factory, think of me. — N.' Excitement poured into the void of Pi's emotions and flowed through him. He had dreamt of Navinda sleeping in the Dream Factory, her storm of midnight-black hair on a white pillow, dreaming, Om's blue light gently pulsing. The dogs slumbering and snoring softly and Tigger — the striped, battle-scarred village cat — on his shelf, keeping safe watch over all; the moon creeping across the purple sky, casting a drifting shaft of light. *If Navinda was here,* Pi thought, *I could begin to deal with all this.*

The bus descended the hill into Dingwell Village and creaked to a halt outside the ancient church. Pi stepped off and pulled up his hood. He noticed the new vicar of Dingwell peering out of his study window. Was he someone to trust? The thunderstorm answered the question. Pi watched the school bus grind back up the hill, children's faces pressed against the rear window. One child waved. It would be his farewell, Pi had decided. *I will not be going back.*

Tigger materialised on the churchyard wall. He stared at Pi, framed by the gothic arched doorway and pagan sundial. A weathervane creaked above the imposing tower and conical black spire. Pi felt comforted; to look at Tigger was to feel a deep bond he could not begin to explain.

Pi shivered. *Get moving,* he told himself. *Not safe in the village.* He hastened down the lane towards the Whodhavethoughtit Pub before turning onto the winding track to Yarmer Valley. Tigger followed him.

3

Ghosts

A char-grilled, tiger-striped trout, laced with Tabasco and stuffed with almonds and lemon, wafted its succulent odours into the willing nostrils of Thomas Clodpole, Dingwell's new vicar. *Well,* he thought. *What a feast!* Thomas gazed appreciatively round the Churchill bar at the Whodhavethoughtit Pub, Dingwell's ancient and atmospheric watering hole. A stuffed badger snarled inanely from a glass case, and a vast taxidermied codfish stared, with typically British stiff upper lip, at the teeming rain that spiked the grassy banks of dizzy flowers in the pub garden. *I could be happy here.* With this simple thought, Thomas set about the pleasing task of filleting the head and tailbone from the trout. The poor creature's face bore a resigned expression with which Thomas empathised. 'It's not your day, Mr. Trout,' he said, a little too loudly.

'Hey, Reverend Thomas. Zat all right for you?' Gideon, the muscular barman, had appeared at Thomas's side, sporting a dazzling cobalt-and-gold apron. An orange T-shirt featuring a

Caribbean sunset, along with a gold earring, completed the vision. Gideon illuminated the oak-panelled walls, solid antique furniture, and soothing hues of the Whodhavethoughtit's bar. If the sun was not shining, Gideon would supply it himself.

'Perfect, Gideon. Perfect. May I call you 'Gideon'?'

'Call me 'Giddy,' man. Everybody does. It's OK.'

'Giddy it is. This looks wonderful.'

'Swiss chard, dill, and parsley, all home grown.'

'Now then, Reverend Thomas, here's your pint.' Tizzy, the aged and bewhiskered pub landlord, had ambled from behind the bar. 'Pint of Methuselah's Old Wrinkly should be fine for thee.'

'Thank you, Tizzy,' said Thomas.

'No point talking to the trout, Reverend. He dead!' Gideon said with a laugh.

'You could eat the whole fish, Reverend. Including the eyes. Miss Cloke does.'

'Miss Cloke?' said Thomas. 'The church-warden?'

'Very same,' said Tizzy. 'Chomps the lot like an old mog.'

'Beyond me, I fear,' said Thomas, slipping the bones onto the spare plate.

'No worries.' Tizzy placed the plate on the

rug by the fire. 'Tigger'll 'ave these.' Tizzy and Gideon headed back to the bar.

Thomas lifted his gaze and caught the yellow eyes, probing stare, and tiger stripes of Tigger, the pub cat, perched on the mantelpiece where he had been calmly observing, with not a little interest, Thomas's ponderous dismantling of the trout. Thomas smiled chubbily at Tigger and saw the strange M shape on his forehead above the yellow eyes and peculiar peppered nose. Thomas absentmindedly started to count the black dots on the pink nose tip. Tigger's ears also disagreed on angles — one neatly upright but the other tilted sharply; indeed a piece was missing. It gave the impression that the cat was eavesdropping on another conversation going on in the snug. And were those his whiskers and lip curling on one side, moving to reveal glittering incisors, sharp as needles? To Thomas the image was of a fiendish grin that was most perturbing to see.

Tigger sprang onto the rug and settled down next to the plate, emitting a blood-curdling purr. He proceeded to pin the fish head and bones to the floor before devouring them with surgical precision.

Thomas wiped his lips with the napkin and abandoned the few remains of his meal, leaving Tigger to gobble up the rest. *Ah, well,* thought Thomas. He wandered thoughtfully from the pub and up to the vicarage, an old Victorian school that rose above the village. The faintly disturbing image of Tigger's inquisitorial features hovered in the air about his head, a feline apparition, as he walked.

Presently Thomas sat at his desk. He caught his image in the mirror — dark-blue fleece, and a pale-blue shirt with his clerical collar; it was a warm, comfortable image, he thought, an image someone could talk to. He smiled at himself. Yes. This fitted. It was how he felt.

His study window framed Dingwell's striking Norman church — All Souls — with its menacing, 'chimneyesque' (Thomas enjoyed the word) tower topped, it seemed, by a witch's hat. It was an unsettling image. The heavy oak doors had withstood shrieking winds, torrential storms, and bloody revolution but were apparently unable to keep out the village cat. Thomas had been distributing hymnbooks in the church and had a creeping intuition that he was not alone. He had turned in trepidation to find Tigger's tiger stripes adorning the altar, where he basked in a halo of sunshine. Tigger had a useful knack for ensuring that if he *were* spotted anywhere, it was always somewhere significant. It meant nothing to Tigger, of course, other than that he was disporting himself in one of his favourite sunny spots. If it happened to be in the middle of the altar, obstructing the view of the crucifix and framed by two gold candlesticks, that was, in Tigger's view, not altogether inappropriate.

Must begin my sermon, thought Thomas. *But what to say?* He sighed. 'What to say . . . ?' He had been in the village for only a month and wanted to make an impression.

The image of Bogle appeared on his desktop. She — if it was a she — smiled. 'What to say?' she said in smooth mid-Atlantic tones, 'That's easy. Say anything.'

Thomas sighed again and stared at the face. It spoke again. 'Can I help you, Thomas?' She always annoyingly pronounced his name as 'Toe-mass.'

'No, thank you, Bogle. I'll find a book,' he said.

'Sure. Good-bye.'

★   ★   ★

In contrast Tigger's day had been altogether less complex. That morning Pi had unlocked the creaking back door of the Dream Factory, and the Springer spaniels — Jack and Jill — had rushed out and raced down to the sea, ears flopping and stumpy tails wagging. The seagulls that had been quietly feeding on the

shoreline, minding their own business, immediately lifted into the air with an annoyed
'aaark,' while the furry buffoons raced about
like toy cars, barked at nothing in particular,
and then remembered it was breakfast time
and raced back again. Meanwhile Pi had closed
the backdoor to give Tigger his breakfast. The
cat flap had swung open, and two floppy
heads tried to squeeze into the gap. Tigger
had reacted by taking his time and eating his
breakfast as slowly as possible; he turned his
head dreamily towards the dogs and licked
his whiskers with evident pleasure. The dogs
yelped and drooled. Now that Pi had come to
the Dream Factory, this was, for Tigger, a
daily joy.

Tigger, like any cat, chose his own
company and marmalised any other cat that
had the effrontery to wander onto his
territory. If you were to ask all the other cats
in Dingwell where Tigger's territory began
and ended, they could not tell you. Tigger's
territory was everywhere, as far as the eye
could see — apart from the beach itself of
course; Tigger was not keen on getting his
feet wet. At low tide all the other cats could
make a dash for the beach and find a pleasant
spot to sit in the sun, free to flick their tails in
peace.

Not that Tigger had everything his own

way. His battered face and tattered ears bore the scars of combat, and in all honesty, you could not call Tigger an attractive cat. Not that he minded, although on occasion he tried to look charming, which, for Tigger, was a challenge.

Tigger dined, courtesy of Pi, at the Dream Factory in the morning and then strolled through the fragrant wooded valley, up Smugglers' Lane, to his other home in Dingwell Village, the Whodhavethoughtit Pub. Here he would occupy his chair by the fire and receive titbits from customers.

Tizzy sported a shaggy mane of grey hair and a splendidly rampant beard. He also had what he called a 'porky pigtail' dangling from the back of his neck. Sometimes Tigger perched on the shelf by the bar and stretched his claws out to grab the pigtail. 'Off with thee, cheeky old mog!' and Tizzy would ruffle his ears and pretend to box with Tigger's paws. 'No respect! Not even from the village mog!' he would tell the locals over a pint of Methuselah's Old Wrinkly.

★　★　★

As the afternoon's cheerful sun retreated before an impetuous thunderstorm, Thomas had chewed his Biro to little purpose. The green school bus roared down the hill and lurched to a halt outside the church. Thomas saw a teenager in a hooded green jacket step down onto the tarmac. Thomas peered, but it was impossible to see who it was. The mysterious figure turned to look at him before heading down towards the pub as the storm broke and rain swarmed over the village. A battered Ford Fiesta swung round the corner and halted by the church. It then careered noisily towards the pub before veering onto the track down to Yarmer Valley, emitting blue smoke from its exhaust. Thomas watched the vapour drift and dissipate as the rain pins bounced and danced on his garden path. He slid the mouse across his desk, and Bogle reappeared.

'Did you think of anything?' Bogle's benign, enquiring smile and artificial eyes filled the screen.

'Yes, I had a brilliant idea,' he lied.

'Write about what you can see.'

Thomas's gaze moved to the photograph of Olivia. He had hesitated before standing the silver frame on his desk with the wooden crucifix. A faded print of Constable's *Salisbury Cathedral from the Meadows* — its spire touching a rainbow — glowed from the wall. *Don't think about the past,* thought Thomas. *Ghosts.*

He and Olivia had thought of having a kitten.

4

Doris Arrives

Doris was in the backseat of her dad and mum's car. Buddy — her black-and-white pup — was on her lap. Buddy was blinking and staring as the old Fiesta swung through the back lanes. The car screeched to a halt in Dingwell by the church.

'Where is this naffin' place?' said Dad. He was feeling grumpy. He wanted to get back home and down to the Dog & Weasel for a beer. 'Where is it?' he snapped again. For a moment he saw the quiet church tower, and a lump came to his throat. He felt guilty about what he was about to do. *Doris,* he thought. *She'll get over it.* It was for the best.

'Down there.' Mum pointed down a steep lane that swung round a corner. The car moved on past the grey cottages and barns. The scudding clouds and cheerful sun had given way to stabbing darts of rain.

Dad peered over the steering wheel as the wipers smeared away the rain, and the car careered down the lane, bounced and weaved past a barn, and emerged into the misty emerald green of Yarmer Valley. The road ended and became a mud track. Doris clung tightly to Buddy, and tears welled in her eyes. She loved her pup. But Mum and Dad said that Buddy had to go. No one was at home to look after him during the day. He just made a mess everywhere.

Doris had said she would take Buddy to school, and she had hid him in her bag. But Miss Prism had seen Buddy's little face peek out of the bag during maths. 'He's beautiful, Doris. Really beautiful,' she had said kindly, peering into the bag. 'But school is not the place for doggies, is it, Doris?' Miss Prism had smiled sweetly.

She nodded. 'Yes, miss, but you see . . . '

Miss Prism had turned to another child, and then looked back at Doris over her little black spectacles. 'Not again, Doris. I *do* hope that is quite clear,' she said firmly.

'Yes, miss,' Doris said with a sigh.

'This is the place. It's safe here.' Dad opened the door, reached in, and grabbed Buddy. Doris emitted a cry, as if something had been ripped from her. She had no words. Her heart was breaking. Dad held Buddy. The pup seemed to give Doris one last look. Bewildered and full of fear, he was in Dad's big, hard hands.

'Go on, Den,' said Mum.

Dad looked at the stream. He was meant to drown the pup, but Doris's cry cut him deeply inside. He was not a brave man. He dashed down the muddy track and placed Buddy under a bramble bush, while the valley held its breath. Dad stumbled back to the car and reversed blindly before accelerating back up the lane, now a river of rain — rain and tears. Doris's cry had given way to long, deep sobs from deep inside herself, echoing out from the space inside herself, the place within of grief and loss, where love had once been.

Mum patted her. 'It'll be all right, Dor . . . be all right.' But Doris was inconsolable, and the sobbing became long and deep. She lay down, drew up her knees, and folded herself together like a foetus, her chestnut ponytail shuddering as she cried.

Pi stepped back into the bushes as the car roared up the track. He caught sight of a child, legs and arms clasped together, and above, a face that was a mask of pain. The cry from the open window of the car wounded him. Pi turned to watch as the Fiesta slithered and scrambled up the slope to the road.

'Shut her up, Jan, for Gawd's sake. Can't bleedin' think.'

'Well, it was your fault, for givin' 'er the stupid pup in the first place. You knew we

21

couldn't look after it.'

She was right of course. Den was a big man with a hard and dirty job to do at the council depot. He lived for football and beer. He loved Doris but did not know how to love her. The pup definitely came off the subs' bench. And so they argued and swore at each other as they drove back to their home in grey Victory Flats.

'Didn't drown it, anyway,' said Dad. 'I left it in the hedge. It'll be all right.

'Hear that, Dor? Dad didn't drown 'im after all. He'll be all right.' But Doris was not listening. Den and Jan did not understand how they had betrayed their daughter.

★　★　★

Pi continued his walk down the lane to Yarmer Valley. He had watched Tigger sneak through the bushes before adeptly scaling the garden wall of the Plunketts' house.

'Up to no good again, Tigger?' The cat turned his battle-scarred features briefly — Pi noted that one eye was half closed — before sliding along the wall and climbing onto a tree branch that provided excellent access to the Plunketts' garden and their bird table. Tigger had been waiting at the Dream Factory when Pi had escaped from his house

— never had he been more pleased to see him. The curtain of rain drew away from the valley, and spears of sun roused the olive and jade hues of Yarmer Valley; fronds and branches of oaks and elms awoke to shake off their rainwater burden. Pi walked onto the simple stone footbridge. Yarmer Stream rushed beneath before making more sedate progress, a glistening thread of light cutting the emerald fields to the sea. Pi looked back up the hill and along the row of houses in Dingwell Lane and saw his home, the Old Rectory, beyond the line of stout oaks that fringed his garden. Pi had seen a new name, *Le Manoir*, daubed clumsily on a gatepost. No. He could not go back. Not yet.

The footpath snaked along the western edge of the valley. Pi paused under the tree line and pulled Om from his jacket pocket.

Om? Think of your smartphone; then think of an elliptical disc, resting in the palm of your hand. Smooth, soft surface, no buttons, no screen but the whole surface illuminating and displaying images and messages in vivid colours.

'Navinda's message again, please, Om,' said Pi.

'You have read it ten times already,' said Om, in his distinctively calm, rich voice. A voice like that of Pi's father.

'Please,' said Pi.

'Same colours? I do have a picture of Navinda.'

'Just the message, Om.' Pi smiled down at Om. He loved this intel unit. He felt so close to his parents when he was using it, and he knew they had been working on the next version. Om glowed a deep azure, and a goblin appeared in the centre; it came running and hurled a bucket of green paint that splotted and slithered down in rivulets, forming Navinda's message.

'That's cool, Om. I like that.'

'Thank you. I like to please,' said Om with undisguised irony.

'Any messages from Mum and Dad?'

'Not yet. I know they are alive, but they are a long way from here.'

Pi replaced Om in his jacket and stood silently beneath the dripping trees. He clenched his fists and felt the wave of anger and pain approaching, like a tube train sliding up his spine. Mum and Dad had been worried. They had said something might happen. Why hadn't they stopped it, done something, run away, taken him . . . somewhere . . . together? 'Must not think like this,' he said to the empty, soothing calm of the valley. Navinda's message, 'Think of me,' drifted upward and seemed to hover before his eyes. A curtain of calm was drawn between Pi and his grief and suffering.

'Think of me,' Pi said aloud to the soft air, and walked on to the end of the path by Yarmer Beach before ascending the steps that led upward along the cliff edge and over the rise. He paused and caught sight of the hawk that endlessly rode the winds of Eastcombe Valley and threaded the trees and bushes of Doctors' Wood with incredible flight lines and precise paths, before soaring upward again to tumble and dive on her prey. Pi trod the zigzag track down into Eastcombe Beach and placed his boots carefully on each of the jutting granite steps that led down to the rushing brook that bound on to the grey calm of the shore.

To the right the Dream Factory clung to the valley's side. Pi's dad had rebuilt the old stone hut and chopped out a rectangle from the rocks and shillet to form a ragged lawn. In the fading afternoon light, Pi stood on this tussocky strip, letting the winds whip his jacket and tousled hair, flowers of pearl-white clover trembling at his feet. *Think of me*. He heard Navinda's voice and closed his eyes. A soft hand was within his hand. 'Think of me.' This time the voice was not in his head but strong and clear by his side. 'Think of me.' He felt a gentle forefinger lay across his lips.

Pi trembled . . . a kiss — a breath upon his cheek. He opened his eyes and fell into the gentle arms and deep gaze of Navinda.

Navinda looked up at him and smiled. 'I told you I had been here.'

'Yes. I never doubted you.'

'There is someone else,' said Navinda. Pi looked round. 'Someone else who needs us.' A little boy with a mop of blond hair was sitting on the grassy bank, dangling his feet into the rushing stream. He had a long stick that he poked into the stones. He turned his face towards Pi. It was tearstained and fearful.

Pi reached out his hand. 'Come with us.' The boy stood up. He scampered through the stream and clasped Pi's hand. 'This way.' The little group walked up the muddy track to the Dream Factory's creaking driftwood door and entered.

★   ★   ★

Doris was put to bed, while Mum and Dad hurriedly put on their coats and dashed to the gaudy warmth of the Dog & Weasel. They returned later, drunk and miserable. But Doris, calm now, lay staring at the photo of her holding Tiger, her tabby cat. Tiger had long disappeared of course. Victory Flats and

Den and Jan Ferrett had held nothing for him. He had no collar but a brown luggage label tied round his neck with the word *Tigger* written on it in vivid colours. Doris had wondered whether there was one 'g' or two in 'Tiger' but thought it safest to spell it with two 'g's. Where was Tiger now? Where was Buddy? Doris slid her thumb into her mouth, and she slept and dreamed. And as she dreamed, Doris arrived in the Dream Factory. She appeared just at the moment that Navinda and Pi were playing chess. She stood before them as Navinda moved her gaze from Pi to Doris. Doris looked at the chessboard on the wooden box, the blue light from Om, and the blazing log fire.

Navinda said, 'Do you like chess?' Doris nodded and knelt by the box. 'I think Pi has cheated. What do you think?'

Doris looked at Pi — his ruffled hair, his crumpled shirt and ragged tie, the cuffs unbuttoned. 'No,' said Doris. 'He wouldn't cheat.'

'I could not cheat you, Navinda,' said Pi.

'If you did,' said Navinda, 'I would call it fair play.'

Pi blinked and shook his head. 'I could not. I never will.'

Navinda smiled and gazed at Doris. 'We know your name, Doris. Welcome.'

'Stay as long as you want,' said Pi. He looked at the board. 'What move should I make?'

'Will you teach me?' said Doris.

'Chess? Yes, and we do writing and drawing and maths and French. Om can teach you anything.'

Navinda pointed to Om, who had been placed on the stone wall and glowed a deep blue. 'I can teach you anything you wish,' said Om. 'I taught Pi his maths,' he continued proudly.

'Ah, but you did not teach Barnie to make an aeroplane,' said Pi. 'I did that.'

'This is Barnie,' said Navinda. A little boy in Crocs and shorts with grubby knees ran into the room clutching a plane made from balsawood. He stopped and looked at Doris. His lips moved to shape a greeting. Then he turned and ran out of the room.

'Barnie does not speak,' explained Navinda. 'I am sure he can speak, but he does not want to. Something has happened to Barnie.'

'Navinda is brilliant at chess, Doris,' said Pi. 'She can teach you now, and then we can take Jack and Jill for a walk.'

Doris knelt at Navinda's side, and her feelings of loss and grief departed for the horizon.

* ★ *

Tigger was there when Den placed Buddy under the bush. Tigger was watching from the bird table in Mr. and Mrs. Plunkett's garden. He liked to stop at the Plunketts' house on his way to the Whodhavethoughtit. The Plunketts had put the bird table in to stop Tigger from chasing the birds away, and it was meant to be cat-proof. Tigger enjoyed proving this was not the case. The bird table was excellently positioned for him to gaze over the valley in a lordly fashion. In fact Tigger was so well fed that he never felt the need to chase anything and felt birds were altogether rather trivial. (Except for the sparrow that had pooped on him while he was sunning himself on the Plunketts' roof. Tigger had suffered the indignity of being bathed by Tizzy after that, before drying off furiously in front of the fire.) He settled down to watch Mr. and Mrs. Plunkett as they ate dinner. Today Tigger was in for some spectacular entertainment.

'That blasted cat!' A red-faced Mr. Plunkett exploded with fury as he caught sight of Tigger gazing pleasantly from the bird table. He stood abruptly, knocking over a huge glass of claret, staining the Chinese lace tablecloth and fluffy white carpet dark red.

29

'Oh, Wilfred, that was Mama's tablecloth!' shrieked Lavinia Plunkett before giving him the most terrible talking to. He scuttled off to the kitchen for a cloth and a stain remover, muttering about mangy moggies and mingy mamas. If she wanted her tablecloth, he could tell her where she could put it. The Plunketts' border terrier, Willy, was in the kitchen and began to bark. Mr. Plunkett opened the kitchen door, and Willy came scampering through. He saw Tigger and yapped and snarled and jumped up and down on his little legs. Willy could even sit upright on his haunches, paws aloft, like a meerkat, snapping and yelping as Tigger gazed calmly down at the mayhem.

Lavinia Plunkett was on all fours, mopping the carpet with her hanky. Wilfred returned in haste. The door swung open and impacted against Lavinia's ample posterior, and the old lady was propelled into the fire irons. Willy barked even more.

Wilfred looked at his wife, trying to disengage from the coalscuttle. Enough was enough. The time for action had come. Ignoring his wife's wailing about her carpet, he burst through the back door with Willy in hot pursuit. He had seized a toy cricket bat, and his face was the colour of the wine he had just spilled. He failed to notice his grandson's skateboard, lethally positioned outside the back door. Wilfred was suddenly hurtling across the crazy paving towards the garden steps. It was a superb performance. He vaulted the first step and bounced off the second before he and the skateboard parted company. For a moment Wilfred was airborne, and he just caught sight of Tigger before descending into the pond with a tremendous splash. Tigger shut his eyes, as the air was full of pond water.

A spluttering Wilfred Plunkett rose from the pond like an old walrus, his hair and moustache draped with weed. He shot Tigger a vengeful look. Willy decided to make himself scarce.

'I'm not having a pussy on my bird table,' he gurgled.

'And I'm not having you in the pond,' said Lavinia, and shooed the sodden old man across the patio. 'You can't come into the house like that. Take your clothes off here. I'll get you a towel.'

Wilfred summoned up his last reserves of pride. 'I will not be naked on my own patio in front of that cat!' he squeaked, removing a piece of weed from his ear. The old man sought sanctuary in his potting shed. He stood shivering, wrapped in a towel and imbibing those rural smells of decomposing compost and hessian sacks. After all that noise at the Youngs' place the other night, this was all he needed.

And so it was from the bird table — it had a most pleasing oriental pagoda to provide shelter for one's fur — that Tigger watched the scene of Buddy's expulsion from the Ferrett family. He saw Buddy scuttle back up the lane as the car drove off and heard the little yelps. He saw Buddy look about him, lost and — he thought — alone. Tigger watched as Buddy crept beneath the wrought-iron gates of the Plunketts' and observed him disappear into their garage, to find some shelter and warmth on an old car blanket. Tigger saw the luggage label around Buddy's neck. Something stirred in his memory. Meanwhile the Plunketts and Willy were trying to resume normal life. *Time for dinner,* Tigger thought, and leapt almost gracefully from the bird table, before heading for the Whodhavethoughtit.

★ ★ ★

Dusk was falling, and a completely pogged Tigger was padding gently down the valley towards Eastcombe and the Dream Factory. The stars blinked, and the Eddystone Lighthouse winked from the horizon. A few clouds hung in the sky, ships becalmed in a sea of pink and purple. The twilight skies even made Tigger wonder whether there was some omnipotent creative force in the sky greater than him. He doubted it. The shifting sea kept its secrets and the cliffs and trees their mysteriousness, and Tigger's tummy was full to the brim.

Tigger slipped over the stile in the bluebell woods and meandered along the track. Rabbits, mice, and voles all hid when Tigger was strolling home. There was no need, of course. Even the thought of hunting for food was just *so* much effort. Then Tigger had that feeling you sometimes get when you walk down a country lane — the feeling that you are not alone, or even that you are being followed.

Tigger stopped. He flicked his tatty ear back to listen. He heard scuffling behind him. Hmm. He wandered on then slipped into a bed of wild garlic just off the path. Tigger waited. A small, frightened, hungry pup was creeping down the path. Buddy saw Tigger and was full of fear. Tigger blinked and yawned expansively, making sure his sharp teeth were seen by the young pup. Buddy rolled onto his back in surrender. Tigger spotted the brown luggage label round Buddy's neck. Now where had he seen that before?

Navinda lit the lantern on the Dream Factory's wall. The light said, 'Come home. It is safe and warm. Bring your friend.' A fragrant Tigger wandered on, and Buddy followed at a respectful distance.

Tigger slipped through his flap and looked at Navinda. She knew at once and opened the door. She lifted the fearful puppy from the step and cradled him in her arms. To Tigger's barely concealed annoyance, Navinda offered Buddy the leftovers from Tigger's breakfast. Buddy ate them gratefully and crawled to the warmth of the fireside. Tigger flicked his tail grumpily but was soon purring on Navinda's lap. She sniffed. 'I think Tigger has been eating French food.' Navinda looked at the label tied around Buddy's neck. 'Pi, look at this.'

Pi glanced up from the balsa pyramid he was building with Barnie, who already had blown the first one down and giggled uncontrollably.

Navinda held up the brown luggage label. 'Buddy' was written in bright colours on the label, but whoever had written it had second thoughts about 'Buddy' having two 'd's. One was crossed out.

'You remember the label around Tigger's neck?' said Pi.

Navinda nodded, and fondled Tigger's tatty

ears. 'I remember. Do you remember, Tigger?'

Doris stood in the doorway, mesmerized. 'I remember.' Her voice trembled. 'I remember Tiger.' She lifted Tigger onto her lap. 'And I remember Buddy, too.' Buddy had finished his meal and he scuttled to Doris's side. He received a hiss from Tigger but Doris hugged them both. She tried to control the tremor in her voice. 'How . . . how . . . ?' she breathed.

'Questions are good.' Navinda spoke calmly. 'Just believe the evidence of your eyes.' Doris sat open-mouthed then moved to Navinda's side. Life would be transformed; a soothing balm to Doris's wounds of anger and betrayal.

Later she would lay in her bed, as the firelight flickered, Buddy warm at her side.

A blush of deep red moved over Om's surface, casting a pool of crimson light on the stuccoed wall. 'Pi. Someone is trying to contact your parents at the Old Rectory.' This time Barnie shook the table, and the pyramid collapsed. He chuckled once more and fell off his stool.

'The call was from an e-phone, reminding your dad he had a dental appointment in Queensbridge.'

Pi frowned. 'But dad doesn't have a dentist in Queensbridge.'

'Yes. And why call from an e-phone? The dentist would use a landline,' said Om.

'Who took the call? Can you play it?' Navinda held Doris's hand, and they joined Pi and Barnie at the table, bathed in a crimson hoop of light.

Om glowed. 'Never heard of you. Don't waste my time!'

Pi shivered. It was a voice he recognised.

5

Enigma Cottage

Miss Cloke had been looking forward to a quiet dinner in the pub. One of Dingwell's most cantankerous residents, the old lady had come striding back from the Whodhavethoughtit, thoroughly annoyed with Tizzy and 'that blasted cat.' A neighbour of the Plunketts, she was all in favour of the mass extermination of every cat on the planet, and particularly any in her garden, and especially that tatty, stripy little monster of a pussy in the pub. Except her own cat, of course, Pandora. She was different. An Apricot Point Siamese, specially chosen to complement her cream Lloyd Loom chairs and Eileen Gray couch. No, Pandora was a real cat, not some moth-eaten, freeloading lump of fur.

Miss Cloke loved, adored, and drooled over liver and bacon, a dish from her childhood that had been a very special treat. Tizzy's chef, Gideon, cooked it perfectly, and the red-onion gravy was, well, sheer bliss. 'Here you are, Miss Cloke,' said Tizzy. 'Just the way you like it. No garlic, as requested. Giddy has mixed some of his special Dijon mustard.'

'Thank you. No,' said Miss Cloke. 'You cannot trust the French!'

'Oh, ah. Some English then?'

'Of course, Tizzy. Thank you. It does look magnificent.' Miss Cloke already had supped two London gins, by way of getting into orbit.

'*Bon appétit* — er, sorry. Enjoy your meal.'

What a silly man, she mused before sighing with pleasure at the aroma of seasoning, bacon, and onions. *Mmmmmm.*

Mmmmmmmmmmm, thought Tigger. Perched on his cushion in the Churchill bar, he yawned and stretched. Then, like the Bisto Kid of Miss Cloke's youth, he mooched dreamily to the snug, where Miss Cloke was savouring each morsel and smiling seraphically. She was overcoming her prejudices with a splendid glass of Nuits-Saint-Georges. She was in a romantic mood and recalled the past, the past she had to remember *not* to talk about. Sometimes, at Christmas, she had forgotten herself after a couple of sherries before suddenly remembering her vow of silence on the subject. Miss Cloke was watchful, secretive. Never missed a thing, 'The smallest detail can be vital or cost your life, or that of your comrades,' she had been told.

Miss Cloke had been a siren beauty, a debutante in her youth. Above all she had been determined, charming, and had an intelligence that had frightened the life out of potential suitors. A Swiss finishing school had added to her flair for languages, and she had been an ideal recruit. Her world had been tumbling out of Lysanders in French fields, documents to be delivered but not read, missions about which she knew nothing. 'This is your task. Do it, Miss Cloke.'

And she would do it, unfailingly, brilliantly. Bewildering enemy soldiers with her fleetness of foot, skills of tracking and deception, and ability to charm enemy officers with her perfect French. One lovelorn lieutenant, a nice young man, she reflected, had come to a sticky end. 'It had to be done,' she murmured, and gazed at the twilight, and through the window she could just see Enigma Cottage in the last rays of the sun. Earlier, from her fragrant garden, Miss Cloke had spied through her binoculars the eviction of Buddy from an unfamiliar car. Strange. She would mention it to the police.

Tigger had memories too, mainly about his last dinner. He was concentrating hard on his next. Miss Cloke saw him. 'Psssshhhh. Sssssssssssssstttt,' and she waved her napkin at him. 'Pish, pish, pish,' she hissed. Tigger blinked before silently climbing onto the sideboard where he could study Miss Cloke's dinner, much to her discomfort. She was getting annoyed.

'Go a-*way*, you *ghastly* creature. Pish! Pish! Pish!' The fur rose on Tigger's back. 'Tizzy! Tizzy! I want the manager,' she shrieked.

Then Tigger yeeaooooowled. He cater-wauled. Tigger normally saved his caterwaul for scaring other cats. He had done it in the pub a few times, to the amusement of regulars guzzling pints of Methuselah's Old Wrinkly. Tizzy even had asked him to do it as a way of announcing closing time.

It was certainly closing time for Miss Cloke. Nothing, absolutely nothing — not bombs, grenades, the fear of discovery, or terrifying parachute landings in the pitch dark of a French night — could match the bloodcurdling effects of Tigger in full cry. The old lady shot out of the pub and beetled back to Enigma Cottage.

Tizzy and Giddy rushed from the kitchen. 'Miss Cloke? What happened?' said Tizzy. Tigger put on his innocent gaze. 'Oh, well, Tigger. You'd better have this.' Tigger tucked in.

You see, Tigger felt it was his duty to keep order in the valley. Any new cat in *his* valley had to be shown which way the fur was flying around here. Apart from the odd bit of fisticuffs — which Tigger rather enjoyed

— the other cats accepted that Tigger was in charge. Life was easier that way. Even the dogs, daft as brushes, were content to be told what was what. Mind you, with a dog's memory, ten seconds later they would forget anyway — water off a dog's back, really. Tigger had spied a newcomer to his territory, and a not altogether unattractive one. An orange-coloured cat was unusual in these parts.

After his unexpected treat of liver and bacon at the Whodhavethoughtit, he decided to stretch his legs and pay a visit. Mind you, the onion gravy repeated on him a little. Tigger had to pause occasionally to recover his composure. As he strolled up Dingwell Lane into Doctors' Wood, the twilight was descending; Tigger had a bright idea.

★   ★   ★

Harriet the sparrow hawk was about to dine. She carved the air above the Dream Factory and would drop upon her prey in the bracken and gorse at Eastcombe Beach. Harriet was a maths genius and could calculate angles and trajectories without conscious thought. The air was her world, and she could ride and rise upon the upward gusts from the beach with consummate skill. She had eyesight to match. Honestly, if you were eating

41

your dinner and left one pea on your plate, from a hundred feet up she could see it. Not that she would stoop from the sky for a mere vegetable. No. Birds, mice, and voles were her prey, or leverets. But Harriet was an aerodynamic marvel of creation. Pi and Doris often gazed at her, awestruck as she hovered and stooped, or swept effortlessly across the valley. Now, perched on a log in the twittering twilight of Doctors' Wood, she was about to dine on her prey. She was looking forward to it.

'Harriet! Harriet!' It was Tigger. He had his eyes fixed on the dead mouse, then shifted his gaze pleadingly.

'Yes. Yes. What is it? I'm about to dine,' said Harriet.

'Harriet.' Tigger's tone became softer, and he put on his most imploring expression. 'Harriet, you know I've always said how wonderful you are.'

If Harriet had eyebrows, she would have raised one. Instead she blinked and gave Tigger an intense stare. 'No, Tigger, I cannot ever remember your saying how wonderful I am. Nor, Tigger, can I ever remember your speaking to me before. Or even speaking at all!'

Tigger gulped. He was pushing his luck. 'I need a favour.'

'A favour? What favour?'

Tigger hesitated. 'The mouse.'

'The mouse? You don't need this mouse. I caught this mouse. It has taken me three hours of intense concentration and superb flying skills to catch it. If you want a meal, go to the Whodhavethoughtit.'

Tigger burped. 'I already have. This is different,' said Tigger. 'It's not for me. It's for someone special,' he said bashfully. If Tigger could have blushed, he would have.

'Someone special, eh? And who might this special someone be? Not Navinda, surely. What would she want with a dead mouse?'

Tigger squirmed with embarrassment. 'It's for a friend,' he simpered. 'A very special friend.' He gazed at Harriet with, yes, a tear in his eye.

Harriet stared sceptically at Tigger, who now seemed suddenly smaller, shrunken, no longer the dreaded predator of the undergrowth but a sad little moggy. She then looked down at the dead field mouse. 'Have it,' she said. 'It's gone cold anyway.'

Tigger looked up in baleful gratitude. 'Oh, thank you, Harriet.'

Harriet dropped the mouse from her powerful claws and watched Tigger grab it and trot jauntily up the path. *Hmm. What is he up to?* She was determined to find out. She stretched her wings and cruised low along the hedge line, as much to find more dinner as to keep an eye on Tigger.

Tigger trotted happily back through Doctors' Wood and made a beeline for Enigma Cottage. He had a present for Pandora. He passed the Reverend Clodpole, who was enjoying an evening stroll and looking for inspiration for his sermon at the morning service. WPC Yvonne Bull streaked past him in a blur of sky blue, her blonde ponytail bouncing with each elegant stride. Then he saw Harriet expertly gliding across the twilight sky. 'Magnificent,' he whispered. He'd had an idea.

Tigger emerged from the wood and gazed at Miss Cloke's thatched home, Enigma Cottage. It was bathed in deep-orange light from the sun descending behind Yarmer Cove. Tigger climbed onto the rough stone wall and saw Pandora. Her apricot fur reflected the orange glow of the sky. She yawned languorously and stretched her long elegant limbs before rolling lazily onto her side and flicking her tail. At that moment she saw Tigger. Silhouetted against the sun. Tigger cut a handsome, if weathered, figure — every inch the returning hero from some far-off war, bearing the trophy of a dead mouse for his queen. Pandora was transfixed by the image of this rugged hero. Tigger leapt down from the wall and paused midstride, arrogantly turning his head this way and that. Pandora's eyes widened to the size of saucers. Tigger strode slowly across the lawn, eyes fixed upon Pandora. He dropped the mouse carelessly in front of her. Pandora sniffed this rich offering. Perfect. She purred. He purred. They purred together. Time passed.

Miss Cloke opened the rickety wooden gate. Tigger thought it best to disappear. Mission accomplished. He whisked over the garden wall and headed back to the Dream Factory.

★　★　★

As he entered, Doris and Barnie were sleeping in their little wooden beds, while Om cast shifting beams of azure and emerald upon the oak beams and roughly plastered walls. Pi and Navinda were sitting on the rug in front of the glowing fire, Pi's head resting on her lap.

'How long can you stay?'

'A few days. Not long.' Navinda slid her slender fingers through Pi's dishevelled hair. 'What will you do?'

'Stay here. We have Barnie and Doris to look after now. Tizzy and Gideon will come tomorrow.'

Om glowed. 'Pi, there has been another call to the Old Rectory. Not from an e-phone this time. Someone in the village. Peculiar message.'

Pi sat up. 'Can you play it?' Pi and Navinda sat, their arms clasped about their knees. 'I still cannot believe you are here.'

Navinda smiled calmly. 'Oh, I am really here.' She leaned forward and touched his cheek with her lips. 'Did you feel that?'

'Yes,' said Pi. 'I'm feeling better now.' His arms wrapped round Navinda's shoulders and held her close.

'If we are quite ready,' said Om, with a hint of paternal impatience, 'I think we will learn a great deal from this — not least who is living in your house, Pi.'

Om's light dimmed to only a single white beam. 'Eaglehawk, this is Mata Hari. Organisation Central confirms Ferdinand and Miranda in the labyrinth. Ariel has flown the coop.'

'Mata Hari?' said Pi.

'French spy — double agent, I believe,' said Om. 'You know the others of course.'

'Ferdinand and Miranda,' mused Pi. 'Dad and Mum?'

'Of course,' said Om. 'Ariel is you. And they will want to find you.'

'But who are those people? Eaglehawk and Mata Hari?' Navinda glanced at Pi. He was shaking, fingers clenched.

'I know their voices. Two old folks from the village. They visited our house.' Pi took a deep breath. 'We thought they were friends.' He shook his head and looked down.

Navinda held him. 'Don't be angry. They want you to be angry.'

6

Funny Olde Englishe

Perhaps, even at the age of seven years, I began to think that life had to be better than this. Swallows and Amazons, and The Adventures of Mr. Toad and My First Book of Poetry — even the bewildering visits to the church — all spoke of a life of happy families enjoying picnics in the sun. Or perhaps it was later when my sister left home.

I remember a full mug of hot tea flying across the kitchen — almost in slow motion — before it struck the wall above my mother and its scalding contents rained upon her new perm. Later I was lying in bed, and my mother stood woozily at my door, holding a wineglass.

'Do you know what your sister called me?'

I feigned sleep.

'She called me a bawd.' Mother wobbled slightly as I half opened my eyes. 'Do you know what a bawd is?'

Of course I knew what a board was. But why on earth call her that? Oh, well, a board is made of wood, like a plank; that sounded more promising. But Mother was not giving me any more time to pursue this fascinating theory.

'A bawd is a woman of the streets.'

My image of a plank was replaced by a strange scene of a street occupied by grey women dressed like my grandmother.

'A prostitute! She called me a prostitute!'

Now I really was confused. I knew what a substitute was. I was twelfth man for the school's cricket team and occasionally went on the field as a substitute. Perhaps a prostitute was a superior form of substitute. If I practiced my batting and bowling really hard, I might be promoted to being a prostitute. 'Prostitute.' I murmured the word so as to remember it.

The next day I went to school and looked up the word in my First English Dictionary. But it wasn't there. Perhaps I had gotten the spelling wrong. 'Sir,' I said brightly to Mr. Moore, my English teacher, 'how do you spell 'prostitute'?' Mr. Moore's eyebrows levitated above the rim of his spectacles. He gave me a long stare. 'It's just that my mother . . . ' My words petered out. Mr. Moore was chewing his lower lip thoughtfully, and then he spluttered, 'Excuse me, class' and raced suddenly for the classroom door. A boy said later that he had heard someone laughing in the staff Gents.

I found out later. On the playground. And several other words. From now on a tart was something not merely made of pastry.

When I got home, my sister was carrying a suitcase. She kissed me, and I wanted to cry. She was going to meet that man I had seen her kissing in the park.

Savaric, the ghost, said that my world was not something I could control.

But I could control the world in myself. At least I think that is what he said. He speaks funny olde Englishe.

7

The Whodhavethoughtit

The Reverend Thomas Clodpole stood by the fire in the Whodhavethoughtit Pub, warming his rear and sipping gratefully at a pint of Methuselah's Old Wrinkly. He needed it. The Sunday-morning service had left him a little shaken. Mind you, his idea of using his homemade vin rouge for the communion had been a mistake. Miss Cloke had one sip before grasping the cup, taking a large gulp to rinse her mouth out, and then dashing to the font to spit it out. The rest of the congregation were, he observed, a tad hesitant after that. Miss Cloke always made Thomas feel nervous — her murky past, working as a spy for British intelligence, for one thing. Thomas felt one could have no secrets with Miss Cloke scurrying around the village, and the old lady probably knew a kindly nitwit when she saw one. No, it wasn't just Miss Cloke. Something had happened during the service.

As he began his sermon, Thomas had peered over the lectern and noticed two pairs of eyes firmly fixed on him. At the back of the church, behind the Plunketts, sat a young couple, a very young couple. A slender, sharp-faced young man, with spiky hair, wearing a green coat made for someone twice his size, and a young woman, olive skinned, with dark hair and striking dark eyes. And both of them were staring intently at him and plainly listening to his every word. Thomas had hesitated for a second. He wasn't used to this. He took a sip of water then continued his sermon on 'The Miracle of Flight and the Sanctity of Life.' As he spoke, Thomas warmed to this interest in his message and became more inspired, and his voice suddenly took on an urgency and passion. 'Yes, the most humble of creatures, even a moth that lives only four days, is one of God's creations and bears that same sacredness of life that God has bestowed upon us.' Thomas had gestured passionately to a stained-glass window, and even clenched his fist, while lifting his gaze skyward. The congregation followed his gaze. Thomas paused dramatically, letting the silence hang in the air, before folding his hands together on the lectern and said softly 'Thanks be to God.'

'Vicar must have had something in his tea this morning,' grumbled Mr. Plunkett to his wife, as they shuffled down the aisle. Thomas stood by the church door, shaking hands with

52

the parishioners as they departed, and elated with his own performance. It was so good to say something that he really believed. Miss Cloke clasped his hand enthusiastically.

'Excellent sermon, Mr. Clodpole. For an idiot like you, that was extremely good. The sanctity of life. Quite right. By the way, did you manage to poison the moles in your garden?'

'Um, er, so nice to see you, Cynthia,' he said, ushering Miss Cloke out of the door before she could embarrass him further. The Patels paused by the door with their daughter, Lucinda.

'Lucinda wants to show you something, Reverend.'

Lucinda opened a matchbox. Inside it was a spider. 'Oh, how splendid,' said Thomas.

Lucinda beamed up at him, 'Should I set him free?'

'Oh, I think so,' said Thomas. 'That would be a kind thing to do.'

'Come, Lucinda,' said Mrs. Patel. 'It is time to let Percy go.'

They departed, followed by the Plunketts and an elegant, tweed-suited Count de Boodle. He doffed his green alpine hat and thrust a fifty-pound note into Thomas's hand. 'Splendid sermon, Monsieur Thomas, *le cure!* I always like to pay for fine thoughts, *monsieur. Bon mots*, indeed.'

'Er, *merci* . . . Thank you,' Thomas replied. Count Henri de Boodle's habit of speaking Franglais in a faintly Germanic accent always confused Thomas. The count had been an occasional visitor to the village but had now moved into the Old Rectory. Thomas felt uneasy about the count. He looked at the note in his hand. It was as if he had made some pact with . . . with . . . what? The count strode through the door. Thomas extended his hand in farewell, expecting to find the young couple walking behind the count. But there was no one left. Suddenly Thomas was disappointed. He had so wanted to meet them. Crestfallen, he looked around the empty little church. They must have left early. *Pity*, he thought, and closed the door.

'You were in fine form today, Reverend,' said Tizzy. Tizzy was behind the bar, smiling through his whiskers. 'You was inspired, I'd say.'

Thomas smiled modestly. 'Thank you, Tizzy. It's always nice to see new people in the church. And young people at that.'

'Oh, ah? Young'uns eh? Who be they?'

Thomas's face took on a perplexed expression. 'I don't know. I saw them during my sermon. Boy and a girl. Never seen them before.'

'Boy and a girl?' said Tizzy.

'Well, no. Teenagers, I think. Looked young. They seemed to be listening to every word. Perhaps I imagined it. I looked for them after the service, but no sign. They had gone. Must have left through the vestry. Most unusual.'

Tizzy poured a beer. 'Perhaps they was too quick for you, Thomas. We're all gettin' on.'

'I don't see how they could. Miss Cloke was manning the collection plate. She said no one had passed her. Pity. I so wanted to talk to them.'

'Young couple, eh? Boy and a girl?'

'Yes.'

'Oh. Ah.'

'Young man was tall with spiky hair. He wore a green coat that was much too big for him.'

'And the other?' Tizzy paused with a beer glass in his hand. Then he carefully placed it under the tap.

'Oh, she had dark hair.' Thomas thought for a moment. 'Remarkable eyes. Both of them had. As if they were seeing right through me.'

They probably were, thought Tizzy. Why would Pi and Navinda come to the village? Odd. And even odder that Thomas Clodpole, of all people, actually could see them.

'Did anyone else see them, Reverend?'

'No, er, I don't know. I don't think so.'

'P'raps you imagined it, Reverend?' Tizzy looked at Thomas carefully. Had he really seen Pi and Navinda? If he had, that changed everything. Thomas was clearly not the fool everyone took him to be.

'I'm sure they were real. I'm sure I . . . ' Thomas hesitated and shook his head. 'I'm sure.'

Tizzy finished pouring the beer. He concentrated, slowly pouring the last drop, until a thin head of foam lay on the surface. The thing was, Tizzy liked Thomas. You could trust him. OK, Miss Cloke and all the other villagers tried to make out that, for a vicar, he wasn't the brightest candle on the altar, but to Tizzy that didn't matter. Thomas was a kindly man.

Tizzy handed the beer to a customer. 'There you are, Nigel. Pint of Meths. Pâté and toast coming right up, and a basket of chips for Pearl?' Nigel nodded. Tizzy motioned for Thomas to come into the snug. 'Wait 'til closing, Reverend. Gideon and I will have a word with thee.'

Tizzy bustled back to the bar, leaving Thomas in the snug confused and trembling. Who were these people, and why did he so want to meet them? Why had they left the church so suddenly? He looked at an old yellowing poster on the wall. It was about a shipwreck. The shipwreck had happened two hundred years ago, and suddenly he felt that time meant nothing. It could have happened yesterday. Why did he feel like this? Thomas walked back into the bar and watched the rest of the parishioners chatting, heads nodding like hens. The Plunketts and the Patels. Count de Boodle and Miss Cloke. Yvonne Bull, Dingwell's young policewoman, stood in her blue tracksuit, chatting to Gideon, who was exuberant in orange shades and Bermuda shorts. 'You should come Hashing, Gideon.'

'I don't mind running, Yvonne. But doin' what you guys do, tear-arsing through forests, crossin' streams ain't for me. Dry — I like to be dry, not facedown in a bog. You dig?'

Yvonne laughed. 'Come with us early Tuesday. We've got our annual fancy-dress morning run through Stoggies Farm, followed by a dip in the sea at Eastcombe. Then back to the campsite for a breakfast barbecue. The old farm track is OK. You'll love it.'

'OK. Maybe I will.' He smiled. 'And, hey, you lookin' good, baby. Great tan. Been away?'

'France,' Yvonne said with a sigh. 'It was terrific. She leaned towards Gideon and whispered, 'Have the Youngs left Dingwell, Giddy?'

'They gone.' Gideon frowned and spoke quietly. 'Nobody know where. One night they just gone. Now the count live in their house. Somethin' not right, Yvonne.'

'And Peter?'

There was a shout from the kitchen.

'Gotta go, Yvonne. Catch you later?' Gideon headed back to the kitchen. Yvonne stood quietly. Peter had meant so much to her. She was his 'big sis.' She really missed him.

Hairy Nigel and Pearl Furkiss were sitting in the window seat. They never seemed to speak to each other in the pub, although Nigel routinely passed her peanuts while studying the Racing Post. Pearl Furkiss laughed like a donkey and retreated to the garden every few minutes for a smoke. Famously Thomas had been treated to a view of Pearl Furkiss's bottom when he had seen her hanging out the washing at Tidy Cottage in a fur coat and flip-flops, and there was a sudden windy gust. Funny people. Lucinda had been pestering the locals with her matchbox, and Miss Cloke had feigned horror when she had seen Percy. She was an odd cove. She had caught Thomas in the act of inspecting his mole traps while walking round his garden in green wellies and carrying a spanner. Miss Cloke had wondered what the spanner was for and watched as a molehill rose up before Thomas's eyes; Thomas promptly fell to his knees and bashed the molehill repeatedly with the spanner. Then, afraid he might actually have clobbered a mole, he poked the soil to one side before peering down the hole. The mole was long gone, but Miss Cloke wasn't. Thomas, nose covered in earth, caught sight of Miss Cloke and suddenly felt extremely silly. It was a feeling Thomas was used to. It happened all the time.

Thomas sat down in the snug. The coal fire bathed the room in red and orange and poked out little tongues of flame. The brass horseshoes and copper bed warmer glimmered, and as he gazed into the depths of the fire, he supped his ale and felt warm inside. Ah, well. What mysteries life held for him!

'That was brilliant, Reverend.' Thomas looked up and found himself staring into the blue eyes of WPC Yvonne Bull. 'I always enjoy your sermons,' she continued, while Thomas began to feel somewhat overwhelmed. 'So good to think about life. Was that fifty pounds the count gave you?'

'Yes, it was. Most generous. It will go to the church restoration fund of course,' said Thomas hurriedly.

Yvonne leaned against the doorway of the snug. She gazed fondly at Thomas. 'But you don't feel entirely happy about it, do you?' She smiled.

'No. I don't. And I don't know why,' he confessed.

'There's something I need to talk to you about.' Yvonne looked about nervously. 'A private matter.'

'Of course,' said Thomas. 'But not here. Miss Cloke will — '

'I'm going to The Fossils tomorrow. I promised to visit Mrs. Smallpiece — known to Pearl as Miss Bonkers. She was also my old piano teacher. Perhaps after that.'

'Why call her Miss Bonkers?' said Thomas.

'Oh, you know. Feisty lady. A bit mad but mind as sharp as a tack. Had a stroke a few weeks back, so she can't speak. But she can write. She can really write.'

'Bet she keeps them on their toes.'

'Oh, yes. And a bit wicked too. Once, she even pretended to be dead. Frightened the wits out of her son. When the paramedic arrived, she gave him a very naughty wink. Great teacher, though.'

'I must meet her,' said Thomas.

'She'll be suspicious of you. And what has happened to Peter?'

'Peter?'

'Peter Young. And his parents. There is someone else living in their house.'

Thomas looked flummoxed. 'Oh, was he the lad I saw getting off the bus?'

'Probably. Bell ringing Monday. Don't forget.'

Before he could reply, she was gone. If Thomas were a younger man, he could have loved Yvonne. To see her jogging through the village in her blue tracksuit, blonde hair bobbing, lifted his spirits. It wasn't just that she was attractive, it was . . . it was . . . as he so often did, he reached for the right words but could not find them.

Tizzy and Gideon joined him, and the threesome sat in front of the fire. Tizzy looked at Gideon. He nodded. 'Tell him, man,' said Gideon. 'Tell him. It's OK.'

Tizzy scratched his whiskers. 'Reverend, it's like this. Them young'uns you saw in the church . . . '

Thomas looked away from the fire, beaming. 'Yes?'

'You wasn't imaginin' nothin'. They woz there.'

'Who woz — er, were?'

'Pi. Pi and Navinda.'

'Pie? Did you say, 'Pie'?'

'His name is Peter. Peter Young. Pi. See? Well, he changed it to Pi,' said Tizzy.

'So his name is Pi, short for Peter?' said Thomas, baffled.

'Yep. And Navinda.'

'Navinda? What is that short for?' said Thomas.

61

'Nothing. Navinda is Navinda. It's her name.'

'That's a relief. So she is just called Navinda?'

'She has a family name. I dunno what it is. Do you, Giddy?'

Gideon shook his head. 'No, man. Hey, what other name do she need? Bright lady. She shinin', man. An' Pi. Cool, cool.'

Thomas looked flummoxed. 'Why did they disappear?'

'Dunno, man. I do not know. But if they came to your church, there was a reason. A good reason.'

'Look, Thomas. It's Sunday afternoon. And we need to take a walk,' said Gideon.

'We take a walk to a special place,' said Tizzy

'I see,' said Thomas, now completely baffled.

'We want you to come with us,' said Gideon.

'It's important. It's important you know,' said Tizzy.

Tigger had appeared in the doorway. He had finished his lunch of leftover pâté de foie gras. He blinked at Tizzy and eyed Thomas.

'It's OK, Tigger. The reverend will be coming with us,' said Tizzy. Tigger turned and padded through the kitchen to the back door. He waited while Tizzy and Gideon put on their rucksacks. 'Reverend, take this. Lightens the load.' Thomas looped a canvas bag full of bread over his shoulder.

'Ready?' Thomas and Gideon nodded. 'Reverend, what you are about to see is not a secret. It's just that if you tell it to someone, they won't believe you.' Tizzy opened the back door of the Whodhavethoughtit, and Tigger led the way through the pub orchard to a battered wooden gate.

8

The Dream Factory

As Thomas followed Tigger through the gate, he felt something inside him change. The Thomas Clodpole he knew, whose clothes he wore, had dropped from him like a discarded skin. He did not feel he was being brave. He just had to know why his life suddenly was changing, and yes, he wanted to know something that the other villagers — particularly Miss Cloke — clearly did not know. That would certainly make a change. There was a deeper meaning to life he always had known about instinctively — that the reality of everyday life had almost destroyed. He, Thomas, would come to know.

Tigger padded down Smugglers' Path, between the lines of windblown, misshapen trees. Bushes and shrubs projected leaves and saplings like tongues, eager voices to be heard. The branches shuddered and shook, making a strange shifting music, and the hedgerows suddenly bristled with life: slow-worms and rabbits and weasels fiercely active and their rustling adding to the strange rhythmic music of the woodland. Harriet curved overhead. Thomas heard the airborne hiss and 'shhhhhhh' of her flight curve. This was not a world of garden gnomes and genial villagers and sermons and parish councils, but a trembling, urgent refrain of the undergrowth and elements.

Tizzy and Giddy cheerfully yomped on behind Thomas. 'Hey, man, you see Miss Furkiss? Fur coat, man. Why she always wear dat?'

'I'm just relieved she does, Gideon,' Tizzy said with a sigh. Thomas agreed.

Gideon laughed. 'The village have some wacky people'

'That it does, eh, Reverend?' said Tizzy.

Thomas felt comforted and nodded. 'And call me Thomas — no, Tom. No one's called me Tom since I was at school. Call me Tom.'

'Can't do that,' said Tizzy. 'You're *Reverend*. That's who you are.'

'In the village I suppose I am. But it's not *who* I am.' He paused and thought. 'Not here anyway.'

'OK. Giddy, call the Reverend 'Tom' from now on.'

'Reverend Tom. No problem.' said Gideon.

Thomas smiled. 'Just Tom,' he said.

'Tom it is. No problem, Reverend — er, Tom.'

This part of Doctors' Wood was new to Thomas. He had wandered through the wood many times but never seen the old Smugglers' Lane hidden beneath this tunnel of wild and twisted trees. Ahead Thomas saw the shafts of twilight sun breaking the canopy, and the path swung right and down a slope past the roots of high oaks, and they were in the twilight calm of Yarmer Valley. The tiny Yarmer Stream cut and snaked through the woodland and pasture. They paused on a granite bridge. 'Let's have a breather here, Reverend.' Tizzy put down his rucksack and breathed deeply. 'Not as young as I was.'

'How old are you?' said Thomas.

'Truly, Reverend, I don't know. Not something I've ever worried about. You OK, Giddy?'

'Am I OK? Hey, I'm muscle. I'm fit, man. You wanna run the rest of the way?'

'No, thanks,' said Thomas, suddenly alarmed. He walked on ahead with Gideon. 'What brought you to Dingwell, Gideon?'

'Good question, Reverend Tom. I know *how* I got here but still thinking about *what* brought me here.'

'Go on,' said Thomas.

'Well, I was doing my student thing, you know. Not much for a Bajan boy to do 'cept wait tables and stuff, and smile a big smile at the customers, and cadge tips, give tourists a ride on a cat. Told my old man I'd had enough of that.'

'And?'

'Got my scholarship to the uni in St. Augustine. But I wanted to see the world. So I travelled all over — Oz, Thailand, India — waiting tables and cooking all the way. Happiest time when I was walking along a track in Lesotho. Been teaching kids to canoe and swim in the big lake. Kids was afraid of the water snake — they said it would come up from the dark and snatch them down into the depths to die. They said the silver trail on the lake was the sign of the snake. I said, 'That's the moon, shining on the lake, kids.' They shook their heads and backed away from the bank. I said, 'I'll show you.' I dived in the water, and I heard them all scream as I entered the water. I came up, and shouted, 'There ain't no snake. Come and join me.' Then they all looked at each other, daring each other to jump in. 'Come on,' I said. 'Come in.' Then they all grabbed a little girl and pushed her in. She screamed and stood up. I swam over to her and picked her up and held her. We ducked under the water together. She just laughed. Then I chucked her up the air, and she fell in . . . splash. She come up, laughing. Then she put her hand on my head, and I let her push me under. Suddenly all the kids were in the water, jumping and splashing and swimming and laughing. Then all their mums and dads came to collect them. I remember them all staring and pointing at their kids, having a great time. We played so long that it was getting dark before we came out.'

'Amazing,' said Thomas.

'Kids all went home, and I stood there under the stars. Then I realised I had no money. All my dollars had washed out of my pocket. I was wet and soaking and had nothing but my skin and the clothes I was wearing. Best moment in my life. I knew who I was.'

Thomas felt a pang of personal regret. Why had he not done that? He hadn't travelled the world, taken a risk, lived on his wits. He felt a deep admiration for Gideon. 'Why Dingwell?'

'I was gonna go back home but just had to do the coast path here. Could have been any-where. Got off the bus in Dingwell and walked into the Whodhavethoughtit and asked for work.'

They stepped over a wooden stile and looked back along the path. Tizzy lagged behind and was puffing beneath his canvas rucksack. Perspiration beads dribbled down his forehead.

'Don't you want to go back to university?'

Gideon glanced back at Tizzy before turning to Thomas, the sunlight conjuring tones of deep copper and umber from his face. 'Feel I am at university. It's just a different kind. When you find wisdom, you tend to want to stick around.'

'I see,' said Thomas. 'Tizzy just seems timeless.'

'You know, he don't need much sleep. Every night he's at his desk. Writing.'

'What does he write?'

'Says it's his diary. His 'little gift' to the world.'

'Thought you boys was going to run all the way,' shouted Tizzy, as he finally caught up. 'Seems you got a bit puffed. Slow and steady is best.' He winked at Gideon.

Gideon grinned. 'The tortoise and the hare.'

Thomas looked along the valley. 'Where next, Tizzy?'

'Oh, just follow Tigger, but if you needs to know, follow the track to Yarmer Beach. Then we climbs up and over to Eastcombe. You'll see it there.'

'See what? The only thing there is an old stone shed.'

Tizzy looked at Thomas. 'Reverend — er, Tom. Depends what eyes you're looking with.

69

Don't it? Thought p'raps you'd already realised that. Lead on, Tigger, you lazy old mog. Show us the way.' Tigger rose from his comfortable seat on a stone pillar and stretched before descending to the track once again.

Thomas gazed at Yarmer Valley, which was bathed in light from the setting sun. He had seen it before, but now it was different, its colours deeper, stronger, and teeming wildlife suddenly visible as he paced along behind Tigger. An adder flicked across the path, its markings vivid. 'See that, Tom?' Tizzy said. 'Not normal this time o' the year.'

'No, indeed not,' said Thomas, his eyes drawn by a dog fox breaking cover beneath the bracken. Tigger had increased his pace, but Thomas strode forward vigorously. He was enjoying this journey, feeling his senses switched on and alert. He felt awake, truly awake, as if for the first time in years. They clambered over a stile and stood on the soft sands above Yarmer Beach. Burgh Island lay becalmed in the glassy shifting sea, and the Eddystone Lighthouse flashed on the horizon.

Tigger had begun the climb up the cliff path to a bluff of grasses and blasted trees. At the top Thomas could look down the whole coastline of grey and silver cliffs, and Harriet was displaying her superlative flying skills, swooping across the valley and diving, spinning towards the earth then upward on the soft winds. Thomas was like a child again, wishing he could fly to dizzying heights and perform amazing stunts without a trace of fear. Harriet climaxed her performance by swooping low over Thomas's head and abruptly landing on a fencepost as Thomas walked past. She blinked at him. He blinked back and smiled in awe. Harriet accepted the compliment and jetted off across the valley to look for food; all this exhibition stuff was making her hungry. The path down to Eastcombe Beach was steep and zigzagged. Thomas heard Tizzy puffing behind and Gideon saying, 'C'mon old man.'

'Less of the 'old'!' said Tizzy. They had to help each other down the last step before reaching the stream that bound out from the valley.

Thomas looked at the beach. 'Where now?'

'Just back along,' Gideon said.

Thomas turned and looked. He held his breath. The ruined stone shed was now whole and strongly built, and a storm lantern cast a warm glow on the driftwood doorway. Smoke from the chimney told of a joyous log fire, and a young man was hurling a ball up the grassy slope for some dogs to chase.

9

Le Manoir

Thomas's journey to the Dream Factory had not gone unnoticed. Count Henri de Boodle was sitting in a Lloyd Loom chair on the balcony of *Le Manoir,* the old Dingwell rectory. The son of a German army officer and Constance, a French aristocratic mother, great-granddaughter of Prince Raymond of Toulouse, the count had royal blood surging in his veins. Constance's love for 'liberty, equality, fraternity' was outgunned by his stern father's darker ethics of 'work, family, fatherland.' He slowly extended the lens of his Wetzlar pocket telescope to its fullest extent.

'Ah. Interesting, Miss Cloke. Just as you said.'

Miss Cloke put down her teacup and plucked her binoculars from a wicker basket.

'Have I ever given you false information, Count Henri?'

'No, my dear Cynthia. You have not.' The count smiled affectionately. 'It seems so strange after all these years that we are on the same side.'

Miss Cloke focussed her binoculars. 'Perhaps we always were, Henri. We just did not know it.'

'So many years wasted. Ach! *Quel dommage!*'

'Sunday at fifteen thirty hours, precisely. They go to that ruined hut in Eastcombe.'

The count shrugged. 'But why? No one lives there.'

'They take food. And that blasted cat leads the way.'

'Tigger? That pub cat. *Ce vieux chat effroyable.*'

'The very same.' Miss Cloke put down her binoculars and contemplated a date-and-pecan meringue. She was wearing a floral Ralph Lauren dress the count had given her.

'You look adorable in that dress, Miss Cloke.'

'Thank you, count. Most kind. This is a very fine house. A good choice. Most appropriate. The Young family residence, *n'est-ce pas?*'

'Indeed, yes, Madame.' He lowered his telescope. 'The troublesome Young family . . . '

'Captain and Mrs. Young and their son.'

'They were both captains in the service, Miss Cloke. He was — is . . . no, probably *was* — a gifted engineer and designer. But the mother had the real gift. An intelligence more than mere intelligence.' Miss Cloke noted the jealous contempt when he said the word *mother*. But Miss Cloke was not a leader; she was a provider of information to those who led. After all this time, it was in her DNA.

'They are both dead?' Miss Cloke put her hand to her mouth as if shocked.

'The Organisation has them, I believe. I have not met them, but my superiors assure me they are no longer a risk.'

'But their son . . . ?' Miss Cloke gave a small smile.

'Ah, yes, their son. We would like to meet him. Very much.' He shifted his gaze to his black Doberman pinscher, Odessa. The dog yawned and stretched on the terrace in the evening sun.

'Young Peter has flown the coop, disappeared from school. It is not just what he knows but what he *is*, Miss Cloke. Though, God knows, if he knows a tenth of what his parents knew, it would be dangerous enough.'

Miss Cloke studied the count's features: the track lines of age crisscrossing the jutting jaw of a once handsome warrior, his glittering eye that of a master spy, the neatly combed and parted hair that of a gigolo — a ladies' man of another age. A man who could never quietly retire, as she could not.

'Living in their home,' he said, 'I feel, as you say, as if I am a cuckoo in their nest. I find it deeply satisfying. When I touch a chair or a cup, I feel I am replacing their scent with mine. Every time I open a window or close a door, I am victorious.' He nodded slowly and smiled. 'But the son, Peter. We do not have the son. We must have him to feel secure.'

Miss Cloke delicately sipped the remainder of her tea and slowly placed the Limoges bone-china cup on the gleaming saucer. She crossed her hands in her lap and leant towards the count. 'He is here,' she whispered.

'Here? In this godforsaken village?' The count had shifted his gaze to her and was concentrating hard.

'At least I think he may be here.' She spoke slowly, enjoying the tension.

'Maybe here? Maybe? Take me to this 'maybe.'' The count slid his hand into his pocket in search of his Luger. 'How do you know, Miss Cloke? Tell me.'

'That idiot of a vicar told me about a young man and a girl who were in the church service Sunday morning. Slim, large jacket, spiky hair . . . just like the boy.'

'Could have been anyone.'

'Not in this village.' Miss Cloke leant forward again. 'Here?' She smiled. 'They are all older than a hundred!'

'Find him anyway, and I will kill him, whoever he is.' The count stared about wildly. 'Where is he? He could be here in this house.'

Odessa raised his head at the urgency of his master's voice.

'How could he be here?' reasoned Miss Cloke. 'We would see him — unless he is hiding of course. But he would leave a trail. Don't you agree?'

'And with a girl? Who is this girl?' The count resorted to a brandy and breathed deeply, eyes fixed on the setting sun. 'I do not like there being a girl with him.' He glanced at Miss Cloke, who noted a sense of fear in his lined face. He looked suddenly old and weary. 'There are things you do not know, Cynthia . . . about the Youngs . . . what they were doing.'

'Tell me, Henri,' she whispered gently. 'Your secret will be safe. Don't you trust me?'

The count rose from his chair. 'Esther Young was a scientist who believed in God. Can you think of such a thing? Preposterous.'

'Quite possible, Henri. But do go on.'

'She and her husband did not just design artificial intelligence. They went further. They created it. They created a mind that could speak and think and feel and support itself. A mind that did not think it was a human but thought *like* a human. A mind that could live from the air around it. They went beyond creating a robot — a robot is simply a higher form of imbecile anyway. No, just give this mind — like a crystal — a home in any device, and it would learn quickly how to use it to communicate. And it would alter the device to enable it to do other things.'

'Dear God,' gasped Miss Cloke, unwittingly speaking for the Almighty.

'It can garner energy from its surroundings, never needing any source of power.' He turned and looked intently into Miss Cloke's eyes. 'The implications, Miss Cloke, the implications.'

'But you have the parents, so you must have the secret.'

'Miss Cloke, they have lost their minds. They stare. We do not know if they are alive or dead.'

Miss Cloke tutted.

The count continued, 'There were other things . . . other strange ideas that we heard about.'

'Indeed?' Miss Cloke said, already amazed.

'Yes, probably stupid things, but well, there was a rumour they had found a way of leaving the body and being somewhere else.'

'Like death.'

'Well, yes, in a way. I don't understand these things. I do not understand or know enough. However much I find out, I seem to know less.' His voice trailed off, and he sank into his chair. 'A girl involved. *Nom d'un chien!* If the little bitch has made him feel . . . complete . . . ' His voice faltered. 'I am tired, Miss Cloke. My old bones ache.'

Miss Cloke placed a soft kiss on his forehead and bade farewell. She paced down the darkening lane in her little white shoes and pottered back to the comfort of Enigma Cottage and Pandora. Come to think of it, Pandora had been behaving strangely, hiding in wardrobes and the like. More mystery. Evidence was Miss Cloke's mission in life. And she needed more.

10

Just the Car for a Killer

Thomas was walking back through Yarmer Valley with Gideon and Tizzy in the moonlight. He heard them chatting and laughing, but he had no need to speak. He walked as in a dream. Perhaps he was dreaming and would wake up to the cold reality of his life and work — he prayed that he was not dreaming.

When they had arrived at the Dream Factory, Pi was running the dogs, Jack and Jill, in the back garden, a garden strewn with a joyful mix of wildflowers and vegetables. Tigger would have you believe it was his creation. In a way it was. Tigger always could get things done without any effort himself. He would tap the ground with his paw and sniff, and Jack and Jill immediately would rush to the spot and start digging, showering earth in all directions. Eventually, with this brilliantly simple solution, the entire garden had been dug over, and Pi shooed the dogs down to the beach for a much-needed wash. Meanwhile Navinda produced several packets of flower and vegetable seeds and had given them to Doris and Barnie, who, naturally, opened them all and ran laughing round the garden scattering the seeds randomly. Result? Nasturtiums bloomed by spring onions, and marigolds among artichokes, and busy Lizzies with Webb's Wonderfuls.

And so it was that Thomas had broken bread by the log fire with Pi and Navinda, eating feta, mysterious pickles, tomatoes, and tangerines, and sipping Pi's homemade ale.

' 'Tis a good brew, Pi,' said Tizzy, and raised his glass as if to toast the occasion. Pi and Navinda raised their glasses too.

'Dad's recipe,' said Pi.

'How long will you be staying?'

'We don't know,' said Navinda. 'Do we?' She turned to Pi, who smiled.

'There was nowhere else to go that felt right when Mum and Dad were taken. I dreamt that Navinda would come here too. And she did.'

Thomas wanted to ask 'How?' but something stopped him. The normal rules of reality were clearly on hold.

'And Doris?' said Gideon.

'No, Doris just fell out of the sky one day,' said Pi. He looked across to the little bed beneath the window. Doris was asleep with her thumb in her mouth and Buddy nestled under her arm. 'I don't know how long she will be here. She ought to go back really soon. I hope so.'

'Where did the pup come from?' said Tizzy.

'He just turned up the other day. Tigger brought him here.'

'Oh, ah,' said Tizzy. 'Apparently Miss Cloke saw a strange car down Yarmer Lane. Battered old car it were. Man gets out and puts a pup under a bush. Drives off in a hurry. Yvonne was asking if I'd seen the car.'

'Doris just adores Buddy,' said Pi. 'There was a label round his neck with his name on it.'

Thomas looked at Navinda. Her dark eyes focussed on him. 'Where were you before . . . before . . . being here, erm . . . ' He stopped. Navinda smiled.

'I was standing in my school uniform in a queue, waiting to receive a prize.' She paused. 'My mother, Alena, and my three brothers were sitting in the front row. Saeed, my father, was away in London. He could not make the prize giving.' Navinda frowned at the memory.

A stream of questions went through Thomas's mind.

'You want to know what happened, don't you?' Navinda continued. 'Suddenly it was all too much. I closed my eyes and went outside

81

myself and came here.'

'Went outside of . . . ' stuttered Thomas.

'Yes. Have you never done that?' Navinda stared intently at him.

'Erm, well, yes, er, I . . . maybe . . . erm . . . in a way,' he spluttered. Thomas suddenly realised that all eyes in the room were fixed on him, including Tigger's. 'No,' he said more decisively. 'But . . . I have wanted to.'

'I had met Pi before. We were on different teams at a mock trial competition in London. He spoke to me . . . ' She paused, then spoke slowly, looking at Pi. ' . . . eventually. In the cafeteria during the break. He told me about the Dream Factory. I told him he was mad, although I had dreamt of it before.' She laughed and turned to Pi, who smiled shyly.

'Will you go back?' said Thomas.

'Possibly,' said Navinda. 'Possibly. Right now I am happy here. With our funny little family. Barnie is missing his mum. I am sure he will go back very soon. He still has not spoken a word. But I worry about Doris. She needs to forgive — something I cannot do easily.'

'Do you never hear from your parents, Pi?'

Pi looked at Navinda.

'It's all right, Pi. Thomas is someone you can trust,' said Tizzy.

'Yes. I get messages through Om.' He

pointed to an elliptical blue disc on the wall. 'When I read the message, I can hear their voices.'

'Did you know that your parents would leave?' asked Thomas.

'They had prepared me. I knew they might have to leave. They were taken one night.' He shivered at the memory. 'I heard Mum shout. They wanted to take me as well. I knew what to do and ran. The next day I came home from school and got off the bus. I remember walking along the lane. There was a strange car in the drive. I tried my door key, but it did not work. A dog started barking.' Pi's voice trembled. Navinda touched his hand.

'What did you do?' said Thomas.

Pi breathed deeply. 'I came here. I knew that was what I should do. Om had a message from them telling me to stay here, and if I needed anything, I should ask Tizzy and Giddy.'

'Did you phone the police?' said Thomas.

'Cops ain't interested, man. Think he's playing a game. It ain't no game,' said Gideon.

'You need to stay here,' said Tizzy. 'Wouldn't go to the village if I were thee. That Miss Cloke, always pokin' her nose. And the count living in your house. They're as thick as thieves.'

'Pearl Furkiss says they're sweet on each other,' Gideon said with a laugh. 'Imagine that.'

'Trouble is, I can imagine it,' said Tizzy. And I doozn't like it!'

'Miss Cloke did not see you at the church, though,' Thomas said to Pi and Navinda. 'I asked her.'

'You asked her?' Tizzy sounded alarmed.

'Yes, I asked if she had seen the two young people at . . . ' Thomas trailed off into silence. Tizzy was stroking his whiskers. He looked a worried man. 'I mean I did not know . . . '

'No, you wasn't to know, Reverend Thomas. Still, 'tis a worry. Best you young'uns stays here then. If you needs anythin', just send Tigger with a note. And Thomas, you 'as one of they computer thingies?'

Thomas nodded. 'Erm, yes.'

'Careful how you uses it. Don't use Bogle. 'Tis important,' said Tizzy.

'Right. OK,' said Thomas.

'Do you use Bogle?' Tizzy looked at him intensely.

'Yes, I do,' said Thomas.

'Have you written anything on your computer about us?' Navinda asked, looking at Thomas.

'I keep a diary,' said Thomas, now deeply worried.

'Don't write anything about us if you use Bogle,' said Navinda.

'Use Sunrise,' said Pi.

'And Splutter,' said Navinda. 'Good for messages.' She smiled. 'I will send you a Splot, Thomas.'

Thomas stopped and looked back to the sea. Shafts of moonlight speared through the clouds onto the restless, shimmering waters. Thomas thought of the eternal sea, the sea that cleansed the earth and cleared the mind, the sea of peace, the sea of tranquillity. For a moment he felt a mad impulse to go running fully clothed into the silver waves — and then he thought better of it. (He couldn't swim.) Ah, well.

Presently he was back in the vicarage, gazing out at the starlight through his study window. What was it Pi had said?

'Who took your parents?'

'The Organisation.'

'Who are they?'

'A sort of brotherhood.'

Thomas did not know how to get rid of Bogle. He would buy a new computer; that would be the answer. He stared at the computer — it suddenly had become an enemy to him. Who were these people, and was Miss Cloke one of them? It was certainly true that the Youngs had lived in the Old Rectory, before Thomas had come to Dingwell.

Thomas's gaze moved to the photograph of his wife. Where was Olivia now? She had left him when teaching had changed him. Thomas had come home from school, having had a terrible day. A shaven-headed boy had yelled, 'Sod off, nob 'ead!' And there was a note from Olivia. It was the last time Thomas had cried. He recalled kneeling on all fours, sobbing uncontrollably. He had lurched out of his backdoor to find the lady next door staring at him over the fence. She knew all along. Her children would know. It would be all round the school. It was the end.

From teaching, Thomas had fled into the clergy to heal his wounds and seek out the lost fire of his youth. Now he had begun to find it. He thought about who he was now, changed beyond all measure from the heartbroken man and hesitant, podgy, nervous clergyman. He said his prayers, as he always did — prayers for others, not for himself. Tomorrow he would go into All Souls Church on his own to think. Thomas did not know how dramatically life in Dingwell would change.

★　★　★

Nor did Miss Cloke. She had fed Pandora and was sitting on her sofa with a cup of Horlicks. Tomorrow she would visit that old shed by the stream in Eastcombe and find out what was really going on. It would be an excellent test of her field craft!

★ ★ ★

'Good poem,' said Om.

Navinda and Doris were asleep, but Pi was restless and had left his bed to sit at his desk and write. Tigger yawned and stretched by the fire.

'Thank you,' said Pi. 'It was meant to be private.'

'Navinda liked it too.'

Pi stood up. 'You showed it to her!'

'Of course. It was meant for her, wasn't it?' said Om.

'Yes, but ... oh ... I can't believe you showed it to her,' he hissed, shaking his head in disbelief. 'When did you show her?'

'When you were out with Doris and the dogs.'

'What did she say?' said Pi, trembling.

'She said nothing,' said Om.

'Nothing?'

'Not a word. She just smiled. She had written one about you.'

'About me? Show me. Show me!'

'No,' said Om. 'It's private.'

'Private? Why wasn't mine private?' Pi paced the room. 'You wretched machine!'

'Machine? What an insult.'

'Can't believe you did that. What did she say? Tell me. Tell me!'

'Sorry. Can't do that,' said Om, enjoying the moment.

Pi frowned. 'Did she say . . . good things . . . about me?' Pi had stopped pacing and looked pleadingly at Om.

'Navinda is someone you most certainly do not need to worry about.' Suddenly Om reminded Pi of his father. 'I am here to look after you. Your parents made me. Remember that.'

'Has there been another message from them?'

'Yes.'

Pi's heart missed a beat.

'Do you want to hear it now?'

Pi breathed deeply. 'Yes . . . now, please.'

'I want to hear it too.' Navinda had appeared at the door. 'Can I?'

Pi nodded. He was beginning to understand what Navinda meant to him. She sat with him by the fire. Colours in the room changed as Om turned a deep and brilliant blue. Then Pi heard and felt the voice, the touch of his mother.

★ ★ ★

Far, far away, Detective Sergeant Sarah Raine closed the green manila folder. It was marked, 'The Organisation.' Sarah preferred paper files. There was too much loose information flying around in Special Branch as it was. She liked things all in one place. 'Someone is protecting them, Charlie.'

The young sergeant shifted in his chair. 'Why not use the computers?' Charlie's dark eyes and mop of black hair enquired.

'Because every time we do, another door closes. No, Charlie. This is one for good old pencil and paper, and a good nose.' Sarah tapped her own nose. Her raven hair and hazel-green eyes gave the impression that she could see right through people, read their minds. This made her slightly unsettling company for younger officers, who had nicknamed her 'Tarot.' Sarah had felt flattered by the moniker when Charlie had told her about it. 'It was my suggestion,' Charlie confessed.

'Better than being called, 'That black bitch,'' Sarah had retorted, and smiled. 'What were the other suggestions?'

'Scout, Wicca, Phantom, Gypsy, Tais.'

'Tais?' Sarah's eyes enquired.

'Gaelic word for ghost.'

'No one sees where I'm coming from, eh Charlie?'

'I liked Tais as well. But Tarot is good. The

team reckon you can read the runes.' Charlie smiled.

'Great gran was Irish,' said Sarah, surveying the white walls of her new office. 'Married a US army captain.'

Charlie really liked DS Raine. As a senior officer, she was smart, really smart. A real 'mentalist,' which frightened the life out of other senior officers. All of which meant she would only ever work with a small team. Others always wanted to know what 'Tarot' Raine was thinking but rarely had the courage to ask her outright. Techies and nerds also derided her distaste for technology. In truth Sarah disliked what technology did to people, but as a tool for her job, she used it like anyone else. Now she stood, tall, dark, and slimly silhouetted against the window. Outside, the new recruits at Bluford Camp tramped the parade ground, and gulls whirled in random arcs and loops.

'What do we have?' said Charlie.

'Cars, Charlie. Your favourite subject.'

Charlie nodded. 'I like cars,' he agreed. 'Real cars.'

'We are talking real cars, Charlie. Not the antique rust buckets from which you derive some weird pleasure while rebuilding.'

'Those are real cars, ma'am.'

Sarah grinned. 'No. Real cars are shiny and

have an engine that goes when you turn a key. And don't call me 'ma'am.''

'What should I call you, m . . . Detective Sergeant?'

'Call me what you call me when I'm not in the room.'

'I call you 'Tarot.''

'DS Raine or Tarot. Take your pick.'

'DS Tarot it is. Anyway, what cars?'

Sarah flicked open the file. 'A Daimler double-six V12. Last seen at Oxeter Services. Owned by one theatrically named French count.'

'French? Sounded German when he answered the phone. Still, nice wagon,' Charlie said with a nod.

'Wagon! Show some respect for a divinely smooth machine, you ruffian.'

'Yes, DS Raine. And?'

'Better still, Sergeant. Something to awaken the tiger in you . . . '

'Can't wait.'

'A Mercedes E-Class coupe!'

'Tin can with knobs on!' said Charlie.

'With a five-point-five litre bi-turbo V8 engine? Come on, Charlie. Class.'

'OK, OK. Obviously people with taste,' concurred Charlie.

'Owner, one Mr. Rosencrantz. Probably a fictitious name.'

'Shakespeare,' said Charlie. Sarah looked at

him quizzically. 'Rosencrantz was a flunky hired to find out what was afflicting Hamlet. In other words, a spy. We need to talk to him?'

'We do.'

'Just the car for a killer.'

'Did you finish reading *The Periodic Table?*' said Sarah.

'I always do my homework, DS Raine.'

'Primo Levi. Did you read the story that's a surreal conversation between him and the commander of the extermination camp?'

' "Vanadium." ' Charlie nodded. 'It left me wondering if it was just a story — just invention.'

'Or did he just walk through the wardrobe and appear in the ex-commandant's office?' Sarah returned to her desk and rested her chin on her hands. 'Esther and John Young are scientists working in the service. Or were.'

'Were?' Charlie had opened the manila folder. 'Are they dead?'

Sarah sighed. This young sergeant was a clever boy but he had plenty to learn. 'You won't find this stuff in the file, Charlie.'

Charlie closed the file. He blinked and folded his hands on his lap.

'We don't know if they're dead, but we suspect not. They created a device code-named 'Om' — an intel unit that makes your e-phone look about as clever as that bloody Ford Capri you've been rebuilding.'

Charlie smiled. 'OK. But in its time . . . '

'Yes. OK, Charlie. I get it. In its time. But this is now.' She rose from her black leather chair and sat on the edge of the grey desk. She looked down intently at the young sergeant. 'But they went further. Something that could be planted inside the human body and could interact with the senses.'

'Holy smoke!' Charlie whistled. 'Amazing.'

'Precisely, Charlie. Vary apt . . . incidentally. Don't write any of this down, Charlie.'

'Why bother to write it down?' he smiled. 'Who would believe it? So why has Count Henri de Boodle suddenly decided to move into an obscure English village and become a member of the squirarchy?'

'Dingwell was the Youngs' home, Charlie.' She spoke quietly. 'These are nasty people. Really, really nasty. They want Peter Young. Someone is going to be hurt. Very badly.'

11

Death of a Hawk Moth

At *Le Manoir,* Count de Boodle ushered Odessa out through the back door onto the moonlit lawn. He shivered. The silent trees unnerved him, and the moonlight cast long stark shadows of strange and threatening figures across the back of the house — giant bony hands, limbs, spears, and headless creatures. These ghostly images recalled his broken marriages, children he never saw, grandchildren for all he knew. Relics from a strange, disordered world that he could not control. At night he saw their faces, heard their voices and laughter. It was the only time he felt fear. Fear was normally his friend. He could control events by fear. But this fear was of the unknown, the future beyond his control. He figured that if he kept moving, this fear would never find him.

He would not remain here for long, he decided, and longed for the plainer angles and lines of city life with its corridors of power, secret meetings, and closed societies and clubs. That was his world. Airports and first-class carriages and taxis. He glanced at his Daimler parked in the drive like a noble ship docked at the quayside. He would wait for Miss Cloke to report back on her mission to Eastcombe. He wanted the boy. Dead. Then he would be gone from this forsaken, unnerving place.

'Odessa! Oder!' he shouted. The great dog bounded in through the back door and into the scullery with its high windows that overlooked the garden.

The count could not bring himself to sleep in the Youngs' romantic bedroom, however. He felt their presence in the room and, for the same reason, rarely ventured into their study just down the hall. Instead he built up the fire in the scullery and settled down on a large sofa, covering himself with a blanket and quilt. He adjusted the cushions beneath his head and made sure his Luger was within reach. As he and Odessa dozed and twitched in slumber, the drama of the night was beginning. At that moment Pi was closing the latch at the Dream Factory and stepping into the night. Tigger was with him.

Tigger led the way in the moonlight over the hill from Eastcombe and down into Yarmer Valley. It was a path they had walked many times, then up through Smugglers' Lane to the pub. But this time their route would change. Tigger slipped through a wooden gate onto an overgrown track that led to the ruined mill. Pi had to climb over the gate, the barbed wire snagging his jacket. The moon illuminated their path. Cows stood as silent witnesses — motionless, expressionless pieces of scenery in an impending drama.

As they neared the mill, the sound of the rushing Yarmer Stream grew louder. Pi and Tigger knew every inch of the ground. Pi had played hide-and-seek and sardines in the mill many times with Mum and Dad. Then they would say, 'Time for tea, Peter' and grasp his hand, or Dad would pick him up and put him on his strong shoulders. Now, as he knelt, his hands felt the old stone wall, and he heard his mother's voice. 'The loose stone at the end, Peter. You will find the key.' Pi's fingers located the loose cob and grasped the key, and he slipped it into his pocket. For Pi this was no game. He knew what he had to do.

A steep and stony footpath draped like a rosary round the mill before leading upward, towards the houses on Dingwell Lane, whose facades shone a ghostly white. A few lights still shone from The Fossils old people's home, but the Plunketts' house was blank and silent, and next to it was the Old Rectory — or *Le Manoir* as the count had renamed it. As the count and Odessa slept, Pi and Tigger slid like phantoms to the edge of the garden. Pi's hands felt for the spikes he had hammered into the trunk of the oak tree behind his garden wall. He climbed up and clambered along the branch across the wall before dropping onto the old compost heap. Odessa heard the faint sound of the impact, and his eyes startled open.

Tigger, as usual, had an easier task. He simply walked through a dry culvert at the bottom of the wall and stood patiently, waiting on the lawn for Pi to join him. Pi surveyed his former home; for a moment feelings of anger shot to the surface of his being, but he quickly subdued them. He would not be diverted from his purpose. There were no lights on, but he could see the glow of flames from the fire in the scullery. Good. That meant the count would be in there.

If the count had been looking out of the window, he may have seen the shadow of a young man skirting the perimeter of the lawn before disappearing round the side of house. As it was, the count slept a dreamless sleep. But Odessa's eyes were open, and his ears pricked. As Pi slid the key into the lock of the cellar door, Tigger took centre stage with devastating results.

Tigger has some unpleasant habits. He

specialises in catching and eating moths. It is horrible to watch. The hapless creatures are attracted by light, and they remain transfixed and helpless on the windowpane. Then Tigger appears, reaching up on his hind legs and spreading out his front paws on either side of the creature. And he just gobbles it up. If you're watching from inside, you see the poor thing fluttering his last before he disappears down Tigger's throat.

There were several moths on the scullery windows, attracted by the light of the blazing fire. From inside the room, Tigger's silhouette in the moonlight was made more vivid by the leaping red and orange flames that created a demonic vision akin to a messenger from the devil himself. Odessa already had emitted a low growl as Pi had entered the cellar and headed for the wooden steps that would lead into the hall.

Tigger's timing was perfect. Odessa immediately barked ferociously, leaping and snarling as Tigger's mouth closed on his victim. The count startled awake and goggled at this vision from the bowels of hell.

'*Douce mère de Dieu!*' he cried, as Odessa leapt at the window and sent a series of brass pots and ornaments crashing to the floor.

Pi emerged into the hall. The scullery door was to his left and was closed, with the key in the lock. Pi turned it. 'Quickly, Pi,' said his mother. 'In the study.' In a breath Pi was there. 'Bottom drawer, the Apocrypha.'

The count seized his Luger and scrambled off the couch. He pulled the trigger as Tigger leapt from the window ledge and Pi opened the book to find the tiny crystal taped inside the last page.

The bullet cut a neat O in the glass before continuing its journey into the Plunketts' garden, where it made an equally neat feature in the pagoda of the bird table. Now Odessa was snarling and growling at the scullery door, as she had the scent of Pi's arrival in the hall. The count struggled into his dressing gown. 'Silence, Odessa. Silence.' Pi had heard the crack of the pistol as he dropped the book and strode towards the hall.

The count seized the door handle. 'Locked. Damn him. He is here,' he hissed, just as Tigger began his encore. This was a particularly lurid repeat performance involving the consumption of a black-and-grey Privet hawk moth. Beneath the window was a canteen of silver cutlery that Odessa dislodged and scattered across the stone floor as she barked and leapt ferociously at the window. All this while the count, in bare feet, was to be seen performing a strange and contorted version of the hornpipe as he attempted to avoid potential laceration by the sharp knives and forks that danced around him. He failed. His right foot had an unwanted rendezvous with the carving knife and bled copiously. In desperation the count hurled himself onto the sofa.

'Silence, Odessa. Silence!'

Tigger leapt from the window as the count found his gun and aimed for the scullery door. He fired three times at the lock. The third bullet ricocheted across the hall, into the wall behind Pi's head as he bounded for the cellar door. The count struggled into his shoes and strode to the door. He kicked the scullery door open as Pi descended the steps to the cellar. In the gloom the count saw two eyes fixed on him, and put a bullet into the amiable life-size portrait of the former rector of Dingwell, William Twitten. He fired down the hall and decapitated a suit of armour that had been patiently guarding the stairs.

Odessa leapt into the hall. The count raced for the cellar door and flung it open. The dog descended the steps in time only to see Pi as he shut the outside door and escaped into the night.

The count strode out to the lawn, his prey long gone. 'I will kill you, *jeune homme, tu peux en être sûr.*' He hissed the words into the night air. '*Jeune Peter, tu mourras.*'

12

Some Old Fruitcake from Dingwell

Sergeant Heffer yawned and stretched his legs onto a table and leaned back in his chair. The phone at the Queensbridge police station was ringing, but he was in no hurry to answer it. *Perhaps it will stop,* he thought. But it didn't. 'Can't even catch forty winks. What a life,' he groaned, and lowered his feet to the floor, before trudging wearily across to his desk, jabbing the 'off' button on the TV as he did so. 'Queensbridge police station,' he drawled, barely stifling another yawn.

'Oh, is that the police?' spluttered Mr. Plunkett.

'Well, sir, most police stations do have police in them,' said Sergeant Heffer dryly.

Mr. Plunkett had no time for wit. 'Damn it man, we're under attack. Some bugger has shot my bird table.'

'I see, sir.' Sergeant Heffer licked the end of his pencil and flipped open a notebook. 'A person or persons unknown have shot your bird table,' he said slowly. 'Is that it, sir?'

'No, that bloody well isn't it, Constable!

Bloody bullet hole in the pagoda,' he barked.

'Bullet hole in the pagoda,' repeated Sergeant Heffer. 'Anything else, sir?'

'We want you to do something about it, Constable!' yelled Mr. Plunkett.

'This is *Sergeant* Heffer, sir. Now can you tell me your name, sir?'

'Plunkett, Wilfred Plunkett, from Dingwell Village.'

'I see, sir. And can I ask where you are right now?'

'I'm under the kitchen table with my wife!'

'Under the kitchen table with your wife,' repeated the Sergeant carefully. 'Anyone else there, sir?'

'Yes. Willy. He's trembling all over.'

Rosy-cheeked PC Dave Rabbetts wandered into the office and looked enquiringly at Sergeant Heffer, who put his hand over the phone's mouthpiece. 'Just some old fruitcake from Dingwell, Dave. I'll deal with it.'

'Are you there?' squawked Mr. Plunkett.

'Yes, I'm here, sir. What exactly happened?'

'Well, I was taking Willy out for his last widdle and — '

'And Willy is what, sir?'

'Our dog. What the hell did you think it was?'

'Thought it might be a pet name for something else, sir. Do go on.'

'Suddenly there was this crack, like a pistol shot, and a zinging sound, and bang! Bloody bullet embedded in my bird table.'

'In the pagoda, sir?'

'Yes, yes, in the bloody pagoda, Sergeant.'

'Any other shots, sir?'

'Well, I turned and ran for the bloody house, I can tell you. I think there were two more, at least. Grabbed the memsahib and took cover.'

'Are you sure these were bullets, sir?'

'Yes, I am bloody sure. Nearly shot my nose off. I know a bullet when I hear one, Sergeant!'

'It couldn't have been your neighbour watching a cowboy movie?'

'No, it bloody wasn't!'

'No need to swear, sir. It really doesn't help,'

'Sorry, Sergeant. But we are very frightened.'

'Why would anyone shoot your bird table, sir?'

'I haven't the faintest bloody idea!'

'Do you keep any particularly unpleasant birds as pets, sir?'

'Such as what, for God's sake?'

'Vultures? Eagles? Condors have a huge wingspan of twenty-five feet,' said the sergeant, recalling a particularly fascinating programme on the Feathers and Flight Channel.

'No, I bloody well don't! Now are you going to do something?'

'Is it all quiet outside now, sir?'

'Yes, sergeant, it is. Oh, there was some shouting after the gunshots. Hell of a commotion next door. No idea what it was about.'

'Right, sir. We'll get a car over to you as soon as possible. I suggest you go to a friend's house and stay there for tonight. Leave it to us.'

★ ★ ★

Pi slithered down the stony path until he reached the mill. He replaced the key behind the loose stone and paused. He heard his heart beating. No one had followed him. Ahead he saw a moonlit Tigger perched calmly on the little stone bridge, Yarmer Stream rushing beneath. Pi soundlessly paced along the track and climbed the wooden gate before dismounting and joining the cat. 'You are amazing, Tigger,' he said, and stroked Tigger's back. Tigger just stared straight ahead — Navinda was motionless on the stone steps at the end of the footpath. She turned as Pi approached, and her gaze breached the dam of his emotions. He buried his face in her dark hair. She turned her head and held Pi's face in her hands.

'Don't be afraid of me,' she said. 'It's what

is wrong with the world.' But Pi could not speak. 'You can kiss me.' She drew his face down to hers, and their lips softly met. In truth the only girl Pi had ever really kissed was big Marjorie at the primary school, and that was because he'd wanted her Gobstopper. But now Navinda's hand caressed his hair, and she pressed him farther down. He kissed her deeply and energy returned to his arms; Pi held her strongly and softly. His hand seemed to fit perfectly into the small of her back.

'You are not afraid of me, are you?'

Pi shook his head. 'No, I am not. I'm really not. If I am afraid of anything, it is finding that you have gone.'

'Don't be afraid of that.' She pulled him tight to her. 'Let there be no fear.'

'It's just who I am now.' He paused and gazed into her dark eyes. 'More than I have ever been.'

'I am not leaving. Not yet. I will have to leave when this is done. But I will come back.'

Pi reached into his jacket pocket and pulled out the crystal. 'At least the Organisation does not have this.' He placed it in Navinda's hand.

'I can feel it tingling.'

'Alpha is reacting to your hand. It is not

really a crystal. It is a living thing, waiting to live. Waiting for a home.'

'Like Om.'

'Om was the first. I am not sure I could bear to live with two Oms. They might disagree and argue,' said Pi.

'I read your poem,' said Navinda. 'Do you really feel that about me?' She stared at him, trying to read his mind. 'Do you really?'

'Yes, I do. I think I . . . ' Navinda placed her finger across his lips.

'Don't say it. Don't say the 'I' word. Until you know. Until you really know.' Navinda suddenly embraced him tightly. 'Not until we are certain.'

'Yes, not 'til then.' They turned and ascended the hill above Yarmer, then carefully stepped down the steep path to Eastcombe Beach.

'It feels safe, here,' said Navinda. 'But I am not sure we are. The count must know it was you.'

'Yes, he knows it was Tigger too. I don't know what Tigger did, but he caused mayhem. You know the count tried to shoot Tigger?' Navinda gasped. 'At least I assume it was Tigger he was shooting at. Another bullet just missed me in the hall.'

'So we are not safe here,' said Navinda. 'They will be looking for you.'

'And you too,' said Pi. They glanced at the

Dream Factory. A curl of smoke drifted in lazy circles from the chimney. 'It's our little home.'

'With our little family,' said Navinda. 'But they might come here.'

Pi looked steadily into Navinda's eyes. 'They might.'

'Tigger?'

'By the fire in the Whodhavethoughtit, I expect.' Pi smiled. 'He lives by his own rules.'

'Promise me you will smile more often.'

'With you I have reason to.'

'We must decide what to do,' said Navinda. 'Barnie and Doris have to go back.'

'Barnie might. I'll talk to him. But Doris is still too angry.'

★   ★   ★

Tizzy had some late guests at the Whodhave-thoughtit that night. He opened the old oak door to find a dazed and shaken elderly couple standing in the moonlight in their pyjamas with a bewildered Willy. 'My stars, folks. What's happened to thee?' Tizzy ushered the Plun-ketts into the hallway and put the lights on in the snug.

'Oh, it's been terrible, Tizzy. I was just taking the dog out for his last wee-wee and . . . and . . . '

'You just sit down there Wilfred and Mrs. P.' They sat down, and Tizzy poked the fire into fresh life, adding a piece of driftwood. Willy settled on Mrs. P's slippers. 'There you are m'dears. Have a sip o' that,' he said, handing them a small glass of whiskey each. 'That will settle thee.' They sipped gratefully, and for the first time since he had known them, Tizzy pitied this grumpy old couple who now looked so frail and helpless.

'I heard a shot, then another and the zing of this bullet. It went *thump* into our bird table.'

'Lord, no,' said Tizzy.

'Then there was another, and I ran for cover. Lavinia and I hid under the table. And there was this shouting. It was frightening. Some chap screaming in some foreign lingo — French, I think. About killing someone.'

'Oh, ah? Where did this come from?'

'The Old Rectory, I think,' sniffed Wilfred.

'*Le Manoir* — where the count lives?' said Tizzy.

'They used to be such a lovely family,' Lavinia sobbed. 'What happened to them, Tizzy? Where did they go?'

'Where indeed?' muttered Tizzy. 'Where indeed?' He stroked his beard thoughtfully.

'We phoned the police,' Wilfred said. 'They said they would send a car over. We should

108

leave everything to them.'

'Right. In that case you folks stay here. When you're ready, go and lie down in the old drawing room. Good bed in there. And don't worry or nothin'.'

Wilfred and Lavinia nodded then rested their heads wearily. Tizzy walked back into the hall. Gideon came down the stairs.

'What's happening, man?'

'I'm not sure, but I doozn't like it one bit. Wilfred and Lavinia reckon someone was using a gun at the Old Rectory tonight. Heard shoutin'. Someone yellin' in French about killing someone.'

Wilfred Plunkett appeared in the doorway. 'I've just remembered, Tizzy. What I heard. It was *'Jeune* Peter,' I think. Yes, *'Jeune* Peter. *Tu mourras.'* ' That's death isn't it?'

'Want me to go take a look?' said Gideon.

'No, Giddy. Let the police 'andle it. Thanks, Wilfred. You have a rest with Mrs. P. You need it.'

Wilfred wandered back to the fire. Gideon and Tizzy went to the kitchen.

'I don't like this, Giddy.'

'Reckon Peter went to the house. Bet he wanted to get somethin'.'

Tizzy nodded. 'Makes sense. Must be a lot of things in that house that belong to Peter. And some stuff he don't want the count to

109

get his hands on, more like.'

'Did Peter get away?'

'No worries. The count wouldn't have been shouting otherwise. You get some sleep, Giddy. I still got one or two things to do.'

Gideon ran back up stairs. Tizzy wandered through the main bar. A small wooden door in the corner bore the battered pub dartboard. Tizzy turned the brass handle and entered his tiny study — a haven of peace lit by a single skylight. Now the moon beamed into this space, and a fire flickered in the small grate. Tizzy only smoked in this room — an aromatic tobacco he mixed himself that gave comfort to his aching bones and tired eyes. His father's gnarled shepherd's crook stood in the corner, its carved oak handle gleaming black. A dainty coronet of gold worn by Chariclo, Tizzy's mother, glimmered from a glass case above his desk. This was Tizzy's inner world, a place where he pondered the day's events and wrote his journal, whose leather volumes — on creaking wooden shelves — lined the walls with glimmering maroon and russet.

Tizzy undid the string tie that bound the beautiful leather book. Its pages were of pure cotton, white as flowers of clover. Tizzy's face, as creased and tanned as the journal's cover, frowned thoughtfully. What did it mean if you gave your love white clover? Tizzy, scratched his beard in thought. Ah, yes. 'Think of me.' Affection flooded Tizzy's features. 'Think of me.' Navinda's message to young Peter. That was it. Tizzy reached for his Sonnet fountain pen.

'Think of me' appeared in elegant italic script on the new white page, and Tizzy composed a simple sketch of Pi and Navinda standing in the doorway of the Dream Factory.

Tizzy put down his pen. He lay back in the leather chair and closed his eyes.

★ ★ ★

Constable Rabbetts and Sergeant Heffer were deciding what to do over a mug of cocoa and chocolate HobNobs. 'Strange folk in Dingwell,' said the sergeant, and licked his fingers.

'Yeah, but gunfire at two in the morning,' said the constable. 'Can't believe it.'

'Neither can I.'

'What are you going to do?'

'Nothin'.' Sergeant Heffer stirred his drink. 'Dave, just in case, put a message on Yvonne's voice mail. She's to pay a visit in the morning. Tell 'er to take care mind.'

★ ★ ★

Yvonne Bull returned to Cosy Cottage in Dingwell. She closed the door, put on the hall light, and hung up her coat. Her lips were still smouldering from Alison's goodnight kiss. She trembled blissfully at the memory. They had been to see *The Forbidden Planet* and afterwards embraced outside the theatre, like two slender willows entangled, bending together in the wind and rain under the night's dark canopy. Yvonne closed her eyes again and revisited the kiss, savouring the moment. She removed her crocheted French beret, bejewelled with rain diamonds, and draped it over the ears of a tall oak statuette of a cat that loyally guarded the stairs. It had been a present from Alison from their holiday in Honfleur. Yvonne had called it 'Tigger,' and Alison had laughed. 'Are you naming this perfect piece of wooden art after that mangy cat?'

'Tigger is lovely,' Yvonne had replied. 'He belongs to the village. He *is* the village.' She smiled at the memory and looked down at her ring finger, which was adorned with a simple diamond eternity ring that Alison had slipped into her hand. The diamond shimmered like the beads of rain on her hat. Her eyes moved to the mirror of the hallstand and stared hard at her own image, with the slim silver necklace and tiny crucifix her mother had given her. Alison's loving eyes and auburn hair beamed from Yvonne's portrait of her, composed in sumptuous oils. 'I will talk to Thomas about Alison and me. Soon,' she decided, and turned toward the stairs.

She was stopped by a green light flashing on her answering machine. She pressed the 'play' button, and Constable Rabbetts's soft, rural voice floated into the air. 'Oh, ah, hello, Yvonne. This is Dave from the station. (Dave had a crush on Yvonne, and she knew it.) Hope you're OK an' stuff. Erm, Sergeant asked me to give you a call. Some old muffin called Plunkett phoned up complainin' someone 'ad shot 'is bird table or somethin'. Probably nothin' in it. Sergeant wants you to pop round in the mornin'. Take care mind. Lots of l . . . Er, sorry. Cheers. Byeee.'

Yvonne collapsed onto the hall chair, shaking with laughter. 'Dave, you silly wally.' She wiped a tear from her cheek. 'Not a very professional message, Constable Rabbetts, but I shall do as you suggest,' she said to the answering machine, then gave it a salute and headed for the bathroom. Dear old Dave, with his curly hair, funny teeth, and big ears —Yvonne was briefly touched by the thought of Dave's unrequited love. Tomorrow was her day off, but she would take her morning jog past the Plunketts' house.

Count Henri de Boodle had tried to sleep amid the debris of broken ornaments. Having bandaged his foot, he shook the quilt and found a broom to sweep the cutlery and shattered pottery into a heap at the end of the scullery. But sleep would not come. He hated this accursed place. All he needed would be for the local police to sniff around and ask damn-fool questions. No, there were people he needed to speak to. It was time to make himself scarce. He would see Miss Cloke later. And so, in the dead of night, he ushered Odessa into his car, and the Daimler slid quietly out of Dingwell.

13

Miss Cloke's Reconnaissance

The dawn rose in a miasma of purple and peach hues in the east, and the sun's rays first slipped their gaudy spears through the curtains of Enigma Cottage. But Miss Cloke was already awake. Miss Cloke always slept flat on her back, and her eyes popped open like twin alarm clocks, always at dawn. She had much to do.

'Reconnaissance, Sergeant Cloke, is a mission to obtain information by visual observation, or other detection methods, about the activities and resources of an enemy or potential enemy.' Miss Cloke recalled the cut-glass voice of her SIS commander, Sir Ranville B'Stard. 'Know your enemy, Miss Cloke. Study him tirelessly, look for his strengths, his weaknesses, his vices, what he drinks, where he sleeps and who with; know his lies and his truths, his faith, his dreams, his obsessions; know him like you know your own skin, Miss Cloke.' She remembered the tobacco smell on the breath of the commander as he stood close to her and hissed the words into her face. 'You know what to do, Miss Cloke.'

Miss Cloke stood by her scrubbed kitchen table and gazed at the equipment she had laid out the night before. This would be a simple area reconnaissance — 'the observation of, and information obtained about, a specified location and the area around it.' Miss Cloke leafed through the yellowing old SIS agent's manual that she had kept all these years. It listed the equipment she would need:

binoculars — check
flashlight — check
evidence canister — check
pencil and pad — check
first-aid kit — check
pistol — check
suicide pill — check

Miss Cloke lovingly ran her fingers across the black contours of the Smith & Wesson Sigma pistol, its hand guard removed for faster firing. *Beautiful weapon*, she thought. She had no intention of shooting anyone on this mission, but 'one must be prepared for anything, Miss Cloke.' To the list of equipment, she added a thermos of coffee and some shortbread. All this, with a spare hanky, tissues, some anti-mozzy cream, and a copy of *Woman's Own*, fitted into an old canvas camouflage bag that would loop over her shoulders.

Her little walking boots stood dubbined at the ready by the back door. But first she had to feed the cat. 'Pandora, Pandora,' she trilled. 'Come along, poppet!' Miss Cloke tore open the seal from a pack of Cleopatra's Cat's Cuisine and tipped the contents into Pandora's dish. 'Pandora . . . Oh, where are you?' Pandora had been behaving strangely, finding various places in the cottage to hide. This time Miss Cloke found her in the wardrobe of the spare room, frantically licking her 'nether regions,' as Miss Cloke preferred to call them. 'Now what are you doing there, you funny cat?' She left the bowl by the wardrobe door and toddled back to the kitchen and looked in the mirror. All set. Grey military socks atop her walking boots, camouflage trousers, a green parka, and a green rain hat completed the picture. Miss Cloke hung her glasses around her neck and picked up her bag. It was time.

She crept down the footpath to her gate. Good. It was early. There was no one about. Excellent. Miss Cloke fastened the gate and scurried along the lane and slipped into the chirruping dawn and bustle of Doctors' Wood. From there she would plot her way through a maze of footpaths until she had uncovered the entrance to Smugglers' Lane by pulling aside some giant japonica leaves.

But Dingwell had some other early risers. Tigger spied Miss Cloke's departure from a monkey-puzzle tree in her garden. He carefully slid into the long grass before slipping over the wall and into the wood. At that moment, WPC Yvonne Bull slid back her curtains to catch sight of the sprightly old lady heading down the lane. She spotted the canvas bag. 'Hmm. Miss Cloke is on a mission. Now what is she up to?' And above the wood, Harriet stretched her wings and cruised through the fragrant morning winds, rotating this way and that and keeping the old lady's little rain hat perfectly in view.

★　★　★

Pi and Navinda managed some sleep while Om kept watch, blue light pulsing gently. As Miss Cloke entered Smugglers' Lane, Tigger arrived for his breakfast at the Dream Factory. While Doris fed him, Pi took Jack and Jill and Buddy down to the beach with Barnie. Barnie held Pi's hand, and Pi experienced those emotions that fathers feel — what it is like to be trusted, for someone to depend on you. They sat on a rock and paddled their feet in the cool waters of

Eastcombe Brook, where it bounded off the land and spread out to make a small estuary that teemed across the shingle to the sea. Higher up Eastcombe Brook, there was a little wooden bridge in the woods. Pi and Navinda had played poohsticks with Doris and Barnie; Barnie had shrieked with laughter and chuckled constantly. He finally tried to win by throwing a whole handful of sticks into the brook, but Jack spoiled the game anyway by grabbing the winning stick and swimming off with it. But still Barnie had not spoken.

Now Barnie poked the stones in the stream with his stick. He pointed at a silver fish in the middle of the stream, motionless except for its gills flicking.

'Barnie.' Pi was not used to breaking bad news to young children. He had no script. 'Barnie, I . . . '

Barnie was looking at him, his big round eyes full of love and trust. He spoke. 'I know,' he said. 'You and Navinda think I have to go back. You think a nasty man is going to come.'

Pi looked down at their two sticks resting on the bed of shingle. But there was no one holding Barnie's stick. He had gone. Pi looked at the space where Barnie had been. His life suddenly had an empty space within it. 'I will see you again, Barnie,' said Pi to the empty air. How he had loved teaching Barnie simple sums and the messy fun of glue and paper and sticks and paint. For the time being, that was over. Miss Cloke had arrived at Yarmer Beach. She began to climb the stone steps.

★   ★   ★

Yvonne was in her hall once more, arranging her hair into a blonde ponytail. She laced her Nike trainers and opened the front door. She did some stretches in her tiny front garden before placing her left foot on the garden wall and flexing on her other leg to stretch the hamstring. She repeated this with her right hamstring and set her race watch. Probably no point in trying a PB this morning, as she would be visiting the Plunketts. She was a good runner with an even, rhythmic stride that quickly consumed the miles on the hilly lanes around Dingwell. She was planning to do a half marathon with Alison in the summer. Let us follow her. Down Martyrs' Lane from Cosy Cottage, past the front of the Whodhavethoughtit — she always waved to Gideon, who was recycling several boxes of green bottles. Now to put some power on as she attacked the hill leading up to All Souls

Church before turning the corner onto Dingwell Lane. On, past the graveyard and the meadow, where a lonely bull stood tethered to a post, then *Le Manoir* (Yvonne still called it the Old Rectory). A further burst of speed brought her to the Plunketts' residence. Yvonne stopped and caught her breath.

The Plunketts' ancient Humber was parked in the drive. But Raffles, their beautiful granite-and-timber house, showed no signs of life. Crimson and russet ivy entwined the ancient walls, and cascades of scarlet alyssum, climbing snapdragons, and pansies trailed from baskets or erupted from vast Mediterranean terracotta pots. Cherry blossom and mimosa trees added bolder splashes of vermillion and gold to the myriad dots of flowers that drifted and quivered in the soft breeze. Yvonne paced up the drive to the oak-panelled front door and clanged the brass ship's bell. No answer. She walked through the wrought-iron gate and onto the patio — the scene of Wilfred's encounter with the skateboard. She noted the half-submerged object protruding from the pond and a discarded cricket bat lying under a jacaranda tree. Beyond stretched the immaculate emerald lawns, dazzling blue azaleas, peach rhododendrons, and blood-red viburnum and a line of stately oaks sheltering the garden. Through the trees Yvonne saw the glitter of the sea at Eastcombe. All was peaceful, with insects busy and swifts darting through the fragrant air, catching thrips and hoverflies on the wing.

So where was the bird table? It was a thing of ornate elegance whose graceful Chinese curves endowed this most English of gardens with a hint of empire. Yvonne approached it carefully, skirting the perimeter of the pond. The roof had graceful curved elevations that reminded her of a Chinese teahouse she once had seen in Hong Kong. The pagoda's surface was a single piece of beautifully carved mahogany. Yvonne ran her fingers over its surface. She reached her hand under the pagoda onto the bird table and gathered a handful of cat fur — *Now I wonder whose this is*. Her fingers moved to the end of the pagoda and felt a roughened edge. She examined it closely. There was no mistaking this. A single neat hole, the breadth of her little finger, was punched into the engraved image of a dragon on the fascia. Yvonne slipped off her eternity ring and held it over the hole. She could not see the bullet and assumed that it had become embedded in the dense mahogany of the bird table's roof. If a gun had been fired, where had the bullet come from? To the right was *Twitten Towers*, an eccentric nineteenth-century folly that was now a retirement home. The locals had given it the cheerful nickname of 'The Fossils,' and the name had stuck. But there was no doubt that the bullet had come from the east — *Le Manoir*. Yvonne noted a carton of fish food that had been dropped by the bird table, and a handsome young olive tree in a pot lay toppled on its side. She reasoned that someone had been in the garden when the shot was fired; probably poor old Mr. Plunkett, who had come out to feed his fish and give Willy one last turn in the garden, had heard the shot and then ran for his life. *He must have been terrified*, she thought. Who fired the shot and why?

Yvonne moved towards the slatted wooden fence that separated *Le Manoir* from the Plunketts. Surely no one would be standing out in the garden of *Le Manoir* just to take a potshot at the Plunkett's bird table, or even Mr. Plunkett. He could be a grumpy old codger, but Yvonne couldn't imagine anyone wanting to shoot the poor old soul. And why shoot him in his garden? Why not shoot him in his house while he was listening to *The Archers* or writing yet another letter of complaint to the parish council. No. The bullet must have come from *Le Manoir*, from the house itself. She headed for the drive once more and closed the gate.

Yvonne had loved the Old Rectory. As a girl she had babysat for the Youngs and read stories to Peter. They would welcome other children to the house and hold parties on its sunny lawns and not mind if the kids ran up and down the big staircase or climbed the oak trees or jumped into the flowerbed or kicked a football through the greenhouse window. Now Peter had gone, and the sunshine had gone from the house. Yvonne did not like the new name for the house — *Le Manoir,* which had been crudely painted on the granite gatepost. The house looked unloved, and its once prolific flowerbeds were choked with weeds; grasses poked through paths; and the lawns were ragged and uncut. As she walked up the drive, she noticed that the count's car was gone, and he had left the garage door open. How curious! A strange handcart was parked at the back of the garage, painted in camouflage colours. It had a steel box mounted on it. She examined the embossed label on the side of the box; it read, 'SEP 70007 MP40 Panzerfaust.' A mystery to Yvonne, but she would find out.

She pressed the doorbell then noticed the split casing on the plastic switch and the disconnected wires drooping. 'Well, I tried to do the polite thing.' Memories of the Old Rectory in happier times now flooded Yvonne's mind. At each step as she moved round the side of the house, images of laughing children and playing hide-and-seek in the cellar, hardly daring to breathe, flickered in her imagination like photographs sliding across a table. She passed the stone steps down to the cellar door. Had someone only recently run up those same steps and raced across the lush grasses still starred with morning dew? She saw the indentations, and from the length of the stride, she could tell someone had been running to leave the house. She followed the footsteps across the neglected lawn. Of course. The oak tree. Put your foot in the missing brick on the garden wall, stretch up to grab the overhanging branch, swing your legs up and loop them over the bough, ease yourself up, and scramble down the metal spikes in the tree trunk and escape into the woods. It had been a game she had played with Peter. When he was little, she used to lift him up to grab the branch, his little legs dangling and kicking.

Once, she had walked back to the house with a six-year-old Peter holding her hand. Peter had then announced to his amused mother that he wanted to 'marry Yvonne and live in a tree house.' Yvonne smiled at the memory and leant against the back wall by the scullery window.

She shifted her gaze, her eyes following the line of the sill where Tigger had given the performance of a lifetime. Her eyes focussed on a small but unmistakable hole in the scullery window. In that moment she knew Peter had been here. Her heart bounded at the thought. She looked through the window. The chaos and destruction looked like a murder scene.

Yvonne raced down the stone steps to the cellar door. It had been left open. She snapped on the light then went up the wooden steps to the hall, where she expected to find a body. Instead the scullery door hung twisted and splintered off one hinge and revealed an extraordinary scene. The count's bedcover lay bundled on the floor, and smears of dried blood crisscrossed the stone tiles by the sofa. An array of pots and memorabilia, some broken, mingled with silver cutlery, had been swept into a heap by the fireplace. The canteen had been hurled to the back of the fire, and it still smouldered in the grate. There was an empty dog's bed.

Yvonne went back into the hall. The gently smiling features of the Reverend William Twitten sported a bullet hole between his eyes. The head of the old cardboard suit of armour, made for the village pantomime, lay on the floor, its visor tilted upward and staring blankly at the ceiling.

Yvonne stepped over the debris and walked down the hall into the study. The curtains were still drawn, and she flicked on the light. She noted the open drawer of Esther Young's desk and a discarded book lying open on the carpet. She walked back down the hall. No more blood anywhere else. If Peter had been here, she reasoned, he had almost certainly escaped. The blood in the scullery? The count probably had cut himself and driven off to the local surgery. Still, plenty for the scenes of crime team to pore over. Time to run back home and call the station.

It was a lovelorn PC Dave Rabbetts who answered the phone. 'Oh, 'ello, Yvonne. How are you, babe?'

'Is the sergeant there, Dave?'

'No, my love — 'e's slipped out,' he gushed.

'Listen, Dave. I've been to the Plunketts' house.'

'Oh, is it nice? Got a nice garden, I 'spect. By the way I was goin' to say, do you fancy a drink or somethin' tonight?'

Whatever the 'somethin' ' was, Yvonne was having none of it. 'Dave, you are right out of order. And if you continue talking to me like some sexist nob, I am going to file a complaint! Clear?'

'Oh, ah. All righty. Didn't mean nothin'.'

'Listen, Dave. Tell the sergeant shots *were* fired in Dingwell last night. And the house next door to the Plunketts', called *Le Manoir*, looks . . . well, the scullery looks like Jack the Ripper's kitchen.'

'Oh, strewth! Bugger. You OK?'

'I'm fine. Tell the sergeant to get scenes of crime onto it now. Call me back, and I'll meet them there.'

'Right-e-o,' burbled Dave.

'Oh, and by the way. There's a Panzerfaust RPG, World War Two vintage, in the garage. Interesting, don't you think?'

'Stone the crows. Panzerwhatsit, eh? Is that a lawnmower?'

'No, Dave. It's a rocket-propelled grenade launcher. Bet you haven't got one of those in your potting shed.'

'Friggin' Ada. You're effing joking, aren't you?'

'No joke, Dave. Now get things moving.' She put the phone down. She was worried now. Dave was a Muppet. Oh, well, she would call back later and talk to the sergeant.

★   ★   ★

Miss Cloke made slow progress up the footpath from Yarmer to Eastcombe. She felt a little puffed. At the top of the hill, she

128

stopped. The sea rolled irresistibly into Fairyland Beach below, filling the channels between the rocky spines and just as quickly retreating, drawing a clatter of shingle with it before a fresh wave sent a surge of water into the rock pools and little gorges. In the days of smuggling, this was a wreckers' beach, where ships had been lured by false lights — lanterns attached to horses or held by children who walked up and down the beach. It was called Fairyland because anything worth stealing always would be washed up here.

Miss Cloke took a short footpath inland and stepped through a crumbling slate wall into a ruined shepherd's hut that afforded a perfect view of Eastcombe Beach. The hut's roof was long gone. Miss Cloke put down her pack, unfolded her little stool, and settled down for a rest. She nibbled some shortbread and took out her notebook.

⋆　⋆　⋆

Enemy position consists of stone hut with chimney. Good firing positions from within the enemy's stone shed, but very vulnerable to heavy ordinance fired from Stoggie's Farm on far side of Eastcombe. Can be approached by footpaths from north and south but vulnerable to small-arms fire from the shed. Cannot be approached by normal vehicle. Small-scale seaborne landing possible but only by small boat and also vulnerable to small-arms fire.

★   ★   ★

Miss Cloke put on her binoculars. She picked out the mazy line of a path on the hill opposite that ran from the back of The Fossils, through Stoggie's Farm to the coast. Perfect! Above that she spied a 'hide' used by birdwatchers.

★   ★   ★

The hedge on the eastern side of this footpath is dense and high. Would provide perfect cover. Move weaponry into position at dusk. Then launch dawn attack.

She tucked her notebook into her pack. One hundred feet above Miss Cloke's head, Harriet's elegant voyage through the sea air had abruptly halted. She stooped. A controlled vertical dive performed with pinpoint accuracy. Miss Cloke was just reaching for her binoculars when daylight seemed to disappear, and she was in a maelstrom of beating wings and alarming hooked claws that jagged towards her eyes.

There was no time to scream. The claws

were gone, and the feathered fiend lifted itself into the blue sky. Dangling from its claws, on a broken gold neck chain, were Miss Cloke's spectacles.

The old lady reached frantically for her pack. Without her glasses she was dreadfully shortsighted and groped myopically around the hut for her possessions. *Keep calm, Miss Cloke.* She heard the voice of her commanding officer. *Just retrace your steps and return to headquarters.* A somewhat shaken Miss Cloke put on her pack and slowly found her way back to the footpath. She looked fearfully up to the sky. *Just keep moving, Miss Cloke. Keep your head down and keep moving.*

Barnie was looking at his mother. There was a ripped carton of milk on the kitchen table. It was surrounded by glass from the broken window. Barnie's mum fumbled in the table drawer for a lighter. Now she sat in the light of her son's gaze, wrapped in her orange dressing gown, blonde hair pinned back, barefooted with a silver ankle chain. She drew deeply on the cigarette.

'You going to say something. You ain't spoken for days.'

'I don't like that horrible man.'

' 'E's gone, boy. Won't see him no more.' Barnie rushed forward and climbed onto her lap. She held him, averted her face from him to puff smoke in the direction of the window.

'Are we going to stay here?'

She grunted. 'Victory Flats? Why not?' She looked out at the bleak grey roofs and fearfully up at the leaden sky. 'We just keeps moving, Barnie. Just keeps moving.'

'Why?'

A sudden shower rattled hail on the slates and windowsill. Some shot through the broken window and bounced into the sink. 'We'll just stay here, Barnie. You and me.'

Barnie hugged her tight.

'You squeezin' me hard, Barnie. You strong little tyke.' Barnie grinned. 'Strong little boy. Hey! School tomorrow.'

'Don't want to go.'

She stubbed out her fag and kissed his grubby forehead. 'Love you, Barnie.' She held him again. 'Just you and me. Just you and me.'

★　★　★

Thomas had woken that morning blissfully unaware of the night's dramas. He had toddled off to the loo in the early morning and was surprised to see the powerful headlights of the count's Daimler veering down Dingwell Lane. Thomas saw it swing left at the church and smoothly accelerate up the hill. 'Count's up early,' Thomas said with a yawn and headed back to bed. Now it was a sunny morning, and he waved to Yvonne as she jogged round the corner and on up the lane. Thomas did his business, and presently a freshly showered and fragrant (he used Men of England aftershave) Thomas was seated at his desk, munching toast, glugging tea, and listening to the news. Yes, today he needed to think. He needed to visit the church, talk to God (if the Almighty was available for a chat), and think.

'I am not the person I was,' he said out loud to the wooden crucifix on his desk. 'I am not, sweet Lord, the man who came into your service in order to hide from the world. Hide from . . . who I am.' The crucifix, with its finely carved figure of Christ nailed to the cross, head tilted, garlanded with thorns, listened impassively.

A memory of his conversation with Navinda rose like a spirit before his eyes. 'I left my church to discover more about faith.' This remark had shocked Thomas and left him open mouthed. 'We need to know why we do what we do,' she had said, adding copiously to his self-doubt.

Thomas knew there would be no answers here amid the comforts of toast and *The Archers*. His study window looked directly across Dingwell Lane to the square's fourteenth-century crenulated tower, crowned with a pointed turret like a witching bonnet. Thomas put down his cup of tea and found himself walking slowly across the lane to the kissing gate. His feet took him up the path to the worn stone steps and oak arched door at the foot of the tower's facade. He dragged the iron latch upward, and the heavy door creaked inward. He stepped into the gloomy vestibule and reached for the large brass doorknob. It creaked open.

Cheerful sun had given way to a sudden downpour, and Thomas felt it enveloping the church, dimming the vibrant colours of stained glass and fading the shafts of light from the windows to pale spectral ghosts. 'Lord, we need to talk.' Thomas felt a shock at hearing his voice. Was it *his* voice? His feet led him to the nave and then the inner sanctuary. 'We need to talk.' Past the wooden choir stall to the altar rail, he knelt and prayed. 'Guide me,' he said. He gazed pleadingly up at the single gold crucifix. The Virgin Mary beamed wordlessly at him. Sometimes God was not there. He felt like a child coming to a well with a tin cup and finding the well empty. 'I am here. You be here. Please be here.' His breath condensed in the chilled air as he hissed out the words.

They seemed to be forced out from inside him by some . . . thing. 'Be here!' he cried. 'Be here!' Only silence spoke to Thomas. 'I *will* find you.'

He stood up. A blue curtain was draped across a wooden door in the wall — a door to the tower he had yet to open and enter. Now he would. He swept the curtain aside, exposing the little timber door, and seized the handle. It would not budge. Locked. Where did Miss Cloke keep the keys? He strode to the vestry and opened the old dresser drawers, rummaged among old books, and grasped a set of keys on an iron ring. The first of them fitted. The door opened to expose a curving set of stone steps that spiralled upward. Thomas had to stand on a pew and duck his head under the stone arch, before scrambling up the steps on all fours. He emerged into a small square room with a leaded window that gazed down upon the graveyard with its leaning stones and tumbled monuments. The ropes from the belfry above threaded through the floor by his feet. In the corner was a low stone fireplace with an aperture to the side for baking bread, Thomas assumed. But who would live in this tiny room? A rickety and perfectly vertical wooden ladder, pinned to the wall by iron rails, stretched above him. He would have to climb it. Thomas kicked aside a pewter tankard and plate that lay at the foot of the ladder and began his ascent. The ladder creaked under his weight, but Thomas was determined. Hand over hand, his feet feeling and scrabbling for each rung, he climbed forty feet not daring to look down, the wooden hatch above slowly moving towards him.

He reached the top then pushed upward at the hatch with his left hand. For an instant he lost his footing and was left dangling by one arm, like a hapless marionette, while the shaft below revolved crazily. He slammed himself back against the ladder and gripped with all his strength. He was breathing hard. He moved up one more step and pushed his head and left shoulder up against the hatch. There was a crack followed by a sudden blast of air, and the hatch flew open and thudded onto the floor of the belfry. Thomas eased his body up onto the platform and peered nervously over the surrounding parapet.

Fortunately there were no witnesses to see the ashen-faced vicar of Dingwell peeping fearfully over the stone wall of the church tower only to remind himself that he was petrified of heights. Exhausted, he replaced the hatch, deciding to postpone the terrifying descent while he tried to figure out why on earth he was where he was. He lay back on the wooden floor and stared up at a church bell. Why? Why? He needed to rest and closed his eyes.

Thomas's questions would be answered sooner than he could have imagined.

★ ★ ★

Pi, crestfallen, turned away from the waves and gazed up at the gulls circling and heading inland. There was a storm coming. He strode back to the Dream Factory and opened the door. Om was playing pipe music, and he had projected a hologram of Harriet onto the table. Doris was studying it closely with Navinda. 'Just use fine pencil strokes, Doris. Like this.' Doris carefully watched Navinda as she slowly drew the outline of Harriet on her sketchpad. Doris then did the same. Om was brilliant at producing holograms. Harriet even blinked occasionally at Doris. The bright-yellow eye, the tiger flecking across her breast, the vivid yellow claws, and elegant curled deadly talons were beautifully defined.

'Where's Barnie?' asked Doris.

'He's gone back home,' said Pi. 'It was the only time he ever spoke. He said 'I know. There's a nasty man coming.''

Doris looked fearfully at Pi. 'Is there a nasty man coming?'

'He can't hurt you or Navinda,' said Pi.

'But he can hurt *you*,' said Navinda.

'That would hurt us,' said Doris.

'Anything from Mum and Dad, Om?'

Om glowed vivid blue. 'Not yet. They are pleased you retrieved Alpha from the house.'

'Alpha?' said Doris.

'Like Om,' said Navinda.

Doris laughed and pointed at Om. 'You have a little brother.'

'Or maybe a sister. Or maybe neither. I haven't decided yet,' said Om. 'Is it my decision?'

'I want a little brother,' said Doris. 'Can Alpha be my brother?'

'Only your Mummy and Daddy can give you a little brother,' said Om.

'If I have to go back, can I take Om with me?' asked Doris.

'I need to stay with Pi,' said Om. 'Take the memory of me and Pi and Navinda with you. We will always talk to you.'

'Will you teach me more things? I like it when you teach me to write,' said Doris.

'Writing is art. It is like what you are doing now, Doris. Think of it like that, and it is easy. Words carry a message. Your picture of Harriet will carry a message.'

'Om, can you tell me the Everes and Chariclo story again?' Doris loved the picture-book tale of the simple shepherd and the aristocratic nymph.

'When it's bedtime. Let's finish this.'

Navinda's drawing was captivating, Pi thought. The finest of pencil strokes. Hundreds of them. Thousands. Each one drew his eyes into the picture, into the tiniest detail. It was hard to look away. Her hands were thin, fine, and delicate, yet strong when she had embraced him.

'Stop staring.' Navinda smiled and looked hard at Pi. 'What will you do with Alpha?'

'I'm not sure. Om?'

Om glowed a deep blue. 'Alpha is the next stage of development after me. Pi, you will need to decide whether you want Alpha inserted into your body.'

'What can Alpha do?'

'Alpha is a living organism that requires a host. Different from me. If you put me into any device, I can learn to control it and make it work. You called me a 'machine' the other day, Pi. To an extent you are right. But Alpha is different.'

'But how could Pi have Alpha put into his body?' said Doris.

'I think both Pi's parents had Alpha inserted before they were taken. At the top of the spine, beneath the cerebellum. That is how they communicate with me.'

Navinda stopped drawing and looked at Om. 'But if the Organisation has Pi's parents, why haven't they found Alpha?'

'Because Alpha is an organism, not an implant or microchip. They just cannot see it.'

'So are Mum and Dad still alive?' Pi looked pleadingly at Om. Navinda grasped his hand and drew Doris to her side.

'I think Alpha is keeping them alive. And the Organisation does not understand how. That is why they want you, Pi. You are the enemy they can see, but the real prize is under their noses, and they cannot see it. They know there is some big secret they do not have. The next best thing for them may be to destroy this place.'

'What would they do to Pi?' Doris's voice trembled. She rushed to Pi and clutched his legs.

'Do you know what the Organisation is going to do next?' asked Navinda.

'No. I dare not use any of their networks. It's the same if Pi goes back to school. All schools use Bogle. As soon as he is registered, they will know where he is.'

'What about me and Navinda?' said Doris.

'They do not know about you, Doris. They know about me, but not my name?' Navinda looked enquiringly at Om.

'Correct,' said Om.

'The question is,' Navinda continued, 'can Alpha penetrate their networks undetected?'

'They could be very worried about that if they knew about Alpha,' said Om. 'Pi, if you use Alpha, you may be able to communicate with your mum and dad. It may even guide you to them.'

Pi instantly felt the urge to go and find them. He pictured them at home, sitting on the sofa, draped with newspapers, or playing the piano or writing. He shook his head. No, he could not afford to think like this. He had placed Alpha in a silk pouch and kept it in a wooden box under his bedroom floor. 'How did Mum and Dad have Alpha inserted? They must have had a surgeon do it. I wonder who it was.'

'I cannot ask them,' said Om. 'I have to wait for them, or Alpha, to talk to me.'

Pi thought of his parents' friends. One of them could have been a surgeon.

Navinda took Doris's hand. 'Come, Doris. Let's finish our drawing. No one is coming just yet.' Navinda glanced nervously at the window and saw the sea surging, and rain droplets spattering the glass pane.

14

The Storm

A predatory storm had stalked the coast past Eastcombe and chose to unleash its black rain darts and juddering winds on Miss Cloke as she tottered down the stone steps to Yarmer Beach and headed off on the rain-stained footpath that would lead to Doctors' Wood and the safety of Dingwell. Head down, rain cascading from her hat and shoulders, she was forming a plan with each step. The old stone hut at Eastcombe had to be destroyed. It had to be destroyed because she did not know what was going on inside, and the count seemed to think that it and Peter were a risk to his plans — whatever they were. Miss Cloke did not need to know. As an operative she knew questions were for others. Her job was to execute orders and find the means to fulfil her mission. The intensity of her thinking drove her at surprising speed through the shuddering woodland and across teeming rivulets snaking in silver trails down to the bounding Yarmer Stream.

★ ★ ★

The storm bent the grasses and slender trees around the Dream Factory. It whipped the dancing nasturtiums and magnolias, and cabbages with leaves as big as elephants' ears flapped and swayed helplessly in the garden as rain drilled on the roof. Inside, Jack and Jill and Buddy raised their heads from the fireside rug and glanced at Pi and Navinda for reassurance. But the only sound inside the Dream Factory was of minds working and learning, like leaves unfolding and flowers uncurling and opening.

The storm swept up Yarmer Valley, dragging its grey columns of fierce rain. The wind swept into the belfry and snatched a rope and slammed the clapper against the church bell. Thomas awoke with a start. He gasped in fear and stared as the bell above his head swung. The rope pulled again, and the bell tilted and clanged. Then all three bells chimed. Thomas reeled from the cacophony and rolled across the floor.

The trapdoor slammed open. A head, a very shaggy head with a pigtail and bushy eyebrows, poked through, and a face Thomas recognised fixed upon him. 'Better stay 'ere, Reverend. Down below is not safe for thee.' A pewter jug of ale and a plate of bread and fruit were slammed on the floor. A traumatised Thomas crawled across to the parapet and stared fearfully over the edge. Dingwell appeared to have gone mad. A crowd of women and girls chased geese and sheep up the lane and into a field behind his house. An explosion shook the church, and Thomas stared in horror as a round shot seared into the roof of his house, setting the thatch ablaze. He turned and looked down the muddy track towards the Whodhavethoughtit. Men in breeches and doublets were manhandling what looked like a large metal vase in a wooden frame into position. The neck of the 'vase' was tilted to point over the pub. In a second this Roaring Meg had exploded and fired a huge iron ball filled with gunpowder. It landed in Doctors' Wood and sent up a column of flame and a shower of earth. Thomas thought he heard screams, and he saw birds and animals fleeing through trees or soaring into the sky. Other men came running up the lane from the pub and took up position with muskets behind granite boulders and cartwheels. The church bells continued to chime and add to the scene of impending horror. Farm workers with pikes at the ready amassed at either side of the lane in ambush. The Roaring Meg boomed once again, sending its dark shell arcing over the pub.

Thomas moved his terrified gaze to the west and the length of Dingwell Lane. It was a grisly scene. Palls of belching smoke smeared the horizon, and flames leapt from haystacks and cottages. Thomas heard a rush of air, and an iron ball slammed into the wall of Tidy Cottage and exploded. An inferno of orange and crimson burst the doors and windows, and fire consumed its thatched roof in seconds. Thomas watched as a petrified child, ragged clothes aflame, staggered from the door and collapsed into the lane. All the while the rattling of muskets had grown in intensity, and Thomas saw the red uniforms of the New Model Army swarming up Yarmer Valley. They streamed down Martyrs' Lane onto the narrow track outside the pub, where they were met by a volley of musket fire. Thomas heard the cries and screams above the continuous pealing of the bells. Enough. He must help that child. He lifted the hatch and began the descent down the rickety ladder as the bells continued their deafening ringing above him. The bell ropes danced frenziedly up and down in front of his eyes as he descended. He jumped the last three rungs and landed heavily, crashing clumsily down the stone stairs before bursting through the tiny arched door and into the nave.

Yvonne, Lucinda, and Hairy Nigel were

clutching their bell ropes as the vicar of Ding-well erupted through the blue curtain that covered the belfry door and slid unceremoniously the length of a pew, gathering a harvest of hymn-books as he went, before finally rolling onto the tiled floor.

Thomas staggered to his feet. 'I must help that child,' he cried, a haunted look in his eyes. He careered towards the main door, which he hauled open before stumbling down the church path.

'What's happened?' said Lucinda, stifling a giggle.

'Strange is that!' said Nigel.

'I'll go after him,' said Yvonne. 'Lucinda, can you pack away and Nigel lock up?' She headed for the open door. Lucinda followed. 'Thomas!' Yvonne called. 'Thomas!'

But Thomas was not listening. He stood motionless at the kissing gate as he gazed across the lane at Tidy Cottage. It was not on fire. Its walls were whole and strong, and Pearl Furkiss was hanging out the washing in her fur coat.

'What you looking at, Reverend? Saucy boy!' she trilled. But Thomas was speechless.

'Thanks, Yvonne,' said Lucinda. She looked at Thomas and giggled again before disappearing down the lane.

'Bet you get a bit lonely up in the vicarage

on your own. Billy-No-Mates, I calls it,' Pearl purred, and opened the side gate. 'You can talk to me if you wants to, Reverend. Do you want to?' she gushed.

'Er, no ... I mean, yes,' stammered Thomas. 'Silly. I thought your house was on ... on ... fire.'

Pearl chuckled. 'House ain't on fire. But I can tell thee what is.' She slunk amply across the lane. 'Funny man you are. Needs a woman's touch.' She slid her arm round his waist and stroked his nose with her crimson forefinger. 'Zat nice?' she crooned.

'She's all yours, Reverend,' said Hairy Nigel, bustling past Yvonne, jangling the keys. 'That is, if you wants her o' course.'

Thomas tried to swallow the lump in his throat, which was the size of a cannonball. 'Um, er, bit busy. Got things to ... er ... things to do.'

''Ere you are, Reverend. You take the keys. Marilyn Monroe and I have got work to do at The Fossils. Come on, Pearl. Get yer knickers on. Miss Bonkers will need her dinner. Time for work.'

'You isn't no fun, Nigel. And I've 'ad my fill of Miss Bonkers.' Pearl Furkiss slopped back across the lane to Tidy Cottage.

'Everything all right, Reverend? Looked a bit shaken up in there. I put the hymnbooks back. No worries.'

'Thank you, Nigel. Yes. Had a bit of a fright.'

Nigel nodded and followed Pearl.

Thomas leaned against the kissing gate and took a deep breath. Yvonne was gazing at him, and it seemed to Thomas she knew more than even he did about himself.

'You know what you should do with Pearl Furkiss?' Thomas looked puzzled. 'Give her a huge kiss, smack her on the bum, and tell her not to be naughty. She'd love it!'

Thomas smiled.

'That's better,' said Yvonne. 'I don't know what happened to you up there.' She glanced up at the tower.

'It's hard to explain. If I can ever explain it. I'm trying not to think about it.'

Yvonne moved close to Thomas and clasped his hands. 'Thomas . . . ' She looked pleadingly into his eyes. 'Thomas, I've been wanting to speak with you . . . about Alison and me.'

'Yvonne, right now I am no longer sure that I am the right person you need to speak to. But I will do my best.'

'I know you *are* the right person.' Yvonne pressed his hands.

'If there is love between you and Alison, then be assured that we will find a way. Let's talk tomorrow. After work? Come for tea.'

Yvonne nodded. 'That will be nice.'

'All will be well, Yvonne. Be assured of that.'

She turned and walked down the lane. Then broke into a jog. Then a run. And was gone. Thomas turned towards the vicarage. He had much to do.

* * *

As Yvonne passed the Whodhavethoughtit, the door opened, and a grateful Wilfred and Lavinia Plunkett stepped out into the sunshine with Gideon and Tizzy. 'Now you sure you folks is all right?' said Tizzy. 'Look. Rain's stopped, and sun 'as come out for thee.'

'Thank you, Tizzy,' said Lavinia. 'Oh, hello, Yvonne. We're going home. Hopefully things will be a bit quieter tonight.'

'I'll come with you,' said Yvonne. 'The police team should be next door right now.'

They walked slowly up the lane and turned the corner at the church. Along Dingwell Lane the sun painted their journey with cheerful stripes of sun and shadow, past the Old Rectory and into their drive. Yvonne noticed there were no police cars at *Le Manoir* — just a silver Mercedes E-class coupe (Yvonne knew her cars) parked in the Plunketts' drive behind their Humber.

A man got out and stood up. 'Mr. and Mrs. Plunkett?'

'Yes. And you are . . . ?'

'Rosencrantz.' He had a thin face and a smart, shiny grey suit and steel-rimmed spectacles. 'I am the count's representative. I am afraid he cannot be here right now.' Yvonne noted the smooth, anonymous mid-Atlantic voice. She had heard it before. Where?

'I was expecting a police team here. Scenes of crime,' said Yvonne.

'Well, yes,' said Mr. Rosencrantz slowly. 'As I understand it, the police have already interviewed Count de Boodle, and he has explained everything. He asked me to come here and apologise to Mr. and Mrs. Plunkett.'

Yvonne stared critically at Mr. Rosencrantz. 'There were bullets fired here last night, damaging the Plunketts' property and just missing Mr. Plunkett.'

'Ah, yeees,' said Rosencrantz. He had slim, thin fingers and hands. He wrung them expressively. 'You see, Mr. and Mrs. Plunkett — may I call you Wilfred and Lavinia? — the count's house was burgled last night.'

The Plunketts gasped. 'Yes. The count was sleeping downstairs. He heard the burglar in the hall, and he fired his pistol. The count

150

always sleeps with a pistol under his pillow. An old habit from his days in French Special Forces.'

'Oh, we never knew the count was a war hero.'

'Well, yes, indeed.' Rosencrantz looked down modestly. 'The count was a senior member of the Maquis. He received a medal after the war.'

'But one bullet was fired through the window. It went into Mr. and Mrs. Plunkett's garden,' Yvonne protested.

'Ah, yes, the bird table.' Rosencrantz sighed. At that moment a man in overalls and carrying a tool bag came through the side gate. 'All finished?' said Rosencrantz. The man nodded. 'I think you will find the damage has been repaired to your satisfaction,' said Rosencrantz, ushering the old couple into the back garden to inspect the work. 'Yes, and the count wanted me to explain and apologise most sincerely for all the inconvenience you have been caused. He assures you it will never happen again. Oh, and . . . ' Rosencrantz reached into his jacket pocket. 'You will find a cheque in this envelope for five thousand pounds made payable to the Homeless Hedgehogs Charity. The count admires their work greatly, and he knows they also enjoy your support.'

'Most generous.' Mr. Plunkett whistled and took the envelope from Rosencrantz's thin fingers.

'And the Panzerfaust in the garage?' said Yvonne, studying Rosencrantz's expression carefully.

'Panzerfaust?' said Mr. Plunkett. 'What the hell's that?'

'Ah, yeeees.' Rosencrantz wrung his hands once again. 'The count is a world-renowned collector of World War Two memorabilia.'

'It's a rocket-propelled grenade launcher,' said Yvonne.

Mrs. Plunkett gasped. 'Dear God.'

'Now don't be alarmed, Mrs. Plunkett. Believe me, the Panzerfaust is quite safe and has no explosive in it. The count was storing it here before moving it into his collection at his main home.'

'His main home? Where is that?' asked Mrs. Plunkett.

'The count has a very fine château near Vichy.' Rosencrantz smiled a thin smile. 'And he asked me to tell you that he would be honoured if you wished to visit him there. He will make all the arrangements, and he will collect you personally from the airport.'

'Well, that is most kind,' said Mrs. Plunkett. 'Tell the count we are very grateful.'

'And the blood on the scullery floor?'

Yvonne had continued her intense scrutiny of Rosencrantz's features.

'Ah, yeees. The count sustained a cut to his foot during the burglary. He has received treatment for the injury, and it is not serious.'

'Does the count know who the burglar was?' Yvonne asked.

'The count has a theory certainly. But he does not want to press any charges or waste police time. He feels that any further investigation would be — how can I put it? — somewhat tiresome.' He looked quizzically at Yvonne. 'You really have been most thorough, Miss Bull. Impressive.' He gave an appreciative nod. 'If only all the police were as efficient.'

Yvonne was inclined to agree but said nothing. Rosencrantz's fixed smile had returned.

'In fact, Miss Bull, the count is very impressed by your diligence. He wonders if you would consider joining our organisation. We are always on the lookout for intelligent young recruits such as yourself. You would be very well rewarded.'

'What exactly does your 'organisation' do, Mr. Rosencrantz?' Yvonne's blue eyes were peeling back the layers of Rosencrantz's composure.

'A very good question, Miss Bull. We work for international charities and foreign governments. Here is my card.' He proffered a steel-blue business card. Yvonne hesitated before taking it.

'I like it here,' she said, turning her head towards the sunny oaks and the glittering sea. 'I enjoy my job.' She turned her gaze back to Rosencrantz. 'Do you enjoy your job, Mr. Rosencrantz? Do you feel good about what you do?'

The thin smile returned, and Yvonne saw a line of perfect white teeth.

'Of course I enjoy working for such a distinguished man as the count. Do consider what I have said, Miss Bull. Call me anytime.'

Yvonne returned his smile with an impassive one of her own, neither showing approval or disapproval. 'I think not. But thank you for the offer.'

Rosencrantz blinked, as if surprised. 'One thing I forgot to mention — the count is leaving the village tomorrow, Mr. and Mrs. Plunkett. He may not have the time to say good-bye, but he asked me to thank you for being such kind neighbours.'

He shook hands with the Plunketts and offered his hand to Yvonne. She shook his cold hand without averting her gaze. Rosencrantz stepped into the Mercedes. The silver coupe scattered gravel as it slid like a bullet up the lane and out of the village.

'You aren't going to work for that man

. . . are you, Yvonne?' said Mrs. Plunkett. 'We would miss you in the village.'

'Don't worry, Lavinia. Who on earth would swap all this excitement for a windy, freezing old castle in France? I would miss all of you too.' Having delivered this verdict, she turned and resumed her run up Dingwell Lane.

So Count de Boodle knew who the burglar was. Yvonne smiled at the thought of Peter successfully breaking into his own home and escaping with something the count wanted. She quickened her pace, excited at the thought that Peter was somewhere in Dingwell. But where? She stopped at the stone-pillared gateway to The Fossils. The long slate and shillet driveway, flanked by neat lines of slender birches, snaked down to the main house. But Peter would not be in the old folks' home. She lifted her gaze, following the line of the old track that led through the garden at The Fossils before disappearing through the trees. It wound its way through Stoggie's Farm, with its deserted farmhouse and tumbled-down sheds, and on down the wooded valley to Eastcombe. Yvonne focussed on the beach, and to the side, she could just see the old stone hut. Surely he could not be there? Yvonne's mind leafed back through the years. A picnic on Eastcombe beach with Peter's parents and Yvonne's mum. They had played among the pointed rocks and had run back up to the stone hut. Peter's father had been rebuilding the hut, and each time he was finding more stones and building a new wall, mixing the cement in a bucket, using water from the stream. And Peter's mum, Esther, had said, 'We've got a house already — we don't need another one.' Peter's dad had smiled and said, 'It's just a place to dream.'

The braying of an old tethered donkey in the garden at The Fossils interrupted Yvonne's reverie. She looked at her watch. Past lunchtime now. She had promised to visit Miss Bonkers. Yvonne marched down the drive.

★ ★ ★

A damp Miss Cloke returned to Enigma Cottage to find the count's Daimler parked at the front. There was also a present for her draped around the bust of Winston Churchill on a pedestal by her porch. Her spectacles. She snatched them before some other fiend from the sky could escape with them again. And some infernal creature had pooped on Churchill's head!

The count already was ensconced in front of the glowing fire, one foot propped on the Victorian cast-iron fender. He had helped himself to a Bladnoch whiskey and was beginning to feel comfortable.

'Ah, *madame*! The Coco Chanel of Dingwell,' he exclaimed, as Miss Cloke opened the cottage door and stood dripping on the mat.

'I do not have quite her style, Count, I regret to say. Give me a few minutes.'

Miss Cloke bustled off to the bedroom for some dry clothes. The count flicked through *The Dingwell Parish Magazine* only to find a flattering photo of Tigger staring vainly from page three with a strap line proclaiming, 'Tigger, Lord of All He Surveys.' If Tigger could read, he would have enjoyed that. *Probably wrote it himself*, thought the count. It was followed by a sycophantic account of 'the life and times of Dingwell's best-loved character.' The count found this particularly excruciating and promptly topped up his whiskey.

Miss Cloke returned with a cup of tea. 'Whiskey? So early? Count, you must take yourself in hand,' she scolded.

'I had a visitor last night. Two visitors in fact,' said the count. 'And this is one of them.' He held up the picture of Tigger. '*Ce vieux chat effroyable!*'

'My goodness,' said Miss Cloke. 'And your second guest?'

'Monsieur le Chat's accomplice. A burglar.'

'Burglar? Who?'

'Not just any burglar, Miss Cloke. There is only one person it could have been. Someone who knew the house intimately. And someone who had this infernal agent provocateur to assist him.' He furiously waved the picture again before crushing the magazine with both hands and hurling it into the fire.

'I tried to kill them both. I fired five times. But Monsieur le Chat was too quick for me. The burglar locked me in the scullery and escaped.'

'With what?' Miss Cloke leant forward. 'Henri, what was stolen?'

'I do not know. We searched every inch of the place when I moved in. No disks, no memory cards, no hard drives. Only books. Thousands of books. We could not search them all.'

'So you think something was hidden in a book.'

'Oui, *madame. Je pense. Jeune* Peter, you have tricked me. *Tu m'as dupé.*' He stared into the fire, his gnarled hands gripping the armrests. '*Dupé!*' He spat the word out.

'Did anyone hear the shots?'

'I assume *les* Plunketts did — the ancient azaleas next door.' The count sniffed his whiskey and grunted. He had been made a fool of by a cat and a scrawny adolescent.

Fury simmered through his veins. 'Do not worry about the police, Miss Cloke. I phoned Rosencrantz, and we went to see the Chief Constable early this morning.'

'Not very pleased to be hauled out of bed in the small hours, I imagine?' said Miss Cloke.

'Indeed. But when he realised . . . Everything has been explained. Rosencrantz is handling matters. There will be no questions. He just said, whatever we were doing, finish it quickly.'

'Good advice. We must act calmly, Count. Revenge is a dish best served cold.'

The count nodded agreement. 'Indeed, Cynthia. Indeed.'

'You can begin by reading my notes on the reconnaissance to Eastcombe. You will see my recommendations. We must act quickly but not in haste.' She passed her notebook to the count, who donned his spectacles. They were interrupted by a long wailing screech from the spare bedroom.

The count looked up. 'Not Monsieur le Chat again, I trust?'

'Excuse me,' said Miss Cloke. She bustled off to the bedroom. The count settled down to read the notes, and a plan began to form in his mind.

'Aaaaaargh!' shrieked Miss Cloke. The

count struggled to his feet and headed for the bedroom. Miss Cloke was staring into the wardrobe. 'Aaaaaaaargh!' she yelled.

'What's the matter, Cynthia?'

'The cat! Pandora!'

'She has had kittens, Cynthia. That's all,' soothed Henri.

'Aaaargh! I can see that. But look! Just look!'

The count looked. 'They are just kittens, Cynthia.'

'But can't you see?'

'See what, Cynthia?'

'They are all . . . all . . . stripy!'

In the fireplace Tigger's picture, the one part of the parish magazine yet to be consumed by the flames, gazed triumphantly across the room.

15

Miss B

Miss Bonkers had finished her lunch, and Pearl Furkiss wiped away the last residues of apple crumble and custard from around her mouth. 'There you are, my love.'

Miss Bonkers scribbled on her notepad — just one word, 'Lipstick!'

'Oh, right you are. Now where d'you keep your lippy?' Pearl held up a vast leather handbag. Miss Bonkers nodded. 'In 'ere? Oh, my Lor' . . . There's so much stuff in 'ere.' While Pearl rummaged, Miss B looked through the arched gothic windows of The Fossils. They afforded a clear view of the old cart track as it curved through the grounds beneath the stately oaks and elder trees, and across to the little wood that bordered Stoggie's Farm. She had the same view every day. She liked it. She enjoyed the way the winds swung aside the full-leafed branches of the trees to unveil a fleeting vision of the valley down to Eastcombe. *Will the children come to the woods again today?* she wondered.

Pearl had found the lipstick and did her

best to apply it while Miss B puckered and pouted. In her youth Miss B had scandalised her prim and wealthy parents by appearing topless in *The Daily Splash* — the stable lad had handed a copy of it to her father, she recalled with a smirk. The old man nearly swallowed his pipe. Her next outrage was to be photographed again — which she arranged — dancing naked at the Isle of Dogs Pop Festival with her completely stoned friends, her body painted purple but for a single sunflower growing from where the sun could not possibly shine.

Her colourful career as an art and music teacher concluded abruptly when, under her tutelage, one her students persuaded a thirty-foot-long inflatable penis to wobble ominously through the window behind the principal's head as he was addressing a governors' meeting. She had then married one Timothy Smallpiece, the curator of a tiny art gallery in Sleephaven where she featured her work. One of her sculptures — a wicker basket containing a severed head on a bed of erotic fruits — memorably caused one elderly voyeur to pass out.

As she was ever a woman of lustful pleasures, her husband had passed away from exhaustion a few years before. Now she sat on her Celtic dragon throne chair, propped up by crimson and gold cushions, and spent each day nagging the staff, scribbling incomprehensible poetry, and sailing on a sumptuous ocean of memories and pure invention. It was a constant voyage that she loved. The grandson of one of the other 'inmates,' as she called them, had looked at her and remarked, 'I wouldn't want to end up like that,' before stuffing a cheeseburger into his head. She had thought, *Thank God I never ended up like you*, and that was revenge enough for his insult. She savoured victories of the mind.

Miss B had been enjoying watching the storm's lightning fork the land, and its shifting ghostly drift across the valley and punishing needles of rain excited her spirits. Now the emergence of the sun's balm and kiss on the dripping trees and patient stones of the old house summoned joy from within her. The sun caught the blonde hair of her favourite piano student as Yvonne entered the room. The light faded briefly as Yvonne bent down to kiss her.

'Mrs. Smallpiece. How are you?'

The old lady scribbled, 'Call me Miss Bonkers! Or Miss B! How are you? Tell me about Alison.'

And Yvonne did.

Stand here and watch the rapturous hug she receives. Miss B is scribbling again. It is about the young couple, sitting on the stile by the wooden gate, playing chess. Yvonne rushes to the window and looks back at Miss B, shaking her head, 'Not there now.'

Miss B writes, 'They were there. With a little girl. And dogs.'

Yvonne looks towards the woods, wistfully. 'A young couple. With a little girl?'

We will leave them there in the fading afternoon light, talking among the eclectic scenery of William Morris prints; cushions of tulip, rose, and pimpernel; a carved oak armoire and dresser; deep ruby curtains; the stained glass table supported by a carved dragon; the chess set of nemesis faeries; the ghost mirror; and Caspar David Friedrich's *Angel in Prayer* luminous and exultant above the bed.

★　★　★

At Enigma Cottage, Miss Cloke was unearthing a shortwave radio transmitter and receiver from an ancient leather trunk. She was feeling more than a little weary, but there was still one last part of her mission to be completed. She went in search of her binoculars and passed the wardrobe door, where an exhausted Pandora was feeding her kittens, little stripy digits of fur struggling to survive. They would have to go. Miss Cloke thought darkly about a weighted bag in the pond before walking out into her garden in the fading light. Leaning on Churchill's recently scrubbed crown, she trained her sights on the garden at The Fossils. A blonde woman was walking down the old track towards the gate. WPC Yvonne Bull. She was becoming something of a nuisance. Yvonne had stopped by the old gate and was talking to someone. Miss Cloke adjusted her Kriegsmarine binoculars, trying to make out who Yvonne was talking to. Beside a tree she could just make out a figure standing. Could it be . . . was that a green jacket? So hard to tell. A dog came bounding up to the figure, who bent down to stroke it. She was convinced. It had to be him. Where had he been hiding? Stoggie's Farm? Miss Cloke ruled that out. Too near the village and easy to get to. No, it had to be the old stone hut by Eastcombe Beach. She felt a surge of excitement. The count would be pleased. She would wait until Yvonne had gone before going to the old track herself, and she would open the wooden gates across Stoggie's Farm.

★ ★ ★

Thomas had spent a miserable afternoon composing his letter of resignation to the

165

bishop. He was afraid of Bishop Nonesuch, a spidery, spindly man who constantly clasped and wrung his hands and then asked Thomas questions while tilting his head enquiringly like an aged spaniel. That would be one good thing — he never would have to speak to him again. He imagined a conversation with the withered old stick.

'No, you can't persuade me to change my mind,' Thomas would say grandly, enjoying his brief visit to the moral high ground. 'I have decided, Bishop!'

'But think of your flock, your family, your high standing in the community, the importance of your spiritual leadership, all the people you have saved for Jesus,' pleaded the imaginary Bishop, wringing his hands.

'I know, Your Grace.' Thomas's voice descended from Noel Coward to Orson Welles. 'But I have a higher calling. Good-bye, Your Grace.'

It did occur to Thomas that other than being some incredible 'Master of the Entire Universe,' there could be no higher calling than serving the Lord God, surely. Ah, well. Anyway, Thomas suspected that when the bishop read his letter, his clasped hands would be waving above his head while he danced an arthritic jig of gratitude to the Almighty for the removal of this troublesome priest.

The letter stood propped on his mantel-piece in a white envelope. It was too late to post it now. He had agonised long and hard. No job. No wife. No children. What had Pearl Furkiss said? Billy-No-Mates. No friends either? The problem for Thomas was that what he wanted to talk about nobody else wanted to discuss. Was that true? Tizzy. He could talk to Tizzy. And Yvonne.

Thomas imagined himself in an ordinary job, working in a supermarket, having cheerful coffee breaks with people who were just doing a job without having some blooming mission on their minds. No, their concerns would be their rent, kids, relationships, the dog. That was their mission in life, a mission Thomas wanted but was a million miles away from ever achieving. And if he did work in a supermarket or an office, there would be questions.

'Oh, what did you do before working here?'

'I was a vicar,' he would reply cheerfully, 'and before that a teacher.'

'Why did you give them up?' (Thomas pictured a pleasant lady in accounts chatting over a sandwich.)

'Oh, I found I hated teaching, my wife left me, and I lost my faith.' And the pleasant lady would stare in surprise and lower her coffee cup and suddenly think that she just might be in the company of a lunatic or a defrocked priest who had groped a member of his congregation.

Ah, well. Whatever he did in future, Thomas had decided that loneliness was something he no longer could endure. He could not cope with it. It was like an illness he could not shake off. He would start this very evening. He would go to the pub for dinner and drink beer, and chat to anyone who came in, even if they did not want to talk to him. He would talk to Tizzy, Gideon, Tigger, even Miss Cloke, and scan the newspaper and chortle and read aloud bits of news he thought amusing, and tell witty anecdotes — and if he could not think of any, he would make them up! Tomorrow he would go online to a dating agency! To be truthful, Thomas already had flirted — if that was the right word — with the eHeavenly dating website. He had listed his interests as 'life, fate, and stopping moles digging up my lawn,' which he thought some equally lonely soul would find intriguing. He also had set aside the minor fact that he was still married.

Nevertheless it was a comforted and more cheerful Thomas who later put on his coat and toddled happily down to the warmth and comfort of the Whodhavethoughtit. It was to be a truly unforgettable evening.

★　★　★

Meanwhile, the count had returned to *Le Manoir*, where he went quickly to work in his garage. The Panzerfaust required some attention. He opened the metal box mounted on a two-wheeled carriage and lifted the weapon as if it were an infant, wrapped in oil cloth, and placed it on a workbench. '*C'est magnifique!*' he exclaimed, unwrapping the cloth to reveal the smoothly crafted steel tube of the grenade launcher, with its leaf sight and deadly trigger. A rack of grenade rockets, smooth fins beneath a steel grey explosive chalice, topped with a deadly coned detonator, fitted neatly inside the steel box. There were six — more than enough, thought the count. From a range of one hundred metres, the weapon generated volatile gases as it travelled, which added an explosive power sufficient to disable any tank. However, the count had a rather different target in mind. He oiled and cleaned the weapon thoroughly, loving the military smell of fuel oil and ordinance and its sheer perfection and simplicity. He once had watched it rip into the flank of a Sherman tank and set off a series of explosions that sent its crew desperately trying to escape through the turret, only to be gunned down amid tongues of flame, their bodies slumped like ragdolls. 'Perfection!' he murmured, and smiled at the memory. '*C'était il y a longtemps*.'

He replaced the Panzerfaust in the steel box and manoeuvred the cart to the front of the garage in readiness and was presently back in the scullery washing his hands and forearms with coal tar soap. Excellent! The count checked his Luger. Six bullets — enough to gun down anyone who escaped and have one left over. It was a shame. The dog would have to go. Odessa sat obediently by the count as he dried his hands — bright-brown eyes, elegant head and coat of chestnut, loyal, loving, and powerful as a racehorse. The count looked into his eyes and felt no guilt, only admiration. Odessa would complete his mission and be shot by the count in the back of the Daimler. He already had removed the dog's collar and tossed it onto the scullery fire, together with his spare clothes, including his black suit and the green alpine hat he always wore to church.

The heap of garments steamed on the fire as the count struggled into his ancient fatigues, having donned a grey army vest with an eagle motif. A grey field officer's cap, with silver piping, completed the outfit. But this was no mere costume. To the count this was his other skin, his preferred identity, with its dark philosophy made manifest by cap badge and button, belt and bullet. He caught sight of himself in the hall mirror and saw briefly the younger idealistic man he once had been. But this was now who he was.

'*Oder!* Odessa!' The great dog strode obediently to the front door and into the drive, before leaping into the backseat of the Daimler. The count reversed the car towards his garage and opened the door. He paused in the near darkness. No one was about. He wheeled the Panzerfaust on its carriage to the rear of the car and lowered the coupling onto the tow bar. Finally he stuck gaffer tape over the rear lights and did the same with the headlights, leaving only a vertical slit of light to illuminate his path along the track.

He climbed into the driver's seat and hummed an old military song, '*Maréchal, Nous Voilà!*' his leather gloves gently drumming on the steering wheel. He would wait until it was completely dark and Miss Cloke had done her work — he noticed a shortwave radio receiver had been secreted onto the passenger seat. *Well done indeed, Miss Cloke.* Then, in the early morning, this mission would be done, and he would leave this accursed place forever.

16

A Game of Chess

'Who is that?' said Navinda. She was sitting on the old oak stile by the gate to Stoggie's Farm. Pi and Navinda had been walking in the woods with Doris. They each had held Doris's hand and swung her between them as they strolled along the track, their boots kicking up the muddied leaves. Doris had giggled and shrieked merrily as they pretended to drop her into a puddle. Meanwhile Jack and Jill and Buddy jetted through the undergrowth and would emerge momentarily, breath steaming, fur snagged with bindweed and nettles, before tearing off again into the thicket. Navinda and Doris had been concentrating on a game of chess, while Pi hurled sticks for the dogs. 'That blonde woman,' said Navinda. Pi turned to look.

'That is Yvonne. You remember Tizzy talking about her.'

'I do. She looks really young. Does she go running?'

'Every day. I have known her all my life. She used to babysit and read to me.'

Yvonne had been walking up The Fossils driveway before suddenly detouring onto the old track.

'She's coming this way. Should we hide?' said Navinda.

'No, stay there. She may not even be able to see you. I'll hide,' said Pi, and slid behind a stout oak tree.

To Yvonne it seemed unreal and magical to find this strange girl and an even younger girl seated on the stile playing with a tiny chess set, framed by cheerful birches and oaks at the edge of a dark wood, the ground dotted with wild garlic, bluebells, and wood sorrel. *A subject for Renoir*, she thought, and paused for her senses to absorb this shimmering image. *Yes, the garden in Montmartre.*

'Hello, Yvonne,' said Navinda, her dark eyes turning to catch Yvonne's rapt gaze. 'This is Doris.'

Doris stood up and smiled at Yvonne. 'Pi, says you are a friend. You can see us. Pi said you might not be able to.'

'How did you . . . ' Yvonne paused. 'And who is . . . Pi, did you say?' He stepped out from behind the tree. 'Peter Young, as I live and breathe. I ought to arrest you.'

'For burgling my own house?'

'You could have been killed. Come here.' She wrapped her arms around him and looked at Navinda. 'He wanted to marry me once.'

Pi blushed. 'I was only six.'

'And live in a tree house.' Navinda and Doris laughed. 'How could I have refused an offer like that? Still scruffy, I see.'

'The green jacket has seen better days,' said Navinda.

'That was his dad's at uni,' said Yvonne.

'Yeah, look, he was a punk goth,' said Pi. 'It's still a cool jacket.'

'Fallen in love yet, Peter? What do you think, Doris?'

'Well, I think Pi likes Navinda. But she says he's too scruffy.' It was Pi's turn to laugh.

'Count de Boodle was shouting about wanting to shoot you,' said Yvonne. 'He's working with Miss Cloke. She went on a reconnaissance mission into Doctors' Wood this morning. Modesty Blaise in tweeds. Wouldn't mind betting that she's been spying on the Dream Factory for the count.'

'There's nowhere else we can go,' said Pi. 'We would see anyone coming anyway. Tizzy said we should not come to the village.'

'Tigger will protect us,' said Doris. Right on cue, Tigger slipped from the Y of an oak tree and leapt onto Navinda's lap.

'I wouldn't stay there much longer. Look, use Cosy Cottage, but don't let Miss Cloke see you. The count is leaving.'

'When?'

'Tomorrow.'

Pi looked at Navinda. 'In that case we'll stay where we are until he has gone.'

Jack and Jill and Buddy charged out of the undergrowth. Buddy went to Pi and stood on his hind legs while Pi ruffled his ears.

'Peter, where are your mum and dad?'

The question momentarily shook Pi. It was a question that weakened him physically when he thought about. The woodland seemed suddenly darker, and all eyes were on him.

'I do not know. Sometimes I can hear mum's voice. Om sometimes gets messages, but often they are very faint.'

'Om?'

'The micro intel unit that Mum designed.'

Yvonne smiled. 'So good to see you. I went away on holiday three weeks ago, and when I return, my little brother is gone and his mum and dad too. Why didn't you call the police?'

'I did. I should have spoken to you.'

'Who did you speak to?'

'I don't know. It was the next day. I saw Tizzy and phoned from the pub. I said I was hiding and my parents were gone. I don't think they believed me. Doesn't even sound real to me now when I say it.' Pi looked down.

'What happened?'

Pi sat down on the stile with Doris on his lap. 'Mum and Dad always told me something might happen and what to do if it did. I knew there was some big secret, something they had created. We often had visitors, men in suits. There was a man from the government — the 'minister of something.' I don't know what . . . '

'Go on.'

'I remember Dad saying, 'Son, we may have to go away, be away for a while. You can cope, can't you? I said, 'Yes, of course.' Thought it was exciting. Could skip school. Mum and Dad said Tizzy knew and that he and Gideon would help me. But I did not expect it to happen like this.' He glanced at Navinda; she reached for his hand, and he took a deep breath.

'I was asleep in the cellar — well, not asleep. It was all too exciting being down there with all our old stuff, thinking of the games we had played. There was, well, noise, cars, banging of doors. Dad was shouting, and there was a struggle in the hall, right outside the cellar door. I heard them shout, 'Get the boy.' Mum screamed out, 'Run, Peter, run.' I heard boots running upstairs. You see, my room was being redecorated. That's why I was in the cellar. That saved me.'

Yvonne stood spellbound. Even Tigger was giving matters his full attention.

'I ran out of the cellar. I saw a Mercedes in the drive. Mum and Dad were being dragged into a big car. There were lots of men.'

'What did you do?'

'I locked the cellar door and ran. You know where to.'

Yvonne nodded. 'Yes. I know.'

'Over the wall and down to the old mill. Hid the cellar key and found the key to the Dream Factory. Jack and Jill came with me. When I arrived, Tigger was there. I was so pleased to see him.' Pi smiled at Tigger. 'Then I just looked at the sea. Navinda came. After that I did not dare go back to the house.'

'But you did, you naughty *rascally* thief,' said Yvonne, smiling.

'Yes, I did,' said Pi, enjoying the memory. 'Tigger came too.' Tigger attempted modesty but failed.

'Caused chaos, by the look of things. Scruffy, raggedy boy thief with his wicked accomplice,' said Yvonne, and stroked Tigger's head.

'If the count does leave tomorrow, I'll see Tizzy and Gideon and come back to the house then.'

'I'll find out who took your call at the police station and why you weren't listened to.'

'Thanks, Yvonne.' Pi stood up and hugged

her. 'Brilliant to see you, big sis.'

'You've got a little family to care for you now,' said Yvonne. 'Don't need your big sister.'

'Time to go,' said Pi.

Navinda nodded and stood up. Yvonne watched them fade like ghosts into the trees along the track. Tigger paced behind them while the dogs once again crashed through the bracken and saplings of holly and elder. Yvonne breathed deeply. Her vibrant and cheerful world in which she had so much faith had become darker. Blooming useless Queensbridge police. Probably that idiot, Dave. She would find out the truth tomorrow. She jogged back to the village. Miss Cloke concealed herself in the cemetery, as Yvonne's blonde head, just visible above the old stone wall, bobbed past along the lane. Miss Cloke opened the rusty iron gate and headed for The Fossils. She had a mission to complete. En route she had placed the shortwave radio receiver in the count's Daimler. Things were going according to plan.

★ ★ ★

Thomas was the first arrival at the Whodhavethoughtit. Tizzy was arranging the bar mats and slop trays while Gideon was wiping the tables.

'Reverend Tom, welcome,' said Gideon. 'Your usual chair by the fire?'

'From tomorrow it really will just be plain 'Tom.' No longer 'Reverend,' I'm afraid,' said Thomas, walking to the bar. He perched on a stool.

Tizzy stared.

'You joking, man,' said Gideon.

'Tomorrow I am handing the bishop my letter of resignation. Sad but true. A pint of Methuselah's Old Wrinkly will go down nicely. Please, Tizzy. I need it.'

Tizzy slowly poured the pint, as he always did, adding a final drop to the thin head of foam. 'Something happen at the church today, Reverend? Gather you 'ad a bit of a fright in the church tower. Nigel told me you was a bit shaken up.'

Thomas shook his head wearily. 'I just wonder what is real anymore. Have I been seeing ghosts? Are Pi and Navinda real?'

'You met them, man. They gave you food. You felt warmth from their fire,' said Gideon.

Thomas passed some coins to Tizzy and sipped his pint. 'I went into that church tower today. Climbed right up into the belfry. Then there was chaos. Village went mad, explosions, burning cottages. Men with pikes. Muskets. People dying.' He paused. Gideon and Tizzy were staring at him. 'Suddenly the

179

trapdoor slams open, and a man with a pigtail . . . ' He stopped and stared at Tizzy, who smiled slowly.

'Quite right, Reverend. I got a pigtail. Go on.'

'He had a voice just like . . . like . . . '

'Mine, Reverend? Voice like mine?' Thomas sat open mouthed. Tizzy smiled and winked at Gideon. 'Dunno what happened to thee, Reverend, but I tell thee this. In the Civil War the Reverend Twitten was a royalist, see? Organised an ambush on the bridge at Lower Bottom. When the Roundheads came up Yarmer Valley, the villagers hid him in the church tower and gave 'im food. Up there for two year 'e was. Sounds like you had sighting of that.'

Thomas's fingers clung to the edge of the bar to steady himself. 'So was it you that fed him?'

'P'raps it was,' said Tizzy, laughing.

'Man, he's been around a long time,' said Gideon. 'Since the beginning of time.'

Thomas began to feel warmed by the pint of Meths. As he often felt with Tizzy and Gideon, he did not need to know everything, and they did not expect him to. 'You see, I went to the church today for answers.'

'To the church for answers?' said Gideon. 'Man, that's only a place for questions.'

180

'You see, Thomas,' Tizzy said, 'depends what eyes you seeing with. Keep the faith . . . you says that every Sunday. See this clock 'ere. Six o'clock, opening time. Eleven o'clock, closing time. But there ain't really no openin' and closin'. Never 'as been. It's just somethin' we do. You needs to keep the faith, Reverend Tom. Believe what your eyes and ears is tellin' you. There's them that sees and them that can't see. Go keep the faith, and open more eyes. Talk to Navinda. She'll tell thee.'

'I was wondering whether she was real, if I had dreamt it all.'

'She's more real, Reverend, than that bloomin' clock will ever be.'

'I feel better now,' said Thomas.

Tizzy gripped Thomas's forearm. 'We need you to keep the faith. Giddy and I need you. So do Yvonne and Pi and Navinda, and all the little Dorises and Barnies in this world. They needs to grow up *knowin'* they can believe in you.' Tizzy released his grip. 'They needs to know you will always be there for them.'

Thomas breathed deeply. He felt moved. 'I think I get it now. Thank you,' he said softly.

'Think you got your answer, man,' said Gideon. 'Now, Reverend Tom, am I standing here all night or can I cook you somethin' beautilicious?'

'Oooh! Well now. A curry, I think.'

'Hot one?'

'Oh, yes.'

'Disaster Bay chilis? Arugula? Garbanzo beans? Yellow squash and zucchini ragout? Dopiaza sauce with red curried duck?'

'Oh, yes.'

'Hot?'

'Oh, hot!'

'How hot?'

'Oh, very hot.'

'Hot, hot, hot!' Gideon and Thomas high-fived while Tizzy looked bewildered. 'One volcanovindaloo coming right up.'

'Oh, and papadums and the devilish lime pickle,' said Thomas, now drooling. He wandered over to the fire and settled into the old wing chair, resting his pint on the side table. Tigger had spread himself on the rug with, as usual, no regard for the amount of space he was occupying, and Thomas had to adjust his position so his feet could rest on the fender. Ah, well. He was expecting a quiet evening, contemplating the fire.

★ ★ ★

Miss Bonkers closed her eyes and rested her head on a crimson cushion.

'There. You comfy?' said Pearl. 'There's your meds.'

Miss B reached for the morphine, her favourite elixir. It relieved pain but also enhanced her vivid imagination with a strong dash of euphoria. She nodded her thanks to Pearl, who left the room. Miss B touched her reading lamp, and the room fell into spectral darkness, her dressing gown hanging on the door like a ghost. She loved the darkness, telling a bewildered Pearl that she could see more in the blackness. Now it was in front of the same gothic windows that she was to witness a drama. It commenced with the appearance stage left of two eyes, strange eyes, with penetrating darts of light that stabbed the trees. Miss B stared hard at this vision. Two vertical slits emitted intense focussed beams, startling the woodland into surrender. She wondered about her medication and, in particular, how the morphine would react with the LSD tab supplied by her dear grandson, Kevin, in his little monthly present, hidden under the Curly Wurly in a box of Milk Tray. She would not take it now, she decided, but would choose her moment. Instead Miss B concentrated hard on what appeared to be the eyes of a gigantic serpent, sliding, creeping down the old track in the sepulchral gloom. A hand reached across the sky and drew back the veil of cloud, permitting the rising moon to cast an unearthly light on the count's Daimler as it injected the ancient artery of the forest like a virus. What was that strange little carriage jogging and jolting in its wake that seemed to be carrying some kind of box? She leaned as far forward as she could to catch its departure into the forest, like a menacing slow-moving train. What on earth was happening? She thought of the young children she had seen playing chess by the stile and was suddenly afraid for them. What mission did this mechanical serpent have to glide into the forest under cover of dusk and continue its journey with those eerie slits of light piercing, like forked tongues, the forest's protective cloak of darkness?

She touched her lamp into life and began to compose a frantic sketch of what she had seen. And had she seen it? Had the morphine conjured this demonic vision to perform a strange masque before her exhausted eyes? She looked again at the image she had drawn on the pad and added more details. Then more. She lay back and rested her eyes. She slept fitfully, but the fear would not leave her, tapping quietly like some inner drum.

★   ★   ★

Thomas's reverie, wandering among the flame caves and fire tongues in the Whodhavethoughtit's blazing fireplace, was interrupted by two seismic events. The first was the arrival of his dinner — a reverie in itself of scented rice, crimson curried duck, smoking beans, and ragout delivered on a sizzling raclette.

'There you go, Reverend Tom.'

'Oh, wonderful, Giddy,' swooned Thomas, reaching for the napkin.

'An' lime pickle an' mango sauces. Enjoy.'

'Thank you. Thank you.'

Tigger had opened one eye and briefly contemplated the fragrant feast that was now sitting on the side table. He closed it again. Curry was a Tigger-proof choice.

The second event was Miss Cloke's arrival with a large wicker basket that she dumped on the floor, before angrily ringing the little ship's bell on the bar. 'Landlord! Tizzy! Gideon! Where are you?' Thomas glanced up from his meal and received a withering look from Miss Cloke. 'How you have the nerve to show your face in the village, you insufferable and shameless charlatan, I do not know.'

Thomas rallied his defences, removing a rogue spring onion protruding from his mouth. 'Good evening, Cynthia. How pleasant to see you.' He smiled pleasantly, although his heart seemed to be in sudden overdrive.

'And how fitting that you are in the company of this cat, this supreme fraud, imposter, and gigolo.'

'Erm, that's just Tigger,' said Thomas, and pointed gormlessly at Tigger, whose one eye once again was watching events. Tizzy and Gideon arrived in the bar.

'Ah, Tizzy. Since you are the owner of this appalling thief and bounder of a feline, I have a present for you!' She picked up the wicker basket before dropping it pointedly on the floor.

Gideon peered into the basket. 'They are only kittens, ma'am. Not yet weaned. And their mama cat . . . '

'They are all stripy, which tells you that their father is this . . . ' She pointed at the hearthrug. But the subject of her tirade magically had disappeared. Even as Miss Cloke stood open mouthed, gazing at the empty space where her tormentor had displayed himself like some gauche and brazen lothario, Tigger was making his escape through the kitchen door. Tigger simply did not do 'family.'

'But what about these poor kittens, Miss Cloke? Can't leave 'em here.'

'Either keep them or drown them in the village pond. With their corrupted dam as well.'

'I'll put them in the snug for now,' said Tizzy. 'Be warm in there.'

'You're a hardhearted lady, Miss Cloke,' said Gideon.

'At times I have to be, Gideon.' Her outstretched arm pointed at Thomas, whose mouth was now crammed with crispy duck. 'But with what I know now about this imposter, this play actor, this cheat, this chameleon in cassock and surplice, this . . . this . . . ' Miss Cloke ran out of metaphors and stood shaking. 'When everyone knows, *as they will*, I sincerely hope you will be hounded from the village, never to return. Better still, burned at the stake, as we used to do with witches.'

Thomas swallowed and stood up. 'Mith Cloke,' he blurted, and a speck of rice flew from his mouth and managed to fasten itself to the old lady's forehead. Thomas tried again. 'Like anyone I have made mistakes in my life.' He took a breath. 'But I have never, never done anything of which I am ashamed. Unlike you, I suspect.' Thomas held his defiant stare at Miss Cloke, although his legs were now made of jelly.

Miss Cloke snorted with contempt, and with one last look of loathing, she turned on her heel and departed, slamming the pub door as she went.

Thomas sank back to his seat, visibly shaken.

'You OK, man?' Gideon knelt next to his chair and mopped his brow. 'She's crazy, man. We know you ain't done nothin'. What the hell does she know anyway?'

'Reverend Tom, drink this,' said Tizzy. He did. A warm, soft, enveloping concoction of darkest rum with mead and brown sugars.

Thomas sipped it gratefully. 'It's just that when I see hatred like that, it still shocks me.'

'It shocks us all, Reverend. That's why we needs the faith. And we needs you,' said Tizzy. 'When she talks like that, you know it is not you that she hates. It is her version of you that she hates.'

'Man, I think she be talking about herself. Do you want me to keep your dinner warm for you?'

'Thanks, Gideon. I'm OK now. Just that when I see Miss Cloke, my legs seem to turn to rubber. Don't know why.'

'It ain't just you, Reverend Tom. Trust me.'

The bell rang in the bar as Yvonne entered. 'Hi, Gideon. I see you haven't got Tasmanian devil on the menu tonight.'

Gideon smiled. 'Not tonight, Yvonne. Only by special order!'

'I know. I just passed it going up Martyrs' Lane. You can still see the scorch marks on the road. Oh, and Enigma Cottage is up for sale. The board went up this afternoon.'

'Hey, wow. Reverend Tom is maxing out on the curry. Give it a try.'

'I'll think about it. Thomas, may I join you?'

There was nothing Thomas could have wanted more and beamed at the prospect. 'Of course.' Yvonne sat down on a stool beside him.

Thomas had finished his curry and took a cooling sip from his pint. 'We were going to talk,' he said gently.

Yvonne sat beautifully upright in her seat. She smiled nervously. 'Thomas, Alison and I are in love.'

Thomas took her left hand in his. 'Engaged, I see.' He gently lifted her ring finger, and the diamond diffused the soft glow of the fire. He gazed at her lovely face and the kind, modest heart within and felt the well of his own faith refilling. Yvonne lowered her gaze modestly. 'Yvonne, I know that if I was to marry you and Alison, it would be one of the most beautiful and honest things I have ever done. I know that Jesus himself would give his blessing.'

'But the church will not allow it. That is what you're saying. Isn't it, Thomas?'

'Yes. The church will not allow it. It does allow interracial marriage, although that is prohibited in Genesis twenty-four, and sixteen different books of the Bible.'

''Do not lie with a man as one lies with a woman; that is detestable.' Leviticus,' said Yvonne. 'Do you think it is detestable, Thomas?'

'No, Yvonne. I think love is wonderful,' said

Thomas, 'and you are full of love.' Yvonne smiled. 'Mind you,' continued Thomas cheerfully, 'God can only know how some men find anyone of either sex willing to sleep with them. Rugby front-row forwards, for example, with no teeth, shaven heads, and funny ears. But even they end up with somebody.' Yvonne was smiling broadly. 'And yes, even at school or university, I probably did find some men attractive. And probably still do. But I think that's only natural.'

Yvonne looked at him quizzically. 'You are being very honest tonight, Thomas, and a bit naughty.'

'Tomorrow may be my last day as the vicar of Dingwell.' Yvonne's face changed. 'I have written my letter of resignation but have not posted it yet.'

'Don't leave,' she implored. 'Don't leave us. You have set us free.'

'Whatever I decide about that,' said Thomas, 'if you and Alison would like to come to the church at three o'clock tomorrow afternoon, I will give a holy blessing to your love and union.'

Yvonne's eyes were full of light. 'Is there precedent for that?'

Thomas smiled. 'If it was good enough for the royals, then it is good enough for you and Alison.'

Yvonne's hands were trembling. 'Thomas. Thank you.' She leant across the table and kissed his cheek softly. He felt an energy flow through him. He could not wash his face again without remembering this moment.

'Hashers' night tonight.'

'Oh, the runners with all those funny names,' said Thomas.

'You should join us. You would enjoy it.'

'I'm not very fit really. I used to run a lot.'

'A few jars in here tonight. Back to the campsite. Then a six a.m. run in fancy dress through Stoggie's Farm, down to Eastcombe Beach for a swim and back. All for charity. You could do that.'

'Maybe I could.' Thomas pictured himself running joyfully through Stoggie's Farm, dressed as a gorilla.

'We would have to think of a name for you.'

'What's your name?'

Yvonne smiled shyly. 'Fallen Woman!'

★   ★   ★

Tigger had no problem knowing who he was. The line between reality and imagination is a mazy pathway — one that Tigger was happy to walk, and he walked it with certainty. The realities of other creatures' lives would erupt like flares in the landscape around him, or jets of steam from fissures in the earth's surface. He knew also that the stars would rotate in dizzying symmetry, altering the relationship of every living thing within his domain. He knew this and accepted it. But his instinct told him he needed this night, and this journey through the valley, when the sun would descend in a ball of crimson and umber to the west and the cerise moon rose to the east. This day, this night, pinned his little flag in the great scheme of things and gave him knowledge and belief for the next day. Dinner always provided a useful sense of purpose, of course, and he duly headed down Smugglers' Lane onto the footpath of Yarmer Valley, whose gentle slopes seemed especially illuminated for his arrival. Puddles mirrored his image and reflected these soft hues onto Tigger's countenance most pleasingly. He paused more than once to admire the result. The fact that he had fathered yet another litter of kittens was merely a result of his splendour, he felt. The Dream Factory came into view. All this walking made one peckish.

* * *

DS Sarah Raine slammed her pink baseball-booted foot down, and the 1973 Ford Capri RS 3100 responded with a snarl. Ramming the gearstick into overdrive, the car swept into the outside lane. 'Impressive, Charlie. Love this.'

Charlie adjusted his police shades and smiled. 'Nineteen seventies. Those were the days.'

'Yes. Just grab a suspect, kick him in the nuts, and get him to sign a confession.' Sarah smiled as the car eased between a juggernaut and the crash barrier.

'I guess there would have been more time to ride around in wheels like this,' said Charlie. 'You would have loved it.' Charlie inhaled deeply; the huge rear wheel of an articulated lorry was too close for comfort.

'I would. Mind you, I would have hoped to be slightly less conspicuous on a mission for Special Branch. Doing a ton in a purple geezer wagon. Where did you get the furry dice and the hairy seats?'

'Don't forget the nodding dog on the back shelf.'

'Not exactly rock and roll, Charlie. And does it have to wear a Chelsea football shirt?'

'Oh, I forgot. You're a Barcelona fan.'

'Their shirts have more style. And so do the men. There is no contest.' The Capri burst past the lorry, and Sarah shifted to the middle lane. 'There. I've stopped showing off now. Don't want to get nabbed by a bear trap.'

'Are we going to stop for a coffee?' said Charlie.

'In a minute. Read the file first.'

Charlie flipped open the manila file and scanned Sarah's handwritten notes. There was a list of names, including that of a bishop.

'Bishop Nonesuch? Who is he?'

'We don't know much about him. Look at the others. Ring any bells?'

'This one does. Jordan Diskin. Irish advocate, escaped from prison in Belfast after serving nine months for child sex offences.'

'Now thought to be in Baku, enjoying the life of Riley. He was sprung by the Organisation. Diskin's a rich man.'

'Thomas Yekolow. Wasn't he on trial in Africa? Some resistance army full of child soldiers?'

'That was him. Due to stand trial for war crimes in Buganda. The trial collapsed when the main witness unfortunately fell into the Nile. Accident of course.' Sarah smiled and gave Charlie a knowing wink. 'We think he's in Vichy, waiting to be moved on.'

'Moved on? Where?'

'Time for a coffee.' Sarah moved the car smoothly into the nearside lane. A gaudy advertisement for Macdougall's Big Beast Bites sailed slowly past as they entered the car park at Oxeter Services. 'If I'm driving this beast, I'd better order a bacon triple cheeseburger with fries.'

They stopped. Sarah removed her baseball boots. 'Take these,' she said, reaching for her black Token high wedges and Rebel shoulder bag.

Sarah was now several inches taller than Charlie, and he definitely felt the minor player as she strode, with head-turning elegance, towards the Costa Café. From behind his shades, Charlie smiled at his vibrant, sassy companion; he would love to see her in action with a real villain. *Rosencrantz would be on toast,* he mused, *probably with a dash of Tabasco for good measure. That would be a real Big Beast Bite.* They sat by the window, like two sophisticated lovers having an illicit tryst. Charlie stirred his latte while Sarah sipped her ristretto. Mums with strollers parked by the cherry-red tables. A party of ample pensioners weaved unsteadily through the throng at the counter.

'Are we being watched?' said Charlie.

'Doubtful. The Organisation is too confident to care. They just do stuff and get out. With any luck they will be careless.'

Charlie placed the file on the table. 'All these people — priests, criminals, teachers for God's sake.'

'And policemen, Charlie.'

'Mostly men I see . . . '

'Not all. Don't forget Yekolow's wife. The tyrant's diamond queen and human trafficker — oh, and also the chair of Aid to Africa.'

'The Charity?'

'But of course. Charlie, you could go through that entire list and come up with a hundred charities these bejewelled villains are involved with. Perfect cover. Makes them harder to touch and, in some cases, gets them nearer to their particular obsession. And don't be too meek about the involvement of women in all this. These men's wives splash the cash in Hong Kong or Jo'burg or Hawaii. Some are even worse. We just know less about them.'

Charlie whistled and sat back in his chair. 'So the Organisation shifts them. One country to another.'

Sarah nodded. 'When the law looms on the horizon, they fly to another diamond-dripping watering hole.'

'And Dingwell?'

'Our obscure French count is being helped by a former member of the service. The only thing the Organisation is afraid of is someone penetrating their networks. They are all over ours — hence the pencil-and-paper stuff. Esther Young's Alpha gizmo could burrow its way like a weasel into any network on the planet, even the Dark Net. The Organisation cannot risk that, or their house of rogues would come tumbling down. Peter is hiding out somewhere. He's a bright spark.'

'How many on this operation?'

'Four of us.'

'Four. Is that all?'

'Yes, and you are about to meet one of them.'

A head-scarfed woman with a pushchair squeezed against their table. Charlie stared as Sarah slipped her hand under the seat of the pushchair and snatched a copy of *Cosmopolitan*. The woman shoved the pushchair forward and disappeared into the crowd.

'Close your mouth, Charlie. It's rude to stare.'

'But you . . . '

'It's an old way of doing things. But it works.' She opened the magazine and found a brown envelope. She slit the flap open with a crimson fingernail, and looked inside. 'We'll look at these in the car.' Sarah gulped down her coffee. Charlie joined her, and they strode out into the spring sunshine.

'The Organisation doesn't have to be clever, Charlie. That's the most worrying thing about this case. Our team will meet up in Oxeter tonight then travel down in the morning.'

'Could it be that Alpha is keeping them alive?'

The sun gleamed on the purple Capri. The car had drawn some admirers who were peering into the driver's window. Sarah and Charlie paused some distance away. She turned to look at him, the sun refracting from her Cabana Oasis shades. 'Precisely, Charlie. The surgeon was a member of the Youngs' team.'

The little crowd dispersed as Charlie and Sarah approached.

'You drive.' Sarah tossed him the keys.

'Nice car.' A thin young man in a grey suit and steel-rimmed spectacles smiled his appreciation before walking across the car park towards a Mercedes.

'Memorise that guy's face,' said Sarah, suddenly tense, as she settled into the passenger seat. 'Seems I was wrong.'

Charlie studied the back of the retreating figure. 'Why?'

'Because, I think . . . ' Sarah opened the envelope. 'I think we will find a nice picture of him here.' She spilled out the photographs. One image, taken in a hotel lounge, bore a remarkable resemblance.

'Who is it?' said Charlie.

'Well, well. The steely and elegant Mr. Rosencrantz, I do believe.'

'Oh, him. If that was Rosencrantz, why did he make himself known to you?'

'Arrogance. It's their weakness. Let's get going, Charlie. I'm feeling annoyed. The bloody car got more admirers than I did.'

17

The Masque

'Doris, it's time to go.' Doris pulled a face, looked at her plate, and prodded the last portion of Pi's Extra-Specially-Delicious Cauliflower and Broccoli with Cheese.

'I don't want to go back.' Doris sniffed and looked pleadingly at Navinda. Navinda took her onto her lap. 'I want to stay with you and Om.'

'You have to learn to forgive,' said Navinda. 'I know that. I will have to forgive my father. That will not be easy. But I know I have to.'

Doris looked up at Navinda's dark eyes. 'Are you going back too?'

'Yes. Very soon.'

'What will Pi do? Pi really likes you.'

Navinda smiled. 'First Pi needs to go back to his home, if he can, and then try to find his mummy and daddy. Your mum and dad won't understand what has happened to you. They will be scared.'

'Good,' said Doris.

'Doris, you don't mean that,' said Navinda. She looked sternly at Doris, who pouted,

200

then looked at her shoes.

'No. I'm sorry. It's just that I want to stay in this . . . '

'Dream?' said Navinda. 'That is what it is. But all the things you know now are real. We have real lives too.'

Doris clung to Navinda. 'OK,' she sobbed.

'But first,' said Pi, 'we have something to share. Om will show us. Come and sit by the fire.' They sat on a low bench by the dogs.

Om glowed an intense azure. 'We can't start without Tigger.'

As ever, the cat flap rattled, and the 'Lord of All He Surveys' slid into the room and padded across the floor to Navinda's lap, pausing only — as was his custom — to hiss and display his fangs to the dogs. They responded by yawning and rolling over for yet another nap.

'Now that we are all here,' said Om, 'Navinda and Doris have a song for you, Pi. But first, Doris, hide your eyes. We are going to have some special visitors, but you must not peep yet. I need you to picture them. Who do you want to see before you go?'

Doris kept her eyes tight shut. 'Harriet,' she said.

'OK, now think hard about how you see Harriet. Look at every detail. Open your eyes.'

The room became engulfed in a sapphire light. A hologram of Harriet fluttered across the room and perched on a chair.

'Who else?' said Om.

'Everes and Chariclo.'

'Close your eyes tight, and tell me what you see in your head.' Two figures slowly formed within the blue light.

'I can see a man with a dog, like a shepherd. And a lady. He's holding the lady's hand. They have a baby. Everes is holding him.'

'Open your eyes again,' said Om.

Doris looked. The figures of Everes and Chariclo appeared as shifting waxworks, marvellously detailed.

'Om, they are beautiful,' said Navinda. Pi was open mouthed.

'Can they speak?' said Doris. The figures turned their eyes towards Doris and smiled.

'We have come to hear your song, Doris,' said Chariclo, her voice clear and perfect.

'Please sing for us, Doris. Our baby is listening,' said Everes.

'Come, Doris,' said Navinda, picking up her guitar.

Doris stood bravely and looked at Pi. 'I really wrote this poem for Pi. Navinda helped me. It's called, 'The Kiss.''

The summer evening spreads in blue and
   pink.
Last swallows gracefully carve the air.
The light behind the hill begins to sink,
and I begin to think of those who care.

Within our lives we live and breathe,
and troubles fog the once clear air.
But within your busy life, you thought of
   me,
and I felt blessed by your care.

I follow the path of the crescent moon.
The sun hath dropped o'er the bleak
   horizon.
But the sea does breathe upon the land,
as my love doth kiss upon your hand.

There was warm applause from all the guests, which Om multiplied several times over. 'That was brilliant, Doris,' said Pi. 'Thank you.'

'Quiet, everyone,' said Om. 'Chariclo and Everes are whispering. There is something else to do.'

'This is a love song for Pi and Navinda. Om knows the words, Doris. I am sure you will like it too.' Om conjured a string quartet to accompany Everes and Chariclo.

Beautiful she roamed from field to field.
She tasted all the summer's pride.
Then she the Prince of Love beheld,
who in a golden light did glide.

With April rain her wings were wet;
a sun god fired her burning face.
I trapped her in a silken net
and shut her in a golden cage.

Now I love to sit and hear her sing.
Laughing she will come to me,
and as she stretches her translucent wing,
I mock her loss of liberty.

Doris beamed at the singers and imbibed the shimmering poetry of the words. She would read them and come to understand them.

'There we must stop,' said Om. 'Sweet friends, be gone. Well done. Avoid. No more.'

The vision disappeared, and Doris walked into the now empty space. 'Where have they gone?' asked Doris.

'Into the air,' said Om. 'You pictured them. I simply created them. Now they are gone, but their memory is real. Doris, now is the time to go. Pi, there is something evil quite close to us. Not right outside but near.'

'It is time, Doris,' said Navinda. 'Quickly

now. Take this envelope. It has all your poems and your sketchpad.'

'And your maths sheets,' said Pi.

'And French verbs,' said Navinda. 'Hold it tight.'

'Don't forget your storybook and hand-writing sheets,' said Om.

'And the recipe for cauliflower with cheese,' said Pi.

'And how to play poohsticks,' said Navinda.

'And me and Tigger,' said Om.

'I won't forget you, Om.' Om went from azure to blushing crimson.

'Good-bye, Doris,' they all said.

Pi and Navinda sat at each end of the rug with Doris between them. As she turned to them both, a tear rolled down her face. 'Good-b . . . '

Pi reached across the space that was now between them and pulled Navinda to him and held her.

'What is to become of us?' Her hand reached up and turned his face to hers.

'Doris's poem was good.'

'It almost scanned,' said Navinda. 'She worked really hard on it.'

'I will find my parents and see you again, Navinda. I promise.'

'I will stay one more day.'

'OK.'

18

The Old School

I came to visit the old place and expected to see its buildings whole and strong. I knew it had closed. Something terrible had happened. Parents had taken their children away.

Deserted classrooms, the old assembly hall with gleaming polished floor, lines of coat hooks, wire trays, and book heaps stacked high, some toppled. Old RMs and BBC Masters blank and broken, innards yanked out and smashed. The giant roller chalkboards bearing only graffiti and crude scrawlings of genitalia. Outside the silent staffroom, the memorial garden has been gently tended. I even had checked on Google Earth to see if it was all still there.

I expected to see these things.

But now I walk towards the chain-link fence. A red sign. SITE CLOSED. NO ACCESS.

There is a dog hole in the wire. Come with me. Let us see.

There, an old concrete streetlamp, light smashed, a pointless relic amid the desolation. Desultory boys used to congregate beneath and smoke. Everything has gone, each stone ground down to a sterile shingle of concrete and brick. See the dead bonfires of charred drawings and exercise books; chair legs like hacked off limbs protrude from skips. The memorial garden bulldozed, its bonsais and saplings snapped, and vehicle tracks' snakeskin trails across its floral beds and sculpted lawns. The little plaques of commemoration crushed and twisted, flower garlands and wreaths snatched up by reptilian JCBs to be scrunched and minced. Lines of skips, like tanks, await evacuation beneath circles of wheeling gulls and crows.

One low brick wall survives. I used to drink my coffee here, and kids would gather with their crisps to chat while footballs thudded against the tennis-court fence. Follow the footpath to the end and look! Class T3W gather around and sweep as a wave into room seventeen, as the sea floods the rock fissures in Fairyland. The room always bore the stench of wax and disinfectant, a baited rattrap by the door.

Place your hand on the classroom door handle. When you do, everything you planned to do morphs. The lesson you had planned is snatched from your pocket by a piskie. I always have known that from the very first time. I used to get excited at school, sitting in a lesson waiting for the teacher to arrive and the door to open. To walk through that door is to transform who you are, to walk through the wardrobe, to cross the river, to open the trapdoor. Try it.

I remember. T3W flowed into the room — twenty-nine heads facing front, senses switched on, minds alight. I handed out twenty-nine copies of Macbeth. 'Not enough, sir. One more needed.'

Baffled, I rooted out a spare. 'OK, act three, scene four — the banquet scene.' I looked around the room. Fifteen pairs of seats; there should be one spare.

I took a paper register. Twenty-nine 'Here, sir.' No 'She's away. She's miching.' Unusual. There should be one spare seat. I looked up. There were none.

'Is anyone here who shouldn't be? Has anyone come to the wrong room?'

'None of us wants to be here, sir.' Laughter.

'No one wants you here, Elvis — you stink.' Laughter.

'OK, OK. Let's get on.' I paced the room as we read the text. This was getting to me. I stared at each child then looked across the room, expecting to see their double. They all had exercise books. There should have been one without.

When we did the part where Macbeth goes mad, I was reading the lines aloud. My voice did not sound like my voice.

'Bit loud sir!'

'Sssh! Sir's acting!'

I ended the lesson early. 'Cor, cheers, sir!'

'Leave your exercise books by the door.'

I will not tell you how many books were in the pile. You know, don't you?

The senior mistress told me off for letting the class out early. 'You will never make a teacher.' She shook her head.

I sat in the staffroom at the end of the afternoon, staring across the fields to Victory Flats. I could not talk to anyone about what I had seen. I would have to live with it.

I refused to teach in that room again. I said I was allergic to polish.

Savaric said I should not have been afraid. It had happened before. I just had not noticed.

19

Operation Pandora

Count de Boodle's Daimler crawled along the track to the edge of Stoggie's Wood before entering the open farmland. The count could turn off the headlights; so vivid was the moonlight. He was pleased to be out of the forest, where the trees seemed to hover like apparitions and spectres, silent witnesses to his malevolent mission.

The tall hedge on the left-hand side perfectly obscured his view of the valley and the Dream Factory. 'Well done, Miss Cloke,' the count said with a chuckle, as the car gently rolled and swayed along the rutted lane. Ahead of him a small, dark square shed approached. A turning space had been dug into the bank of the hill. The count turned the car into the space and stopped. Silence, save for the sigh and kiss of waves on Eastcombe Beach and the rattle of shingle.

'Excellent.' He unhitched the trailer and manoeuvred it towards the hut, where he propped the jockey wheel on a rock. He removed the fastening strap from the box, carried the Panzerfaust into the shed, and placed it on the bench. He returned for the radio receiver. The count silently lowered the hatch in the side of the shed, and planting his elbows on the window ledge, he trained his binoculars on the Dream Factory. He saw no light from the building. Strange how we see with the eyes that will only see what we can understand. Strange. Of course, there would be no obvious signs of life, he reasoned. His enemy would be holed up inside, too scared to move. He opened the Panzerfaust's box and removed the weapon from its oilcloth. That military smell again. *Wunderbar!* He found the mounting bracket and quickly screwed it to the ledge. He located the weapon securely on its mount, fastened the spring clip, and flipped up the sight. Perfect. The old stone shed was at his mercy, only eighty metres away. He fumbled for his spectacles. Ah, yes. He identified objects, a small wooden box to the left and an old broken cart to the right. Ideal for 'bracketing' the target. He briefly contemplated getting the damn thing over with and attacking right now. *J'aimerais attaquer maintenant,* he thought. *Get it over with. Hmm.* He savoured the prospect, and his finger caressed the trigger of the Panzerfaust.

'Mata Hari calling Eaglehawk.' The radio crackled into life and the count slipped on the clumsy headphones and pushed the 'talk' switch.

'Eaglehawk to Mata Hari. All in position. Excellent planning, Mata Hari, if I may say so.'

'Thank you, Eaglehawk. Most kind.'

'You are quite some lady, Mata Hari. I like — how you say? — the cut of your jib.'

'Thank you, Eaglehawk. *Très gallant, monsieur.*' Miss Cloke tittered. What a sweet man! 'Any signs of life, Eaglehawk?'

'No. Target quiet as the grave. Are you still wearing that Chanel perfume, Mata Hari?' The count inhaled romantically. 'Mmmm, I can sense it from here.'

'Sorry to disappoint you, Eaglehawk. I have just washed in Swarfega and folded my fatigues, ready for the mission.'

'Swarfega. *Wunderbar* on you, Mata Hari, you petite English minx.' Miss Cloke had a brief thought that the impending heat of battle had sent the count doolally. The dear man probably had been inhaling too much fuel.

'Let us keep to the matter in hand. It is now 01.00 hours. I will be in position at the entrance to Stoggie's Wood at 04.30 for the attack at 05.00. Copy?'

'Yes, I copy, Mata Hari. But why not attack now? Get it over with. Kill them in their beds like helpless animals.' The count was fingering the trigger again and enjoying the sweet smell of cordite from the grenades.

'Yes, but that is not in the plan, Eaglehawk. Let me remind you. Once you have destroyed the target at 05.00, you abandon the weapon and drive to Northmoor airstrip.'

'Yes, yes, Mata Hari, but . . . ' The count was fumbling for his brandy flask. His tummy was feeling a little queasy.

'Rosencrantz will meet you at Northmoor to catch your plane at 06.00. In one hour you will be out of the country.'

'Copy, Mata Hari. As you say. Attack at 05.00.' The count swigged some brandy and gasped.

'Are you all right, Eaglehawk?'

'*Oui, madame. Je pense.* Eaglehawk out.' The count took another nip. He really did feel very strange. He picked up the radio and stumbled back to his car, before which he was violently sick in the bushes. On all fours, under the gaze of this heartless moon, he wondered why he was in this damn place. *Not for much longer*, he thought, and groped his way back to the car. Odessa raised his head as the count heaved himself into the driver's seat and fell fast asleep.

★　★　★

Thomas would have sympathised. He was slumped on the lavatory, having had, a little earlier, his head thrust into the bowl, and making a sound like a rhinoceros in labour. The air smelt malodorous in the extreme, and he was perspiring heavily. Mind you, it had been a sparkling evening with the Hashers at the Whodhavethoughtit, and he had met lots of people who seemed only too pleased to listen to him — or so he thought. They were all Yvonne's friends and all shapes and sizes. The mountainous, curly-haired 'Piddler' and his tiny redheaded wife, 'Princess Lay Ya'; she had a beaming freckly smile that warmed Thomas's heart. 'If you join us, we could call you 'Parson's Nose,'' she'd said, cackling and screeching with laughter.

Yvonne had led Thomas round the bar. 'Meet 'Topshelf.' He's a rugby front row,' she said, stifling a giggle.

Thomas studied this short, stout man with missing teeth, a shaven head, and funny ears. 'Why do they call you 'Topshelf'?'

''Cos I reads dirty mags!' he roared, clinking Thomas's pint glass. 'And I really fancies that little 'Late Bloomer.'' He reached out and pulled a woman with an Afro in a long floaty dress and sandals towards him. She squealed. 'You'd better be running faster tomorrow, maid, or I'll catch thee.'

214

'Too fast for that big belly of yours!' she retorted.

'Dunno why they call you 'Topshelf,'' said Princess Lay Ya.

''Cos he's too short to reach one!' screeched Late Bloomer.

The pub was suddenly crammed with cheerful folks in funny hats, and Tizzy and Gideon were frantically serving beer and supplying trays of chips and burgers and sausages, garlanded with mustard and tomato sauce, while an eclectic mix of disco and heavy metal erupted from the conservatory.

Thomas had spent a long time in the company of a short merchant seaman with a thicket of grey hair, curiously dubbed 'Gooley,' and his theatrically coiffured wife, 'Ging Gang.' Thomas had supped several pints of Meths, and as he sat on the lavatory, Ging Gang now swirled before his eyes. She was clasping a large glass of Pinot Grigio and hysterically reciting random quotations from *A Midsummer Night's Dream*. She had persuaded him to dance on the table with her, and Thomas unwisely had accepted, to the raucous cheers and applause of the revellers. As he wobbled and wove clumsily with Ging Gang ('Prom Queen' had lent him a witch's hat), he had caught Yvonne's illuminated smile. To the boom and bang of

AC/DC's 'Highway to Hell,' Thomas had downed a whole pint of Meths and stood milking the applause with beer dribbling down his chin before sliding unceremoniously off the table into the waiting arms of 'The Piddler.' Thomas recalled all this with a woozy smile, including a conversation with that nice Mr. Rosencrantz, who seemed particularly interested in . . . something or other.

Thomas's head hurt, and he now belched decisively, and this persuaded him, in his nakedness, to veer off to the kitchen to make some coffee. Wearing only his socks, he stood next to the kitchen window. All this would have been well if Thomas had, as he believed, been alone in the house. But he was not alone. His secret visitor had been treated to the sight of his dimpled buttocks wobbling down the hall and had opened the window in the toilet, and puffed a toxic cloud of Harpic into the lavatory pan.

Thomas abandoned his unequal struggle with the kettle and wove off to the bathroom, where he stood motionless in the shower, still in his socks, the water drumming therapeutically on his cranium, while the entire bottle of shampoo that he had poured over his head created a private foam party, removing the bodily detritus that had been clinging to him like a separate skin. Minutes later he was sitting in his armchair, fragrant, wrapped in his stripy bathrobe, toasting his slippered feet by the electric fire, and sipping water, waiting for the Nurofen to do battle with the prostaglandins in his body and stop his bloody head from hurting.

He looked at his watch. Past midnight, and he began to feel a little more his old self. He was enjoying the heat on his feet and smelling . . . what was that smell? Faintly acrid, burning. Thomas sniffed. Were his slippers burning? No. Ah, well. For all the light and gaudy warmth of the pub, here he was alone again. That was what pubs did of course. Make the gift of a blanket of softness and warmth to wrap around one's loneliness. And he was beginning to feel lonely again. He thought of dear Yvonne. All she wanted to do was marry the one she loved. It just happened to be Alison. A woman. What was wrong with that? Why wrap the simple warmth of love up in rules from a bygone age that were almost certainly written by men. Probably men who had sinned. Perhaps they were gay men, petrified of what they perceived as their own sin. Madness. Yvonne would make a perfect priest, even a bishop. Certainly better than spindly Bishop Nonesuch, whose only gift, it seemed to Thomas, was to inspire arachnophobia. Yet Yvonne never could be a bishop because that was not allowed either. What was there in the world more spiritual, more redolent of love, what greater fragrance of virtue and . . . and . . . what was that bloody smell? Something burning. Had he left the cooker on? Bugger!

Thomas rose unsteadily to his feet, and waited for the room to stop swaying. He sniffed again, wobbling gently, nostrils twitching. At last the room stood still. He padded off and stood in the hall. Then he heard a clearly audible sob. Thomas's heart went cold. *Dear God*, he thought. *What is going on?* There it was again.

This house that was his home now felt unfamiliar, as though it no longer belonged to him. That sound again, but more a cry this time. In a trance Thomas walked down the hall and stopped by his study door. The burning smell was stronger now; there was the soft muted cry of someone in pain. He pushed open the door.

'Olivia!'

Olivia was sitting in his chair, her curling auburn hair trailing down to her elegant neck, and her eyes of hazel looked up at him beseechingly. A cigarette protruded from a plant pot, a telltale thread of smoke spiralling upward.

'Olivia!' The silver chain necklace he had given her shone on her pale skin. She shivered in a tattered denim jacket, and he noticed a purple stain above her left eye. 'Olivia, how did you . . . ?'

'Don't ask.' She turned her face away.

'You never smoked.'

'You never got drunk.'

Thomas knelt beside the chair and buried his face into her neck and hair and kissed her. She responded and held him. Her sobbing returned, and she shook with grief as he wrapped his arms around her. 'Shhh. No more. No more, Olivia. Beyond my wildest dreams, when I needed you the most, you are here.' He kissed her lips gently. Olivia smarted. Thomas noticed the thin line of a cut on her lower lip. 'What has happened to you?'

Her tired eyes looked at him. 'I have just seen your bottom.'

'Dear Lord,' said Thomas.

'It is much bigger and more wobbly than it used to be.'

'I suppose so. Sorry, I didn't know you were there.'

'I've cleaned the loo. Had to use a whole can of Harpic. Is there no one to look after you?'

'No, no one.'

'Eight whole years, and there has been no one else in your life? No girlfriend. No one?'

Thomas shook his head.

'Not even a housekeeper? Someone?'

'No. I couldn't, I never wanted to.'

'Typical. Couldn't even bring yourself to find someone who might need you. Useless.'

'I know.'

'Someone like me,' Olivia said. 'Like I need you now.'

'Just shut myself away.'

'Useless! Useless!' She cuffed him repeatedly about the head before collapsing into his arms again. Her grief, a jagged blade of pain and anger and pent-up suffering, tearing and ripping from within her.

Thomas weathered the blows. They were not painful, more a series of maternal smacks that might be administered to a maleficent spaniel. Come to think of it, he felt like a simple spaniel. He accepted the blows benignly, head nodding, his limp body absorbing them like a soft debilitating sofa.

Olivia looked at him steadily. 'I know I left you, but you had left me already. In your head.'

'Yes.' Thomas spoke gently. 'I know that now.'

'And now?'

'I don't care about the past. I don't even want you to explain.'

'I met a little old lady in the village,' Olivia said. 'I asked her where you lived.'

'Think I know who that was.'

'Told her you were my husband.'

'Ah, that explains everything.'

'She met the children as well.'

'We never had children . . . '

'I did.'

Thomas stood at his front door in a daze. He looked across at the church. It was bathed in moonlight. All the fear and uncertainty had gone. He would tear up that letter. In the light from his front door stood three cold, tired, and hungry children, each carrying a small rucksack. He ushered them inside, and they stood by the fireside.

'This is Hendrix.'

Hendrix gave a desultory smile. 'Mum. He looks like a dick. Sure he's not the Feds?'

'I'm Page,' said Page. 'Sorry about my brothers. So immature.'

'Die!' said Clapton, jumping forwards, brandishing a plastic lightsaber, as if to prove the point.

'Our daddy hit Mummy,' said Page. *She has her mother's lovely hair*, thought Thomas.

'That will never happen here,' said Thomas. 'You are welcome.'

'We met this old lady in the village. She said we had to help find a bad dude called Peter. She said she would pay us,' said Hendrix.

'Promise me that while you are here you will take no notice of that lady.' Thomas spoke forcefully. He was surprised at his sudden passion. The children seemed impressed.

Thomas was then treated to another kind of music: skirmishing children, bacon sandwiches, the steam and confusion of bath time, mugs of warm milk, hastily making beds, more arguments, a story for Clapton. Later, in his bed, he held Olivia, as he had done years before.

'You kept my photograph on your desk.' Olivia was cradled once again in Thomas's arms, her breath, albeit bearing a soupçon of Capstan Full Strength, like a feather on Thomas's cheek.

'It gave me hope,' said Thomas.

'Did you always believe I would come back?'

'I prayed that you would but didn't believe it. I should have had more faith.'

Thomas gazed at the moonlight, soft on his curtains. 'Thank you,' he breathed.

Sleep did not arrive immediately for Olivia. She lay with Thomas, as two teddy bears in a box, his arm across her breast. He was sleeping, and the rhythm of his sleep awakened the music of their early life together as passionate student lovers and pursuers of social causes. Memories hovered in the half light — huddled in sleeping bags as hail drummed and storm winds tugged on their old canvas tent, wet through from a day's footslogging demonstration outside the Libyan embassy; scaling a fence at a battery farm in Essex to liberate some extremely unpleasant chickens. The furious fowl had scuttled aggressively round the back garden of their student house, attacking the neighbour's cat.

'That feline is a capitalist lackey,' Thomas unwisely had shouted to the irate lorry driver who had banged on the door to remonstrate.

'And your nose is going to be sticking out the back of your effing head!' A fist then obliged Thomas to visit the casualty department.

'Blooming chickens!' he had groaned through a bundle of tissues. 'The buggers didn't even have the decency to lay an egg.' Thomas was sporting a very large one on his head.

Olivia had dreamed of Thomas metamorphosing from the shy, indecisive, principled man she had married into a strong, outspoken political activist who would help her raise a family of loving, intense, creative, and preferably vegan offspring who could speak several languages and fill their lives with music. Instead she had watched Thomas go into teaching and become a fraught, stressed, ashen, and drooping version of a husband, too tired to have an opinion on anything and clutching a shattered libido.

He had tried to be decisive. She remembered him going out heroically into the garden of their tiny house, armed with a gleaming new spade. He dug up the entire lawn and proudly announced that he had planted Devon Reds and Webb's Wonderfuls. Torrential rain turned the whole patch into a quagmire that cats did their business on. 'Ah, well . . . ' Thomas had said. His resigned tone had infuriated Olivia. Enough was enough.

Olivia had left Thomas for the rough glamour of an Afro-haired young guitarist in The Vultures, a thrashmetal band. Olivia had caught his boyish eye in the Victory Inn on 'Local Bands Nite.' Ruben regarded this beautiful woman as something to hang on his arm. Olivia could protect him from the horror of actually having to grow up and make a living. In fact Olivia could do his growing up for him! Olivia worked in bars to support their three children, who had emerged into the world with remarkable rapidity.

Finally she realised Ruben was another man whom she could not change into something better than he was. The more she tried, the madder and more drunken he became. She had come home from the library with books for the children, only to find them watching a rock DVD while their father reclined on the couch slurping Jack Daniels and Coke. He had punched her, cutting her lip, and lurched through the front door, seizing his coat and screaming expletives. It was not the first time. The children had looked at her balefully; Page had cried. One hour later their rucksacks were packed, and Olivia ushered her charges into their battered estate car and drove through the bleak, litter-strewn streets of Greymouth.

She could not face going to her mother's house. A deafening silence would greet her. No, she would protect her children. There was only one place she could go. But would Thomas accept her? For the first time in years, Olivia prayed, murmuring the words as she drove unsteadily from the torment and darkness of her life. In the soft evening air, she had parked the car outside Dingwell's All Souls Church. The peace of the village, with its cheerful cottages and stout oaks, breathed calm upon her troubled mind and her fearful children.

Now she gazed at the moonlight, and the simple square possessions in Thomas's life: the square wooden bed, the solid oak wardrobe, and the plain chair. Uncluttered. She would bring the power of love to dress the plain furniture of Thomas's life with new creative colours and fragrances, billowing romantic drapes to his square windows, serendipity to his regulated world. He would believe in himself because she would believe in him. She realised now that Thomas's love was one that came without conditions. 'Just love me,' it said.

★　★　★

Meanwhile, Miss Cloke had slipped into her tiny bed, having set her Jazz leather-and-chrome alarm clock for 03.30. Across the village in Cosy Cottage, Yvonne had set her smartphone alarm to 05.30 — she had to be up in time for the 06.00 Hash to Eastcombe.

20

Behold — the Birth of a Death Star

The moonlight cast its shafts of light onto the granite crenulations of *Twitten Towers* Nursing Home. No one used its proper dignified name of course — not even Miss B, who had laughed heartily when she heard Nigel referring to 'The Fossils.' Now Miss B was sleeping and dreaming, occasionally turning in her bed. She was hitchhiking with Roger up the West Coast highway of California and standing beneath the towering Mormon temple at La Jolla. 'Disney meets God,' said Roger, the breeze flicking his blond hair in the brilliant sun.

'It's hideous. Let's go.'

They were looking down from Highway 5 to the sea at Oceanside. A vast aircraft carrier was sliding out from the jaws of the harbour.

'Behold, the birth of a death star. Can you hear the bands playing?' said Roger.

They listened to the dah-dah dahdahdah of the gaudily clad marching bands and drums on the deck and the harbour. Miss B's highly charged mind shifted its vision once again to her primary school in Gravesend, and they were marching round the playground in uniforms — dah-dah dahdahdah, dah-dah dahdahdah — and she was back in her room. The lamp was on, and Pearl was drumming her fingers on the table, humming.

This old man, he played nine.
He played knick-knack on my spine.
With a knick-knack paddywhack,
give the dog a bone,
this old man came rolling home.

Miss B's eyes opened only as slits, and she watched Pearl's fingers softly beating out the old children's marching song — a song she had feared as a child. Fear crawled up her spine and swarmed about her head, and she startled awake.

'Oh, Miss B, you gave me a start.' Pearl picked up the drawing pad and fanned herself with it before noticing the drawing. 'Oh, what's that? Looks nice. Do you want to have a widdle?'

Miss B nodded. 'Nigel,' shouted Pearl. 'Gimme a hand.' Nigel appeared and steadied Miss B's ship as she successfully navigated her passage to the gloomy bathroom and did her business.

Minutes later she was propped up in bed.

She nodded her thanks to Nigel, who went out. Miss B motioned towards the pad, and Pearl picked it up. 'You want this?' Miss B nodded frantically. She tapped the sketch and pointed to her window.

'Nice car,' said Pearl. Miss B pointed to the window. 'There's a car in the garden. Oh, you're playing a game. I can't see no cars.' Miss B grabbed her wrist and gazed intently into her face. 'Whatizit? Get off, Miss B.'

Miss B pointed to the picture and gestured again with her hand, with a sweeping motion to show where the car had come from and gone. 'What car? There is no bloomin' cars! Let go. Let go!'

Miss B's grip strengthened, and Pearl's arm waved frantically as the two women struggled. 'Get off! Get off!'

With a grunt of frustration, Miss B dropped Pearl's arm. Pearl rubbed the skin ruefully. 'You shouldn't do that, Miss B. That's not nice. I'm telling the matron.'

But Miss B was writing frantically again and tossed the pad to Pearl.

''Er . . . what's this? 'Fetch Yvonne'? 'FFS, fetch Yvonne'? Swearin' now, is it? Can't fetch her now. It's two o'clock in the mornin'.' And Pearl was gone.

Miss B lay on the pillow, and a tear began to slide down her cheek.

Neither the darkness of night nor the strange-
ness of moonlight held fears for Miss Cloke.
She simply could not understand why anyone
should be afraid of something that patently
was an illusion. Darkness and shadows were
her friends of course. It was much easier to
spy on others and do things in secret at night.
No dreams or visions troubled her sleep, and
she awoke at the appointed time to carry out
her appointed tasks in the appointed way. She
dressed without fuss and avoided turning on
any lights. She did not mourn past mistakes
because she did not make any. Nor did she
regret emotions or attachments that belonged
in the past, whether these were dead lovers,
duped foreign agents, or for that matter, recently
departed pets. The sun rose the next day
merely to illuminate the notes on her pad
about the next mission, be it assassination,
sabotage, or disinformation. This was the single
dimension of spirituality and consciousness
that Miss Cloke travelled. Her packed suitcase was by the door. She picked it up and
carried it out to the boot of her loyal Morris
Traveller. Once again she looped her pack
over her head and felt the Sigma pistol in the
front pocket.

This time she took the direct route down

Martyrs' Lane, past the darkened Whodhavethoughtit and up towards the church. The suddenly created Clodpole family were all snoozing like contented dogs as Miss Cloke crept into Dingwell Lane and paused to catch her breath. At 04.30 precisely, Miss Cloke was in position, sitting on the stile where the children had played chess, her elbows positioned on the rail and her binoculars trained on the old stone hut. She reached for her radio set and pressed the 'talk' button.

'Mata Hari calling Eaglehawk. Come in, Eaglehawk. Over.'

There was no response. Miss Cloke tried twice more. Oh, well. The mission wasn't due to start for half an hour.

Eaglehawk was blissfully asleep, sunk deep into the leather comfort of the Daimler's driving seat. He and Odessa snored in harmony, the dog basso profondo, the count more tenor, with an occasional whistle in falsetto. Meanwhile the night sky above Eastcombe was playing a visual symphony of dramatic light spears, incandescent halos drifting on the breathing sea, and the slow stately swell and diminuendo of the sighing and gasping ocean.

★　★　★

231

Yvonne awoke to the sound of her alarm — one that played the more soothing sounds of birdsong. But this time it was accompanied by the sound of a cat — a very insistent cat, mewing and mawling, but these were low-pitched, long meows. Yvonne opened the window. 'What are you doing here, Tigger?' Tigger's tail was flexing and flicking, his ears forward and eyes wide and focussed on Yvonne. She flung on her gown and dashed downstairs and opened the front door. Tigger would not come inside. Instead he skittered around her tiny garden, tail curving and bristling, and he would not keep quiet. 'Shhh! Tigger.' The phone rang.

'Yvonne, it's Pearl. Calling from The Fossils. We've had a terrible night with Miss B.'

'What's the matter? Is she ill?'

'No, she's just in a right two-and-eight. Keeps scribbling stuff and asking for you. She's been right 'orrible. Grabbed my arm. Says we got to fetch you. She's been cryin an' that.'

'All right, Pearl. I'll come as soon as I'm dressed.' She put the phone down. Tigger was still creating outside. 'All right, Tigger. I'm coming.' Yvonne headed for the shower and emerged in her white police running top and blue shorts and trainers. 'Don't need an alarm with you around.' But Tigger was not waiting and headed off down Martyrs' Lane before taking a shortcut through the pub garden. Yvonne got into her stride, and by the church, she met the early contenders from the Hashers. Princess Lay Ya and The Piddler had climbed into a pantomime horse costume and were just rounding the first bend. They stopped.

'Tell Topshelf and Late Bloomer that I'll be late. Have to go to The Fossils first.' The horse nodded and Yvonne sped on, followed by three pink fairies and a gorilla.

Hairy Nigel answered the door. 'Oh, come in, Yvonne. Thank Gawd you're here. Miss B's gone potty. Keeps crying and rollin' about. Asking for you all night.' He opened the door to Miss B's room. The old lady lay in her bed, exhausted.

'Miss B, Miss B. What's been the matter?' She embraced her. Miss B waved her sketchpad. 'What's this?' Yvonne held it up. It was unmistakably a large car with a small trailer. Miss B summoned her remaining strength and pointed to the garden and made the same sweep of the hand that she had done hours before. Yvonne nodded and went to the window. 'Across here? This car came through the garden?' Miss B nodded frantically. 'During the night? Towards the stile and the gate?'

Yvonne followed the line of the old track,

and she saw two clear lines in the bedewed grass. She followed the track to the right. There, sitting by the gate on the stile, binoculars trained down the valley, was Miss Cloke. Yvonne's heart went cold.

'Nigel, I can't get a signal on my mobile here. Where's the landline?'

'In the hall. What's goin' on?' He followed Yvonne into the hall.

'Someone is going to die.' She looked steadily at Nigel. 'This is serious. Don't tell Miss B.' Yvonne dialled the Queensbridge police station. 'It's engaged! It's bloody engaged. How can a police station be engaged?' Nigel had turned pale. 'Keep trying, Nigel. Tell them I must have backup now. I think there's going to be a murder, and I'm going to try to stop it.'

'What are you going to do?'

'Tell Miss B not to worry. There's one old lady I want to have a word with.' Yvonne looked through the tall, gothic, arched window at the end of the hall. The Hashers were streaming colourfully along the track past a bemused Miss Cloke.

★   ★   ★

Count de Boodle had awoken and immediately made for the hedge next to the hide, where he urinated plentifully. He heard

234

voices. On the other side of the hedge were two large equine ears, bobbing rhythmically as the creature — whatever it was — trotted along the path.

'This bloody well sums up life being married to you,' said the rear half of the creature. 'Six o'clock in the sodding morning, and I'm running along with my head up your arse.'

'Think yourself lucky, girl,' said the forward half. 'You could have ended up marrying Topshelf. And do keep up.'

'I'll keep up if you bleeding well slow down a bit. It's not the effing Derby.'

'You know you love me, babe. I'm more fun. You said so.'

'Not right now you're not. And if you fart again . . .'

The voices faded away. But when the count looked to his left, he spotted three men dressed as fairies and wearing pumps, slopping along the track, which was getting rapidly churned up. Odessa jumped from the car, scuppering the count's plan to execute him. He made a beeline for an oversize cat that appeared to be running gently on its hind legs, chatting to an emu that was puffing on a fag. Before the count could react — he was struggling with his flies — Odessa was off in pursuit of his prey, barking furiously. The cat judiciously climbed into a tree, while the emu

jettisoned the fag and legged it for all it was
worth. Yellow legs as fast as a runaway train, it
streaked along the footpath until it reached
the beach before plunging into the sea. Odessa
had chased it all the way. Now he turned back
in search of fresh prey. The pantomime horse
had stopped and reared ludicrously before
toppling over in a cloud of sand. Odessa gave
it a good barking before turning his attention
to the three fairies, who promptly scattered.
One startled nymph went scrambling up the
cliff; one perched poetically on a rock, waving
its wand defiantly at the dog; while the third
decided that transformation into a mermaid
was the best option and took the plunge.

'Mata Hari calling Eaglehawk. Come in,
Eaglehawk.'

'Eaglehawk to Mata Hari. What the hell is
going on? Why am I surrounded by maniacs
in funny clothes?'

'I know. I tried to warn you earlier,
Eaglehawk. Did you see the pantomime horse
with the pink mane? Rather delightful. Where
is it now?'

'In the sea, doing the backstroke,' said the
count wearily.

'You have missed the hour for Operation
Pandora. I suggest you abort the mission.'

The count inhaled deeply. 'Abort? *Abort?*
I have spent all bloody night in this

godforsaken place. No, Mata Hari. I am going to finish the mission now.'

'But Count,' said Miss Cloke, as a pantomime cow, two pink rabbits, and Desperate Dan jogged past her, 'it's too dangerous. They might all be police officers.'

The count rarely laughed, but he did now. 'Mata Hari, if you are seriously suggesting to me that all these bloody lunatics running around here are police officers, that explains everything about this bloody country. I mean, how the hell did you win the war? Perhaps British forces turned up for Operation Overlord dressed as vicars and tarts. Perhaps that is your secret.'

'Count, there is a pantomime cow with udders heading in your direction right now.'

'With udders, eh, Mata Hari? You English leave nothing to chance.'

'And two pink rabbits.'

'Ha, ha. Excellent,' said the count. 'Perfect cover. I will liquidate our little friends in their beds and escape in the confusion. Eaglehawk out.'

The count took up his position in the hide once more and swung the Panzerfaust into position. He shunted a grenade into the launcher and looked along the barrel through the sight.

Just below the hide, Topshelf had caught up

with Late Bloomer (in all honesty she could have run a little faster). He thoughtfully spread a tablecloth on the ground, and they settled into an embrace safe, so they thought, beneath the hedge. As their lips met, the count adjusted the telescopic sight and placed the crosshairs on the main window of the Dream Factory. The searing roar of the grenade's launch met Late Bloomer's expectations as the shell tore apart the air across the valley before impacting against the still smoking chimney, which exploded and collapsed into the room below, starting fires where the children had played chess and studied the minute detail of Harriet's wings. Topshelf was less enamoured and stared wild eyed as flames erupted from inside the old shed and the boom and smash of the explosion resounded in the narrow valley.

The count's second volley ended whatever amorous inclinations Topshelf had for Late Bloomer. As the next grenade penetrated the main window and ignited Doris's bed, blew to pieces Barnie's balsa aeroplane and Navinda's guitar, and ignited the driftwood seat where the children had sat watching Everes and the nymph Chariclo, Topshelf decided to tactically withdraw. Late Bloomer was treated to the sight of her amour vaulting the farm gate in his pink rabbit's trousers. He failed, tripped, and ended facedown in the mire as the third grenade scorched the air across the valley. The missile entered a fissure in the wall and slammed into Pi and Navinda's bedroom, initiating a firestorm of such intensity that the rest of the Dream Factory was sucked into a vortex of heat that vaporised every cushion, utensil, and book. As birds and animals fled for cover, Late Bloomer leapt the gate, her foot pressing her erstwhile lover's head farther into the mire before joining the general retreat of mankind and beast from the holocaust.

'Good shot, Eaglehawk! Good shot!' shrieked Miss Cloke, as the Dream Factory disintegrated, its structure shivering and shaking like a wounded elephant before smashing finally to the ground, red-hot stones bounding into the stream, firing upward pillars of steam. Miss Cloke danced frenziedly with delight as each explosion pulsed the air and sent shockwaves through the innocent valley. 'Mission accomplished, Eaglehawk. Well done. Time to migrate.'

'Roger, Mata Hari.' The count stumbled into the Daimler and started the engine. It responded as a faithful friend. He turned towards the farm gate. Hashers were still stumbling and scrambling up the farm track, but he didn't care. He crashed through the gate, the great wheels of the car slithering and grinding into the mud. The car leapt forward, snarling, and sent shards of mud, like flying tongues, into the faces of the runners and the trembling, wounded woodland.

Miss Cloke felt a hand grip her arm. 'You are too late, Miss Bull.' Yvonne pressed her face close to hers. 'I am arresting you, Miss Cloke.'

'On what charge, pray?' Miss Cloke sneered, her smile edging the borders of Yvonne's temper. 'Shouldn't you be saving your precious Peter?'

Yvonne turned towards the wood and the tide of exhausted, panic-stricken runners scrambling for safety. 'I'll be back. I advise you to remain here.' Yvonne ran into the wood, ignoring shouts from the Hashers. She bounded through the wood, through one gate then another, until the sound of a snarling engine and the sight of a sliding Daimler slithered into view. The car stopped and the count stepped out.

'Ah, the troublesome Miss Bull.' The count drew his Luger.

'Don't do this, Count. Police are on their way.' Yvonne backed away, her eyes fixed on the gun.

'But they are not here now, Miss Bull. What a pity.' He fired. The bullet entered between Yvonne's shoulder and her left breast. The impact propelled her backward, and she slammed into the mud. A crimson rose of gore, an exploding death star, spread across her white shirt. She gasped and lay still, blinking.

'You see, young woman, the only reason for getting up in the morning is power. You have yet to learn that.' The count stood over Yvonne and pointed his gun at her forehead. 'Such an important lesson to learn, Miss Bull. What a shame you are only learning it now.' But an old enemy had appeared, perched on the bonnet of the Daimler, yellow eyes focussed on the count. He swung round at Tigger's bloodcurdling caterwaul and fired. Tigger leapt from the car and scampered into the undergrowth. 'Aha, Monsieur le Chat. *Disciple du diable!*'

The sound of figures running through the trees persuaded the count that it was time to escape. He left Yvonne's limp body and spurred the Daimler into fresh life and snarled along the track until he was clear of the wood.

Miss Cloke was long gone and feigned tearfulness at all the commotion, exacting sympathy from the Hashers who helped her back to Dingwell Lane. 'Thank you so much,' she twittered. 'The village is normally so quiet.' She skittered back to Enigma Cottage and gave the village one last look. A pall of smoke spiralled upward from Eastcombe. Mission accomplished. She climbed into her ancient Morris and started the engine.

The Daimler barrelled past a trembling Miss B, who stared heartbroken through her window at the rising spiral of flames and smoke, and shuddered at the sound of the gunshots, staring anxiously at the gate and the strange assortment of gorillas, fairies, and cartoon characters staggering for their lives. Count de Boodle's car burst through the gate. A window lowered, and she saw his face.

'Quickly! Someone has been shot. There is a maniac on the loose! Save yourselves!' he shouted to a bemused penguin. 'I would go myself, but I have been injured.' He then drove through the track and up the drive and along Dingwell Lane, weaving between the exhausted and terrified runners. He emitted a throaty cackle of triumph, elated at the destruction and mayhem.

The count gave the village a last contemptuous look before turning left and driving upward through a tunnel of spreading trees and stone walls. He noticed Rosencrantz and Miss Cloke in conversation by a stile. He was taking her picture. A pity about Miss Cloke. She was no longer of any value. He smiled as a police car, pursued by a small ambulance, zoomed past him. He pulled over and set his satellite navigation to the small private airstrip at Northmoor. In one hour he would be out of the country.

21

A Broken Doll

'The count would like a photo of you for old time's sake.' Rosencrantz pulled his e-phone from his jacket pocket.

Miss Cloke tittered. 'Oh, how very kind. But I am sure the count and I will be meeting again.'

'Perhaps if you just sit on the stile, Miss Cloke.'

'Certainly.'

'A little to the left, so we can get in the valley behind.'

'Of course.'

'Hold still. Perfect.'

'Will you send me a copy?'

'Of course. Just one more.'

'Well, if you insist.'

But Rosencrantz was now holding a slim silver pistol. At the moment Miss Cloke realised this, a bullet penetrated her forehead, spinning her body over the stile. Her final vision was of the sun, before — as she always feared — a wave of darkness enveloped her.

Rosencrantz smiled thinly. 'You watched,

Miss Cloke, but saw too little.' He approached the stile and looked pitilessly down at the crumpled body, the face lined with blood, cracked like a broken doll. He turned on his heel. Just one more task. He focussed on the church and its curious witching-bonnet tower. The boy had to be there.

Inside the church Thomas was enjoying the experience of fatherhood. Hendrix and Page were putting out more chairs, and little Clapton was tottering among the pews with piles of hymnbooks and service sheets, scattering them liberally.

The door creaked open, and Rosencrantz stepped into the church. A small boy sprang out from behind the font. 'Die!' said Clapton, brandishing his lightsaber. Rosencrantz instinctively felt for his pistol before noticing Thomas.

'Ah, Mr. Rosencrantz,' said Thomas. 'How nice to see you again.'

'Ah, yeees, of course, Reverend. I was not expecting to see you again, certainly not here.'

'Things change, Mr. Rosencrantz. Things change.'

'They certainly do around here.' Rosencrantz managed an uneasy smile. 'Did I explain we are looking for a very dangerous criminal?'

Thomas noticed Rosencrantz's right hand nestling in the pocket of his grey suit. 'It is very brave of you to search for such a

dangerous man on your own, Mr. Rosencrantz.'
At that moment Page and Hendrix carried
another bench into the church from the vestry.

'Who's that?' said Page.

'You with the Feds?' asked Hendrix.

'Die!' Clapton sprang once again but
skidded on a hymnbook and dropped his
lightsaber. He ran to Hendrix and clutched
his leg.

Rosencrantz bent down slowly and reached
for the lightsaber. Clapton hugged Hendrix
even tighter. 'Here you are, sonny.'

Clapton shrank away from the thin suit and
predatory smile. 'I'll take it,' said Page.

'I do like children,' said Rosencrantz,
calculating the number of bullets in his gun.
If the boy and his girl were here as well, that
would make the odds rather riskier. 'You are
very lucky, Reverend. I did not know you had
a family.'

Neither did I, thought Thomas, his heart
once again beginning to race. 'There is no
one dangerous here.'

'Thomas!' There was a shout from outside.
Olivia came running into the church.

Too many now, thought Rosencrantz.

'Thomas, there's been some trouble.'

'In that case I'll leave you, Reverend,' said
Rosencrantz. 'So good to meet you both.' He
headed for the door and was gone. He strode

quickly up the lane to his Mercedes. Miss Cloke's car lay tidily parked and now ownerless. He looked across at the stile before driving off to the north to rendezvous with the count.

'Thomas, the hut down by the beach is on fire. There have been gunshots. People are running everywhere.'

'Cool!' said Hendrix. 'Where's the Feds?'

'The police and ambulance are here. They have gone straight up Dingwell Lane. We must hurry.'

Thomas looked at Olivia. 'Trust me, Olivia.' Then he looked at the bemused children. 'Don't be afraid. There are two people I want you to meet. Two very important and wonderful people.' He walked over to a pew close to the main door. On the wall there was a blue curtain. He drew it back. There was a small arched door set into the wall. Thomas knocked on it three times. 'I am sure it is safe now,' he said.

The door creaked open. The children stood wide-eyed and snuggled up to Olivia, who clasped them.

'Don't be afraid children. Just believe your eyes.'

A spiky-haired teenage boy in a crumpled green jacket awkwardly descended the steps and emerged blinking, stepping onto the pew and down onto the floor. 'Hi,' said Pi. 'Are these your kids, Thomas?'

Thomas smiled. 'It is nice to have a surprise for you, Pi. Yes, in a way, they are, and I love them deeply.'

Pi held out his palm into the archway. 'This is my friend, Navinda. I hope you can see her.'

A dark-haired girl, in dusty blue jeans and a black leather jacket, stepped carefully down and stood smiling uneasily next to Pi. She looked at the wide-eyed children. 'Hello. I hope you can see me.'

There was a moment of tension and wonder. 'Yes,' said Olivia. 'We can.' And Olivia walked over and embraced them both. She turned to the children. 'Thomas explained to me during the night that he was hiding Pi and Navinda in the church tower. Someone wanted to kill them.'

'Rosencrantz, the man who was with us just now,' Thomas said, 'had a gun in his pocket. He has gone now.'

'Die!' said Clapton.

★ ★ ★

PC Dave Rabbetts swung the Vauxhall Omega onto Dingwell Lane. He and Sergeant Heffer were met by a flock of exhausted and traumatised animals and cartoon characters wandering chaotically along the lane. One panda was clearly being comforted by the front end of a horse. 'What the bleedin' 'ell's goin' on here?' he muttered, weaving through the throng.

'Told you Dingwell folks is all away with the fairies,' grunted Sergeant Heffer, as three nymphs, one with a broken wand, staggered past. 'Look, The Fossils. Down there on the left, Dave.'

★　★　★

Yvonne was breathing. Her eyes opened; then all went dark. She felt so tired. The pain. Perhaps she had died, she thought, then realised it was a mistake to think you had died if you could feel pain. She was moving. She opened her eyes again. The trees and sky swung violently from side to side. There was Gideon. What was Gideon doing? Her head rolled from side to side and sometimes jolted. Yvonne's eyes closed again. Someone had packed bandages inside her shirt. If only everything could be still and she could stop moving and rolling and swaying and . . .

'Hope you can hear me, Yvonne. This wheelbarrow is the only ambulance we can find. Keep with us, sweet lady.

Keep the faith now, Yvonne. Stay with us, baby. Make him wait. Make him wait now.'

Gideon was talking continually, feeding out a lifeline of thought, and Yvonne resolved to cling to it. *Make him wait. Make who wait?*

Through a door, bang, bump, more faces: Pearl, Hairy Nigel, Tizzy. Where was Peter? She wanted to see Peter. Then being lifted upward, hands under her body. Then on a bed. A chandelier of hands and arms grasping candles. Faces. Sergeant Heffer. Constable Dave. Gideon talking to her. Yvonne tried to listen.

'You come back now, Yvonne. Listen to me, baby. Don't leave us. You with me. You with me.' But Yvonne drifted, drifted away, and Gideon's voice faded, faded.

The paramedics quickly fixed up a drip. Yvonne may even have felt it penetrate her arm, or perhaps the injection into her vein, but she so wanted to drift and drift and run away to the sea with Alison and see Peter and Navinda and Doris and . . . and . . .

'At least this one's not playing dead,' said the young paramedic. They all looked at him. 'Last time I came here, an old girl was pretending she'd joined the turf club. I was about to bag 'er up, and she winked at me and licked 'er lips. Was me that nearly blooming died!'

250

'How is she?' Dave Rabbetts's voice was shaky. A tear rolled down his rosy cheek.

'Lost a lot of blood. Bleeding's stopped. We'll know in a few minutes.'

'Oh, Yvonne. Wish I'd got 'ere sooner.' Dave moved his face towards Yvonne, her lovely face porcelain pale and her eyes barely open.

Yvonne drifted away, away into a mist. *Perhaps I'm dying. Perhaps I'm going to see Jesus. Or the angel Gabriel.* Instinctively her fingers searched for the crucifix on her neck chain. *I am ready. I am ready.* And the mist began to part.

'Yvonne, perhaps you just needs a gentle kiss to awake, laying there like a princess.'

The mist was clearing, and Yvonne saw a face. But something was wrong. This was not the angel Gabriel. It had big ears, funny teeth, and rosy cheeks. It was coming towards her.

'Dave,' she breathed softly.

'Yes, babe. I'm here.'

'Dave,' she murmured again.

'Yes, babe.' Dave's lips approached; his eyes were closing.

From somewhere Yvonne found the strength to open both eyes and whisper softly. 'Dave,' she gasped. 'Sod off.' Her head sank into the pillow.

'Right. Let's get her moving,' said the paramedic. They lifted her onto a stretcher. The vaulted ceiling of The Fossils hallway passed over Yvonne, and then she was in the bright sunlight. Two more faces. They bent down to kiss her.

'Little brother,' said Yvonne, 'and his lovely girl.'

'You're going to be all right, Yvonne,' said Navinda.

'The count and Miss Cloke have gone,' said Pi.

'Oh . . . thank God,' breathed Yvonne. 'You can go home now. How is Thomas?'

Navinda smiled. 'He is fine. And guess what? He has a family.'

'A family. How?'

'Best get moving,' said the paramedic. And Yvonne was strapped into the ambulance. Gideon stepped inside.

'I'll call Tizzy soon as I can,' he shouted.

The doors slammed shut. The ambulance roared up the stony drive and disappeared. The villagers and remaining Hashers were silent, their eyes fixed on the space where the ambulance had stood. The soul of the village had departed and left a terrifying space. The little group stood huddled as mourners. A sob broke the silence. It was Constable Dave.

'For Gawd's sake,' barked Sergeant Heffer.

'Not the first time a girl has told you to sod off! Won't be the last!'

'Sorry. Can't help it. Just love Yvonne so much,' he wailed, as Sergeant Heffer ushered the heartbroken Dave back to the police car. As his ululations mercifully receded, the villagers decided it really was time to put the kettle on.

22

Greymoor

'At the end of the road, turn left,' said Marlena, the GPS.

'For you, anything, Marlena.' Count de Boodle obeyed.

He was in an excellent mood, enjoying being free of Dingwell and looking forward to slipping into his private plane at Northmoor and watching the damned English coastline, with its pitiable green-quilted landscape of fields and infantile inhabitants, slide beneath him like a departing dream. He would not be returning, he decided. Spending a few luxurious months in the heat of South America was an attractive prospect. Clever little Peter Young and his girl could not have survived the holocaust in the stone hut. As soon as he landed, he would tell the Organisation to dispose of the boy's parents once and for all.

The Daimler whispered its way northward. Ahead Greymoor loomed like a table mountain, hooded with a lid of dark cloud. But the count had no plans to drive across it.

Just pick up the motorway between Grey-mouth and Oxeter; then a left turn would take him to the northeastern edge of Greymoor and the airstrip.

'In five hundred yards, take the second left.'

The count did so and was aware that he was on a narrow bridge above the motorway. He stopped the car and got out and looked down at the artery of traffic hurtling beneath. Where was the slip road? *Must be farther on,* he thought. *Trust Marlena,* he told himself. But the road snaked onward, rising upward, until the high farmland hedges disappeared. The Daimler rattled over a cattle grid. 'Go straight for the next five miles,' said Marlena.

Oh, well. It's just taking me on a more direct route. The count drove on and turned on his lights. Stout oaks, with their huge tentacular limbs, embraced the lane, while thickets of holly, rowan, and hazel harboured pockets of darkness. Ferns and mosses danced at their feet. Lichens startled the grey with splashes of emerald and amethyst, and treacherous ivy laced the trunks of elms. As the Daimler turned a corner, mist billowed from a tunnel of trees, enfolding a leaping river that crashed down a narrow fissured valley. The car plunged into the billowing shroud, forded the stream, and emerged onto the open moorland, with its lowering gloomy canopy of cloud and misty rain, dragging its columns across the tussocky grass and grey debris of granite boulders. The road had become narrow and meandered and twisted through an undulating landscape of eerie lunar pyramids of white clay waste, and a luminous grey dust smeared the road. The count felt he was travelling through some lost and forbidden country of the mind. 'What hellish place is this?' he murmured, as the ashen shapes floated past like silent ghost ships. A sickly, sterile lake lapped the spoil heaps, its creamy surface streaked with an oily film.

A lamp glimmered ahead through the sepulchral mist. The stark outline of the Greymoor Hotel loomed towards the count as he rounded the bend. He stopped the car and wiped the windscreen with his sleeve. Was that a light? He pulled over, onto the narrow strip of grey tarmac between the hotel and the lane. A lamp glimmered in the strange curved window of the hotel lounge. Was it a welcome? The count got out of the car and strode to the end of the building. As he walked past the window, the light shifted and flickered. He rounded the corner into the empty little car park.

'Hello. Anyone there?' Footsteps running

away. The laughter of children. 'Ha. *Allez en enfer!* Damn all of you. *Disciples du diable!'* He pulled out his Luger and strode round the car park, brandishing the weapon. 'Show yourselves! Damn you all!' But whatever the light had been was gone, and the Greymoor Hotel stood alone and grim. '*Vous m'avez dupé encore,*' he whispered to the silent air.

A granite crucifix gleamed grey in the sombre light, and caught the count's gaze. It towered impassively over him, and he looked along the road to see another, then another, and perhaps one beyond. Motionless, like monks, they marked an ancient pathway that the count was to cross. He stood still, his grey uniform corresponding with his surroundings, comforted by the gun still in his hand. 'I have power, my silent friend. You do nothing but stand until the cock crows.'

'In three hundred yards turn right,' said Marlena.

'All right, all right. I'm coming.' The count strode back to the car. The door was open. 'Thought I'd closed it. Ach. Too old for this.'

The count nestled into the driver's seat — he never wore a seatbelt — for what would prove to be the last time. 'No more fun and games, Marlena. Just take me to the damn airport.' He reset the GPS again and looked at the display. He seemed to be on the edge of some strange white desert with ashen pyramids and peaks, some with flattened tops, with the serpentine threads of streams and becks, blue snakes among the chalk-white undulations of the moor. There was a river ahead. A mile after that, a main road curved around the northwest edge of Greymoor. He felt more comforted. 'OK. Now we go.'

The Daimler came back to life. A simple white signpost pointing to Caed-a-ford slid towards the car. 'Turn right.' The powerful headlights swung round, and the car picked up speed. The count touched the stereo. '*Non, rien de rien. Non, je ne regrette rien.*' The count accompanied Edith Piaf with his strident basso cantabile, his gloved hands drumming on the steering wheel.

> *Ni le bien qu'on m'a fait, ni le mal.*
> *Tout ça m'est bien égal.*
> *Non, rien de rien.*
> *Non, je ne regrette rien.*
> *C'est payé, balayé, oublié.*
> *Je me fous du passé . . .*

He sang, visualising the old Foreign Legionnaires he had served with in Algeria. They were good boys. Great times. Pride surged to the surface of his being and swelled his chest as he sang. The Daimler was accelerating smoothly with the music, devouring the white line in the centre of the lane.

Avec mes souvenirs
j'ai allumé le feu.
Mes chagrins, mes plaisirs,
je n'ai plus besoin d'eux.

Ah, the futility of human pleasures, mused the count, his wrinkled face suffused with affectionate irony . . .

Balayées les amours
et tous leurs trémolos.
Balayés pour toujours.
Je repars à zéro.

His jilted wives and lovers drifted like phantoms across the ashen landscape as he drove and sang. Oh, how he sang . . .

Non, rien de rien.
Non, je ne regrette rien.
Ni le bien qu'on m'a fait, ni le mal.

. . . the count's gloved fist clenching the air . . .

Tout ça mèst bien égal.
Non, rien de rien.

259

Non, je ne regrette rien.

. . . gripping his past by the throat . . .

Car ma vie, car mes joies,
aujourd'hui . . .

. . . and the climax, *le denouement*. The triumph of his life!

. . . *ça commence . . . avec . . . toi!*

The count held the final note long after 'La Môme Piaf' had left the building. He breathed deeply, exhausted by the exhumed memories of his murder of freedom fighters, celebratory drinks in dingy bars, and violent nights with prostitutes. '*C'était un temps merveilleux!*' His face beamed with joy.

'Hi! I know you!' A little boy in shiny shoes, lederhosen, and a green alpine hat with a feather grinned wickedly from the passenger seat.

'Aha,' said the count, shaken from his reverie. 'So you sneak into my car while it is parked at the hotel, uh?'

The little boy grinned again.

'Well, I am going to stop the car, and you can damn well get out and find your mummy.'

'I don't think so!' the boy said with a smile.

The count tried to brake, but the car would

not respond. It accelerated smoothly, con-
suming more of the white line.

'I know you too!' A dark-haired girl with
pigtails and pink bows smiled from his
rearview mirror.'

'So you think you are clever, uh? You bring
your sister too.'

'Don't forget to steer!' said the boy, seizing
the steering wheel.

'Leave it, you little devil!' shouted the
count, as the car lurched to the left.

'Don't forget to steer!' Two more hands
wearing pink gloves were on the steering wheel.
The count gripped the wheel fiercely with his
leather gloves. But now a dozen young hands
had joined his on the steering wheel, and the
car swung crazily across the lane.

'*Non, rien de rien!*' The music had gone up
several decibels as the count wrestled
frantically with the wheel. 'Damn you! Leave
it, *progéniture de Satan*. Damn you!'

'*Non, je ne regrette rien.*'

The little stone bridge at Caed-a-ford rose
up ahead of the car. 'Don't forget to steer.
Don't forget to steer!' Shrieks of children's
laughter rose to a crescendo. '*Je ne regrette
rien!*' They all sang.

'Perform a U-turn when possible!' Marlena's
voice had increased to deafening. 'Perform a
U-turn when possible!' she repeated, as the

261

car rose towards the bridge. The count's face, as ashen as his surroundings, stared. A young couple, hands joined, smiled calmly from the parapet.

'Don't forget to steer! Don't forget to steer!'

'Perform a U-turn when possible!'

'I know you! I know you!'

'*Non, je ne regrette rien!*'

The young hands wrenched the wheel from the count's grasp, and the car veered to the left. The Daimler was airborne as it left the road. It lurched drunkenly before heading down the steep bank towards the river. The count saw the approach of a granite crucifix and screamed. The impact ejected him, like a missile from its silo, through the windscreen, shards of glass skinning his face before slicing the clothes from his body. The count's skull smashed like an egg on a granite rock in the stream before his mutilated body crashed into the water, spinning round like a sheep's carcass in an eddy, before disappearing in a slew of blood over the weir.

The car had vaulted across the river and landed on its back, headlights briefly stabbing the gloom, the music playing on theatrically. The car phone crackled and burst into life. 'Count? Count?' But all Rosencrantz could hear was the gushing of the river, and a cacophony of music and children's laughter. And finally, 'Perform a U-turn when possible!' before the waters terminated the Daimler's performance. Its lights extinguished abruptly. The end brought no applause, only Greymoor's unforgiving silence.

Rosencrantz studied his e-phone. Strange. He slammed the door of his Mercedes before pacing across the tarmac to the count's Learjet — a steel black dart under a leaden sky. Rosencrantz gazed southward, where the sun streamed down beyond the cloud rim.

'We need to go,' he called out to the pilot. 'I'll call the count again later.' The pilot nodded.

Rosencrantz ascended the few steps in his grey suit and fine leather shoes. He settled into the grey airline seat, placing his attaché case and laptop on the table. Croissants, juice, and dark coffee awaited. He slipped his gun into the tray beneath his seat, put on the seatbelt, and relaxed. It had been a stupid plan, he concluded. But the count had insisted. The Old Warrior. The jet smoothly accelerated, trees and farm buildings flying past, before it soared into the clear air. Rosencrantz looked forward to coming back. He liked England.

23

The Old Rectory

Pi was standing in his garden beneath the oak tree — Navinda, slender in his arms, his face buried in the dark storm of her hair. Beyond the tree line, they saw a thin ribbon of smoke threading skyward from the ruins of the Dream Factory.

'They tried to kill us,' said Pi.

'They wanted to kill the dream even more,' said Navinda.

'Why?'

'Power and fear. Fear of something they could not control,' said Navinda. 'They will never kill the world within us. They cannot do that. They will be worried about that.'

Pi and Navinda heard the police searching the house and the garage.

'You have to go,' said Pi.

'Yes, I have to go,' said Navinda. She turned her dark eyes towards Pi and held his face in her cool hands. 'They may come again.'

'I doubt they will come here again. The whole village will be crawling with police. All the Hashers have been taken into custody.

What will you do?'

'I will speak to my father and mother. I will tell them about my amazing friend.' She smiled. 'But I am not sure they will believe me. Term ends on Friday. I have done all my work. So I will meet you.'

'Not in Dingwell.'

'You remember the first time we met?'

'In that cafeteria. I was too scared to speak to you.'

'Are you still afraid, Peter?' She kissed him tenderly on the cheek. 'Are you still afraid of me?'

'You called me 'Peter.''

'I think you should take your name back. Peter Young. It's who you are.'

'It's who I am,' he agreed. 'Always asking me questions. Always challenging me,' said Peter, who knew that his world lay in those dark eyes of Navinda and the trembling, vibrant envelope of her presence.

'I will meet you in that same cafeteria,' said Navinda. 'And be on time.'

'I will be there,' said Peter.

'I will send a Splot to Om. That will be safer. Goodbye, Peter. Hold me once more.'

Peter's arms gently enfolded the slender willow and life force that was Navinda. She turned her face towards him for the final time. Peter stood, his arms still enfolding the space where Navinda had been. He stood motionless then breathed deeply. As still as a granite crucifix. He would not weep. He was there for some minutes before a shout came from the house.

Sergeant Heffer was wandering across the lawn with PC Rabbetts.

'How is Yvonne?' asked Peter.

'OK. Had the bullet removed. Just needs some rest,' said the sergeant.

'She'll be neat as nine pence,' said Dave. He sat down at the garden table.

'Terrible news about Miss Cloke,' Sergeant Heffer said.

'What about her?' asked Peter.

'Dead as a dodo,' said the sergeant. 'Some bloke called Topshelf was by the stile up back o' the village and found the old girl. Been shot.'

'Dear God. I've known Miss Cloke all my life. And the count?' said Peter.

'Last seen driving out of the village, heading north,' said Dave.

Sergeant Heffer lowered his ample posterior into a wicker chair. 'Peter, the scenes-of-crime team will need to be here for some time. Detective Sergeant Raine will want to interview you. So you'll need to remain in the village.'

'Is anyone, like, looking after you?' said Dave.

Gideon and Tizzy had walked through the

side gate. 'I think I'll be all right. If anyone wants me, I'll be at the Whodhavethoughtit,' said Peter. Gideon and Tizzy joined them at the garden table.

'Thanks for looking after the dogs, Tizzy.'

'Dogs, cats . . . like a blooming zoo down at the pub,' said Tizzy.

'Where's Tigger?'

'Oh, he's buggered off somewhere. Too many cats around for his liking.'

'Too many relatives, more like,' said Gideon.

'Pandora can stay at the pub. Tigger will have to get used to having his missus bossing him about. The Patels are going to take two of the kittens,' said Tizzy.

'Reckon Nigel and Pearl will have two as well. We'll keep Jack and Jill and Buddy until youz sorted here.'

'Guess what, man? We found a home for Odessa.'

'The count's dog?' said Peter. 'He's ferocious.'

'Your neighbours say they need some protection,' said Gideon. 'Poor old Wilfred and Lavinia don't reckon Willy's got much petrol in his engine no more. They're gonna change Odessa's name, though.'

'I still can't understand why Miss Cloke was murdered. It's too awful,' said Peter.

'She was involved in some murky stuff,'

said Tizzy. 'And she's bumped off a few herself. One Christmas she got a bit tiddly in the Whodhavethoughtit and started talking about it. Bumped off some poor bloke with a cheese wire.'

'She was a churchwarden and kept cats,' said Peter, shaking his head.

'Miss Cloke never had no childhood like you had,' said Tizzy. 'She were packed off to private school, then joined the SIS. Trained spy and killer.'

Peter looked back at his house. 'Good to be home.'

'It's good to see you at home, man. Back where you belong.' Gideon smiled and clapped Peter on the back. 'You need anythin', you know where to come.'

Gideon and Tizzy rose from their seats. Peter walked with them to the side gate. Tizzy whispered, 'Look, we ain't said nothin' about Navinda. Guess she's gone back. Trouble is, she's a witness. You may have to say somethin'.'

'How many more witnesses do they need?' said Peter. 'They've got all the poor old Hashers.'

Tizzy looked keenly into Peter's eyes. 'Listen, son. You got to tell the whole story.'

'No choice, man,' said Gideon. 'Even if she don't believe you.'

'She?' said Peter.

'Detective Sergeant Raine,' said Gideon. 'Some lady. We explained to her that Dingwell is a bit different.'

Tizzy nodded. 'You can trust her, Peter. She's like Yvonne.'

★   ★   ★

DS Raine stood in the scullery and looked across the garden. Her green eyes shifted and noted that Sergeant Heffer and Constable Rabbetts were taking it easy in the sun on the lawn. Charlie was examining the bullet hole in the window and ran his finger round the rim. 'Something must have happened outside the window to cause all this. What I don't get is why all this mayhem in here?'

'Well, the burglar locked the count in here with his dog. Curious,' said Sarah. 'Really only one person who could have done that.'

Normally witnesses were in short supply. In this case there was an abundance of witnesses — some shocked and traumatised — and a stack of pieces of evidence, all of which would fit together eventually. What on earth would persuade two elderly residents of a quiet rural village to attempt to commit acts of murder and terrorism, using weapons from another era? Not much made sense. The scenes-of-crime team was examining the scullery in minute detail, like dung beetles scurrying across the forest floor. She would leave them to their work.

'Come with me, Charlie.'

The sharp-suited detective left the scullery and descended the stairs to the cellar. An unmade bed lay among a jumble of rocking horses and toy trains. She stepped through the outside door and ascended the steps onto the back lawn. 'There is only one person who could have burgled this house, and he's in the garden right now.'

'Do you want me to arrest him?' said Charlie.

'No. He's the biggest asset we've got. When all is said and done, it's his house.' They marched onto the lawn.

'So who killed Miss Cloke?'

'Figure it out, Charlie. A Mercedes was seen leaving the village after the fun was over.'

'Rosencrantz. But why?'

'OK, Sergeant. You and the constable can get back to Queensbridge now.' Sergeant Heffer and Dave Rabbetts rose reluctantly and plodded off to their police car. Sarah noticed Tizzy and Gideon by the side gate.

'Ah, DS Raine. This is Peter Young. He lives here. His family owns this house.'

DS Raine looked quizzically at the sharp-faced teenager with his spiky hair and green jacket. The boy looked down, avoiding eye contact.

'We'll get back to the pub and leave you to it.' Tizzy and Gideon wandered through the gate.

There was an awkward silence. 'Can we sit down?' Peter grunted, then sat down, looking away, over the lawn to the oak tree.

'I'm DS Raine and this is Charlie.' She leant forward, both elbows on the table. She smiled. 'Call me Sarah.' Peter glanced at her fleetingly. 'So what has been happening here, Peter? Quite a lot, it would seem.'

'I'll show you,' said Peter. He led the way over to the oak tree and pointed over the old brick wall, down to the Dream Factory at Eastcombe. The sight of the smouldering ruins brought a lump to his throat. 'Someone . . . ' he choked out. 'Someone tried to kill an idea.' He swung round to look at Sarah Raine. 'Someone tried to kill a thought. Now one person is dead, and one of the people I love most is wounded.'

'And your parents are missing?' said Charlie.

'Yes.' Peter kicked the turf. He cried uncontrollably, shaking and trembling. 'Yes. And I don't know where they are. And I miss them so much.'

'You've been coping with this all on your own?'

Peter looked down. 'No.' He looked pleadingly at Sarah.

'Go on.'

'I have a friend.'

'Yes?'

'An invisible friend.' He looked away.

'Invisible?' DS Raine looked pityingly at Peter.

'Not invisible. Just that she's not here. Hard to explain.'

'It doesn't matter. You can tell us if we need to interview her. No one else?'

'Just Om.'

'Om?'

'My computer.' He produced the sphere from his inside pocket. Sarah noticed that Om briefly flushed blue. Was this distressed young man mad? She had seen plenty of young people glued to their smartphones, shut in a virtual world. But this boy was not like that.

'He's very different,' Tizzy had said. 'He may not trust you.' That was no surprise. The boy had been hounded out of his own home and forced to live rough. And when he had asked for help, apart from people in the village, no one had believed him.

'We want to find out who did all this and find your parents,' said Charlie.

'And I want to understand. You talked

about killing an idea,' said Sarah.

Peter nodded. 'That is what matters.' He turned to face them for the first time. Sarah saw the sharp-blue eyes beneath the mop of hair; the tense, young face; and the lines of tears. She also saw resolve and strength. Fearlessness.

'Peter, we need to do this properly. Can you stay somewhere very close by?'

Peter thought. 'I was going to stay at the pub.'

'Closer even than that. We need to protect you.'

'Next door,' Peter smiled. 'With the Plunketts. When I was a kid, I used to camp in their garden.'

'Perfect. I don't want you to go anywhere without telling me. I'll be based here. Take anything you need. I'll come with you. Charlie, give me a minute.' Sarah headed back into the house.

'We'll sort this out, Peter,' said Charlie. Peter shrugged. 'We will. I can tell you, DS Raine is the best — *the* best. She can see through walls.'

'She'll need to,' said Peter.

'When this is over,' said Charlie, 'I'd love you to teach me about your computer. That is awesome.'

'It is, isn't it?' said Peter, smiling at last.

'You'll never guess DS Raine's nickname.'
Peter looked puzzled. 'Tarot!'

'Tarot? She can read the future?'

'Yes.'

'Awesome!' said Peter.

★   ★   ★

Moments later Wilfred and Lavinia Plunkett
were feeling reassured. An early morning's
twitching in search of the great crested willow
tit had been interrupted by Armageddon in
Eastcombe Valley. The kitchen table once
again had served as an air-raid shelter, as the
world about them had resembled a cross
between *The Jungle Book* and *Apocalypse
Now*. Yes, they would be delighted to look
after their young friend Peter, and no, they
did not mind one bit about having two burly
policemen at the front door, both armed to
the teeth, and 'Would they like a cup of tea?'

DS Raine left Peter to their tender care. As
she walked down the drive, she heard them
scold Cecil, their recently acquired Doberman, for jumping 'all over Willy.' She took
two more officers with her and marched
down the track that led across the rear of The
Fossils. An extraordinary sight awaited them.
Discarded animal and cartoon-character
costumes hung from bushes or lay in the mud

like the residue of an abandoned pop festival. The Daimler's deep tracks led them quickly through Stoggie's Wood and onto the hill opposite the ruined Dream Factory. They came to the smashed gate that lay on its back in front of the hide. A smell of vomit and cordite still hung in the air. The door to the hide swung from one hinge.

'Look at this,' said the sergeant.

'Careful,' said Sarah.

'What is it?'

'Grenade launcher, I should say.' She pointed to the steel box, still on the small trailer. 'World War Two vintage. Don't touch it, Sergeant. And radio back. I want this area sealed off.'

She looked across the valley at the smoking ruins of the Dream Factory. The little group slipped back onto the footpath that ran below the count's eyrie, stepping on Topshelf's now unwanted tablecloth and heading for the footpath that ran across the rim of the beach.

'Who's that?'

'Where?'

'There! There!' DS Raine pointed. A girl was standing in the ruins of the Dream Factory, leafing through the charred pages of a book. 'Don't move. Can we talk?' Sarah shouted, then ran along the footpath. The Dream Factory rose up before them as they vaulted the stream, a tableau of charred stones and ashes and the scorched residue of toys and simple furniture.

'I saw a girl. Standing here. Now she's not here.'

Charlie contemplated a storm lantern, its glass cracked and wick still smoking, laying on the scorched grass. 'Perhaps you imagined it, Tarot?'

Sarah turned and smiled. 'I think you're right. To understand what happened here, we all need to do the same.'

They stood on the edge of the smoking ruins. Sarah Raine knew the value of hard evidence, but this crime scene stated the simple truth that consciousness and reality follow converging and diverging pathways. She rarely bothered to bring this dimension with her to work in the morning. When she parked her car at Divisional HQ, she also parked these theories. She knew she needed them now. Madness was always rational action at the time, whichever way you looked at it. To try to destroy a small stone hut on a beach with heavy weapons was madness. But it was a decidedly calculated and sane act — planned with the intention of committing murder but also, through the power of fire and brimstone, to stop the evolution of this particular patch of time and thinking. Why?

Because to allow it to continue would be too dangerous for those in power. The consequences of not destroying it could not be imagined; therefore it was unthinkable not to try to destroy it.

The count and Miss Cloke had used the war instruments and ideologies and idols of the past to destroy a piece of future vision. Simple as that. It would be tough to explain in court, but it was the truth. To the count and Miss Cloke, it had to be done, whatever the consequences. Suddenly Sarah was aware of their sense of mission. But who could or would understand it? She wasn't sure anyone would. Discovering all the facts in this case would reveal other truths about all the characters involved, including Sarah herself. The search for truth, she reasoned, is as constant as a heartbeat, consciously or not.

'Charlie, get this sealed off, and get forensics in. The whole valley, footpaths, the lot — closed down. Terry, stay 'til they get here. We'll get back to the Old Rectory.'

★ ★ ★

A blessedly quiet and bird-twittering evening had descended upon Dingwell. The Hashers, after their life-changing experience, vowed never to return, although Topshelf was still ensconced in the small police tent erected at the site of Miss Cloke's demise. He was with Sergeant Heffer and Dave Rabbetts. The sergeant was enjoying himself and decided to apply some third degree.

'Listen, matey, anyone who goes around calling himself 'Topshelf' has got to be a few Jaffa Cakes short of a full packet.'

'But I've told you before . . . My name is Gordon Bennett.'

'Is this your tablecloth?'

'We were having a picnic,' said Topshelf miserably.

'A picnic, eh? You can say that again.'

'We *were* having a picnic.'

'Heard that before,' said Dave. 'But not according to Mrs. Peabody, aka Late Bloomer. She said you had pulled — '

'Look, I was about to offer her a Jaffa Cake when all hell broke loose. Some maniac started firing missiles.'

'So you ran back here and decided to have a widdle over Miss Cloke, whom you had already bumped off.'

'Yes, but I told you I had *found* a body. If I had murdered the poor woman, would I have done that?' pleaded Topshelf.

'You were being clever. Just a ruse to throw us off the scent,' said the sergeant, now leaning over his victim and talking into his face.

278

'I want my solicitor,' said Topshelf. 'This is a nightmare.'

'We phoned your solicitor who happens to be Mrs. Peabody's husband. He went hashing with you today. He said he hopes you get twenty years.'

DS Raine appeared in the doorway of the tent. 'That's quite enough. You can go, Mr. Bennett.'

'Thank you so much,' said Topshelf. 'Just remembered. My wife's taken the car.'

'Oh, I'm sure Sergeant Heffer and Constable Rabbetts will give you a lift — that is, if you don't mind.'

Topshelf gave the policemen a dubious glance. 'Er . . . OK.'

'Misery acquaints a man with strange bedfellows, Mr. Bennett, or should I call you 'Topshelf'?' Sarah Raine smiled sweetly. Perhaps he had suffered enough.

'Indeed, Detective Sergeant. I will count my blessings.'

'A bird in the hand is worth three in a tree,' said Dave.

'We may need to speak to you again about what you actually saw. It may be helpful to try writing it all down before we contact you again. Just wait outside a few minutes.' She turned to the two policemen. 'Well, boys,' she said, settling comfortably into one of the canvas chairs and crossing her elegant legs — simultaneously reducing Dave's limbs to jelly. 'Apart from the fact that there is no possible motive, no weapon, and not a shred of evidence, the case against Mr. Bennett looks open and shut.' Her irony was lost on Sergeant Heffer and a gaping Dave Rabbetts, who was somewhat overwhelmed in the divine presence of Special Branch. 'There was indeed a picnic in a plastic box. Two store-bought sandwiches and a packet of Jaffa Cakes — unopened. For a romantic picnic, not quite enough to start my engine, I have to admit, but Mr. Bennett is not a suspect.'

'No, DS Raine,' sniffed the sergeant.

'While we are at it, Sergeant, the next time a teenage boy phones up to tell you he has been locked out of his house, his parents have been abducted, and he's being forced to live rough, I suggest you do something.'

'Yes, ma'am.'

'Believe it or not, children tell the truth more often than adults. Now do something useful and take Mr. Bennett back to his wife.'

As the police car drove up the lane, Sarah Raine walked out into the soft evening air and breathed deeply. *What a beautiful place*, she thought. But she knew her quarry had long gone, and cast a glance at the darker sky to the north. The police teams would find the hard evidence but would not be able to reconstruct the emotional and moral architecture of these events. That was a darker and deeper mission into landscapes more shadowy and oppressive than these regal skies and sighing oaks and elms. They had enough witnesses to form a symphony orchestra. However, it was obvious the Organisation did not care. That was significant. Tomorrow Sarah would visit Peter and take him back to his home. That was something to really look forward to.

24

There Is No Such Thing as Time

Navinda Eman awoke in her bed to the alarming sight of Dr. Nathan's dark round spectacles and tufty eyebrows. He was fumbling with his prescription pad.

'Hello, Dr. Nathan. What are you doing?'

The startled doctor dropped his pad in shock and clasped his hands, exclaiming, 'Dear God! Erm, God is great. God is Great. Saeed! Alena! Come quickly!' Two faces then joined Dr. Nathan's. Then three more. They were Navinda's selfish, immensely annoying little brothers. Navinda's mother, Alena, in a blue-spotted dress and large hooped earrings, wept instantly; her arms reached into the bed and wrapped themselves around Navinda's shoulders. 'My baby. Where have you been?' She wept and held Navinda's head to her bosom. Navinda's father, Saeed, stared steadily at his daughter, his eyes dark and loving above the line of his brown moustache. He reached for his daughter and held her, murmuring quiet prayers of thanks to God and swaying gently, while — for no reason

Navinda could comprehend — patting her on the back as if she had wind. Navinda patiently watched her homemade driftwood clock and Chinese paper lantern swing backward and forward as she swayed in her father's arms.

'Navinda. For five days. Five days you have said nothing,' wept Alena.

'We thought you were sick. We were so worried,' said her father. He released his gentle hold, and the room stopped moving about.

'Is she OK?' said Jordan, his dark mop of hair and impish face appearing like a hat-wearing sun between his parents. There was a twinkle in his eye.

Navinda felt suddenly energised. 'Well enough to chase you the whole length of Old Rectory Road, and then thrash you at chess, little brother.' Jordan's face disappeared, and he ran out of the bedroom, laughing with his brothers.

'I think you have your daughter back,' said Dr. Nathan, smiling and beginning to pack his Gladstone bag. 'Her blood pressure is quite normal, and she's well in every way.'

'We will call you if it happens again, Doctor,' said Saeed. 'Please God, it will not.'

Minutes later Navinda was munching toast and drinking sweet tea in front of the fire in her dressing gown and purple slippers. Aya, the budgerigar, was having his flying time, and he jetted across the room and perched on the curtain pole. He chirped.

'I have been on a journey in my head. I have done it before but not like this. It was real. Where I have been is as real as this mug, as this fire.'

'Where have you been?' said Alena.

'To a place by a stream, by the sea.'

'It sounds like a dream.' Saeed stared into the fire. He used a black poker to stir the coals and sticks into flame.

'Dad, the reason I went was because I was angry. I remember standing in the queue waiting to collect my medal for languages.' She hesitated. Saeed looked at her nervously.

'And I was not there.' He looked down at his feet and sat, hands on his knees.

'If it had been Jordan's prize giving?' Navinda let the question hang, like a pesky sprite, hovering.

Saeed nodded. The sprite vanished.

'Did you meet anyone in this . . . this . . . dream?' asked Alena.

Navinda smiled. 'I met a boy. The one I had met before in the mock trial competition in London. I told you about him.'

'Peter?'

'He has lost his parents.'

'Oh, the poor child. How?'

'They were taken from him.'

Alena and Saeed looked anxiously at Navinda.

Saeed spoke. 'This is difficult for us too, Navinda. Please understand our suffering.'

'I want to meet him this weekend. In London. It is the end of term. All my work is done. If you want, you can take me.'

'We would like to meet him.' Saeed grasped his wife's hand.

'Of course. I also want to spend time with him. Alone.'

There was silence. Aya flitted, a blue-and-yellow streak, before alighting on top of his cage.

'Dad, when I was born, you were not there, were you?'

'No, Navinda. I have said before that the hospital did not telephone me to say you were on your way.'

'But when I arrived, and you saw me in that plastic cot . . . '

Saeed blinked, and the wonder of that moment sprang up before his eyes. He paused and spoke softly. 'Yes, I remember. It was a miracle.'

'Was there a label?'

'Yes, around your wrist. With your name.'

'Was there a label tied round my neck?'

'No, no. Of course not.'

'If there was, would it have said, 'Congratulations, Saeed. You have a daughter. Unfortunately she will not be able to choose a husband for herself, choose her own religion, or be sufficiently spiritual to become a priest or an imam. Also, even though she is the oldest child, she will have to come second after her brothers and help them with their schoolwork and remind them of all the things they should remember, because they are too spoiled and lazy to remember it themselves. Apart from that your daughter will be normal in every way.'?'

Saeed looked long and lovingly at his daughter. 'It would have been quite a large label.' Navinda smiled and kissed him. 'I will never forget that moment, Navinda — when I saw you. Your little hands, perfectly engineered, a miracle, fingers opening and closing. Until that moment I had never felt . . . real. When I saw you, I knew I existed.' Navinda sat up and looked in his eyes. 'All I had to guide me was what I had known as a child. I did my best but . . . ' He held up his hand ' . . . obviously it has not been good enough. I have not been fair. But the love I felt as a father has lifted me in the darkest of times. Please know that.'

He turned to Alena. 'We will take Navinda to meet her friend. It is important. She must have the time she needs.'

The wood-chipped walls of the room sighed with relief, and Aya chirruped his agreement.

* * *

For the first time since he was a child, Thomas had dined with a real family. Things had not gone entirely according to plan. Page had helpfully posted the letter to the bishop, which had been on the mantelpiece. Thomas had thanked her and then hurriedly phoned Bishop Nonesuch, warning him to expect a strange letter about Thomas's resignation. Thomas had, of course, no intention of resigning, he told the bishop, who had seemed strangely reluctant to believe him.

'But why did you write the letter if you didn't mean it? I really don't understand.'

Thomas had to fall back on invention. 'I had an inheritance of a million pounds from a rich aunt,' babbled Thomas, vowing that this would be the last untruth he ever told.

'Well, my dear fellow, heartiest congratulations. How splendid for you. What good fortune indeed!'

'And I had decided to retire and travel the world and live on the beach in Goa.' (Which sounded rather attractive when he thought about it. Bugger the million pounds.)

'Of course! What a terrific idea — to carry your mission to a far-off land.' *Preferably as far away as possible*, thought the bishop. *How about the moon?*

'But I had a sudden revelation in the garden, Bishop.'

'In the garden?'

'Yes, yes. I saw a little mound of soil growing slowly out of my lawn. Then a little black bewhiskered head with a tiny pointed nose came into view.'

'Yes, yes . . . '

'And I thought, that is one of God's creatures moving the earth itself to find its way to the light.' Thomas's voice plunged once again to Orson Welles. 'How could I be so selfish when life for others — yes, even moles, Bishop — is such a struggle?'

'So what did you decide to do?' said the bishop, bordering on delirium.

'I've given all the money away to the Charity for Homeless Hedgehogs.' There was a strange gurgling sound at the other end of the phone. 'Bishop, I cannot tell you how much better I feel.' Which was, at least, strangely true.

But there was no reply, only a few seconds of silence. Then the bishop's assistant, Miss Parchment, came on the line. 'Oh, hello,

Reverend Clodpole. I'm afraid His Grace has had to leave the room rather suddenly. I'm so sorry. Good-bye.'

That little problem behind him, Thomas had eaten the best meal he'd had in years, and every so often, he caught his beautiful Olivia's gaze and felt a joyful disbelief. He thanked God truly from his heart.

Later, after the children had been settled into bed, Olivia had kissed him and said, 'I want you to go to the pub and see your friends.' Thomas had wandered out into the purple dark and moonlight and sauntered down the hill. He turned back once to see the light illuminating the window of his study. He was a man free of care and fear, and his heart was full.

The pub was strangely deserted when he arrived. 'Folks is a bit scared to go out,' said Tizzy, pouring a pint of Methuselah's Old Wrinkly. 'Enigma Cottage has got police all over it. DS Raine and Charlie have been in for dinner.'

Thomas sipped his pint. 'DS Raine?'

'Sarah Raine, detective in charge. Special Branch, they say. Quite some lady.'

'And how is young Peter?'

'Staying with the Plunketts. Wilfred and Lavinia are glad of the company. They adopted Odessa, the count's dog. Only they call it Cecil,' said Tizzy with a wink.

Thomas laughed.

'It's a beautiful dog, mind. Very affection-ate, it seems.' Gideon came through from the kitchen and sat on the barstool. 'Quiet night, eh, Giddy?'

'Yeah, man. Things are cool. Man, things need to calm down round here.'

'How is Yvonne?' said Thomas.

'Yeah, she's cool, man. She's fine. Alison is with her. Reckons she be bringing her home tomorrow. Doc wants her to stay in hospital, but Yvonne say she missin' Dingwell. Wants to be home.'

Gideon beheaded a Bud and swigged plentifully. Thomas took a good draw from his pint.

'Instant family, eh, Thomas?'

'You can certainly say that, Tizzy. You can certainly say that.'

'Just like Tigger,' said Tizzy, glancing towards the snug where Pandora was stretched out by the fire with her kittens.

'Where's the doting father?' said Thomas.

Gideon laughed. 'Man, now Tigger goes out all the time. He don't do much doting. Not like you, Reverend Tom.'

Thomas nodded. 'They are lively children. A lot for me to learn. Been on my own too long of course.'

'But no longer.' Tizzy smiled, the lines of age creasing his tanned face like shoe leather. 'Must be a good feeling. S'pose you'll be getting back soon? You'll be too busy to have a quiet pint with us two anymore.' He winked again at Gideon.

'Man, you struttin' your stuff with the Hashers. Never thought I'd see the day.'

'You'll probably never see it again, but I'll have another,' said Thomas, pushing his glass across the bar.

'Past closin',' said Tizzy.

'You said there was no such thing as time.'

Tizzy beamed. 'As it's for thee,' and reached for Thomas's glass.

25

There Are No Strangers Here

The sun drew up the eastern sky, raising then shrinking shadows from the long trees and creating a myriad of shifting silhouettes and outlines from Dingwell's romantic barns and thatched cottages. Peter lay in the Plunketts' spare bedroom and woke to the movement of the window's shape across the green flock wallpaper. Voices. Breakfast cooking. A mug of steaming tea was by his bed. He had slept deeply, peacefully. Not without dreams. About Navinda. He tried to recall them but could not.

Having negotiated the ancient plumbing of the lavatory and the shower — both built for a more leisurely age — Peter slipped on his clothes. He touched Om, which flushed green briefly, but there were no messages. He sat on the edge of the bed, sipping the tea. It was good. The green goth jacket dangled from a chair like a recumbent headless monster. Even Peter had to admit, as he slid his arm through the sleeve, that it needed a wash. He slipped Om into his pocket and headed downstairs.

He wasn't prepared for the round of applause that greeted him, like a wave, at the bottom of the stairs. The Plunketts had arranged a joyful breakfast in the garden. Peter hesitated at the ring of faces that turned towards him as he stepped onto the terrace. Tizzy and Gideon and the Patels and, best of all, Yvonne. She gave him a one-handed hug. 'Little brother. Pesky, pesky ruffian and thief!'

Alison had pushed Miss B round from The Fossils, and the old lady beamed, proffering him a note.

'Pearl and Nigel send their love,' said Alison. 'They will call in to see you later.' It was the first time Peter had met Alison. 'Call me 'Ali.'' Peter gazed in awe at this elegant woman, dressed in a purple top and blue jeans. He knew her now from Yvonne's portrait. Now she seemed even more remarkable.

Peter hesitated. 'Oh, are you and Yvonne . . . ?'

'We are engaged,' said Yvonne. 'Well, I couldn't marry you, Peter. All you offered me was a tree house.' They all laughed. 'And you're still wearing that smelly old jacket.'

Thomas stepped forward and shook his hand. Olivia kissed and hugged him. There was a danger of Peter becoming a tad over-whelmed. Then Hendrix shook his hand and 'punched' his shoulder. Page gave him a hug. 'Die!' said Clapton. Even Willy showed his joy by spinning round in circles before peeing expansively on the olive tree. Most entertaining of all was the sight of Cecil — né Odessa — chasing Jack, Jill, and Buddy round the garden before all four plunged into the Plunketts' pond to cool off

'Peter, we have some news.' Peter was finishing his toast when Sarah and Charlie approached the table. 'Just a quiet word. Yvonne, you may want to hear this.' The little group walked over to the gate that Mr. Plunkett had put into his fence. Peter and Yvonne used to come through the gate to play with the Plunketts' grandchildren. The count had crudely nailed it shut.

'Yes, Tarot?' said Peter.

'Cheeky boy. You told him my nickname, Charlie. Out of order.'

'Sorry, DS Tarot,' said Charlie.

'We don't think the count will be bothering you again. He crashed his car on the moors. We will spare you the gruesome details.'

Peter breathed deeply. 'Another death. It's terrible.' He sighed and looked at his shoes and shook his head.

'It is terrible, Peter. We don't really know how it happened, but it did.' DS Raine and Charlie looked at Peter's slumped figure.

This boy is a hero, a genius, and yet he feels all this pain, mused Charlie.

Peter stared at the house that had so recently been inhabited by the count. 'There was one other man. Thomas met him. Drove a Mercedes. Called Rosencrantz, or something like that.'

'We think Rosencrantz has left the country. His car was found abandoned at Northmoor airstrip,' said Charlie.

Sarah gently touched Peter's arm, and his sun-kissed face turned towards her. 'At least it means that something very evil has gone from your house.' Sarah smiled at this extraordinary boy.

Peter looked across at the Old Rectory, which was quiet in the morning sun. 'Can I go home now?'

'Yes,' said Sarah. 'We've finished in there now. There may be an old feline friend waiting for you.'

Peter laughed. 'That's Tigger. Brilliant.'

'DS Raine isn't too fond of cats,' said Charlie.

Sarah sighed and gave Charlie a long look. 'Cats and I have too much in common to be compatible, eh, Charlie?'

'Cats just know who they are.' Charlie looked at the sky.

'Go and have some time on your own, Peter. We'll stay here for a bit. Then we'll talk again.'

Peter reached for the old black handle on

the gate. Wilfred shouted, 'I think you'll find it's open now, Peter. It always will be.' Peter smiled gratefully and pushed the gate back.

The vista of Peter's living, breathing home seemed suddenly revealed to him — the scullery window, the French doors that spilled life into the garden and imbibed the fragrant air of the trees and swaying flowers and bushes. The house had opened its eyes once more. *Welcome. Come*, it said. *Bring your friend*. Peter walked over to the large open French doors and billowing drapes. The sign his father had etched on a brass plate and fixed to the doorpost was still there.

THERE ARE NO STRANGERS HERE, ONLY FRIENDS WHOM WE HAVE YET TO MEET.

A lump came to Peter's throat when he thought of his father and mother. He would find them. There was a buzz from his pocket. Excitedly he pulled out Om.

'Navinda is on Splutter, Peter. She has sent you a Splot!' Peter looked at Om. A tin of coloured paint appeared. The green goblin seized it and threw the contents. The resulting splot formed the message.

'Parents taking me to London Saturday. Meet you at Old Bailey Café. Twelve noon. Dreamt about you. — N.'

'Om, Splot back. 'I'll be there at noon. Dreamt about you. — P'.' Om did so, and Peter saw the new bucket of paint and the mischievous dancing green goblin disappearing into the distance.

Sarah, Charlie, and Yvonne stood by the gate, watching. 'Go inside, Peter,' said Yvonne. 'There's someone you need to thank. I think he's there.'

Peter walked slowly into the empty lounge. The hall door was open. As in a trance, he walked through. All the damage had been repaired, and his eyes followed the length of the hallway and lifted towards the stairs. Tigger sat, relaxed as ever, on the first landing and rose to his feet when Peter approached. In a breath Peter's dream of Navinda returned, and he saw her swimming in an ocean of vivid purple. The waves lapped about his feet and on the sea; hanging webs of charcoal cloud floated like drifting galleons. Navinda's eyes looked skyward as darts of silver fired into the upper sky. She moved away from him across the waters, leaving only a coloured wooden box by his feet. In his dream he had wanted to open it, and he half awoke in the night, thinking the key was somewhere in the room; he foolishly searched under the pillows and through his jacket pockets. He had returned to sleep with a deep sense of loss. Peter picked up Tigger, cradling him in his arms, his sense of loss departed. It was true. The house was breathing calmly again. The evil had departed. Now it was Peter who breathed deeply and wandered across the silent wooden floor of the lounge and emerged blinking into the jubilant sunlight.

'This cat saved my life,' he said, stroking Tigger's ears — which was appreciated. 'I don't know how he did it.'

★   ★   ★

'What a moment,' said Yvonne. 'I thought it would never happen.'

Charlie surveyed the scene. 'How can someone just come to your home and take it? Kick you out and take who you are?'

Sarah led Yvonne toward the gate. 'Yvonne, tell us about Peter.' She looked at Yvonne's clear-blue eyes.

'Brilliant kid — no longer a kid, I suppose. With two brilliant, edgy parents.'

'Edgy?'

'In the last few years,' Yvonne said, 'they weren't as relaxed as when I had known them as a child. I realise now they were probably expecting a knock at the door. Or an important phone call. A bit of tension there.

It may have gotten to Peter a bit. They clearly had prepared him for what might happen.'

'They got away with it, Charlie, because someone in the service helped them. Yvonne, I think your local boys had some pressure.'

Yvonne smiled ruefully at the idea of someone threatening Sergeant Heffer. 'Of course. If they had spoken to Dave, he would have wet himself!'

'We have spoken to the sergeant and Dave, Yvonne. Don't discuss this with them or anyone else.' Sarah strode towards the scullery. She drew a long manicured finger along the sill. 'Any idea why the count decided to shoot the Plunketts' bird table?'

'I think he was shooting at Tigger,' Yvonne said with a smile.

'The village cat?' asked Charlie.

Yvonne nodded. 'Hence the fur.'

DS Raine stood in her black knee-length suit and high heels. She turned her head to the sky. 'Is that a hawk?' Their eyes followed the curve of a dark shape along the line of oaks.

'DS Raine, I had a conversation with Mr. Rosencrantz.' Yvonne had Sarah and Charlie's immediate attention. 'I forgot to mention it. He offered me a job with the Organisation.'

'Did he indeed? And what did you say?' said Sarah.

'I said no of course.'

'And?'

'I've changed my mind. I want to help. I want to go undercover.'

Charlie and Sarah exchanged glances. 'You know what it means, Yvonne?'

'I have an idea,' she said.

'You explain it, Charlie.'

'It means disappearing. It means you will not be you.'

'Have you discussed this with Alison?'

'Yes. We both want to help if we can. Peter means a lot to us.'

DS Raine walked towards Yvonne. 'I want to talk to you both first. We don't have much time. Call me.' She gave Yvonne a card. 'But tell no one else.'

Peter emerged from the house with Om in his hand. 'Navinda wants to meet me in London. I can't wait.'

Om buzzed once again. 'Peter, I think this is a message from your parents. I think it's your mum. Clearer than usual. Shall I play it?'

'Yes, yes, please.' The little group crowded round. Peter placed Om on the garden table. 'Go ahead.'

'Peter, something peculiar is happening here. Everyone seems to have gone. We're in this strange old room with one window. The walls are wooden. There is a stone fireplace, bricked up. There are seven iron rings on the wall. Your father is across the room. He is lying on a table. He is not speaking, but I think he is breathing. I won't say what is keeping us alive — they may be listening. We have been alone for . . . how long? A day? Days? I don't know. I know we are both very weak, but we are still here. Where 'here' is, God alone knows. But I am sure we are alone.' Esther Young's voice hesitated. 'So tired, Peter. So tired. If you hear this, ask Om to send a pulse back. We love you . . . ' Esther's voice faded.

Peter gripped the edge of the table. 'They're alive. They're alive.' He put his head in his hands and looked at Sarah. 'Help me find them.'

'This changes everything, Charlie. We have to move fast.'

'Om,' Peter said. 'Send a pulse.'

'It's done,' said Om.

'Was that a safe thing to do?' asked Peter.

'No point in secrecy now,' said Charlie. 'Can you get Om to play that message again?'

'Yes. Why?'

'I heard something. Very faint. Could be nothing.'

'What did you hear, Charlie?'

'It was just a sound. Reminded me of something.'

'Om, amplify the background sound,' said Peter.

'I'll play it without your mother's voice,' said Om. They huddled around the wooden table. Om glowed a deep crimson. The Old Rectory garden held its breath. They listened. Charlie closed his eyes and placed his hands on the table, listening intently. Om emitted a low rumbling sound.

'Om,' said Charlie, 'play the last ten seconds of that rumbling sound again.'

Om glowed once more, colours rolling in waves across its surface.

'Got it! Got it! Once more Om.'

Om played the low droning sound again. But there was another sound — one that Charlie knew.

''My redeemer liveth,'' he murmured. ''I know that my redeemer liveth.' From an aria in Handel's *Messiah*.'

'That faint bell?' said Sarah.

Charlie nodded. 'Four bells. I remember it. My folks had a council flat in Lambeth. I used to hear it.'

'And the rumble?'

'The tube. It ran beneath our block. If I built a house of cards, it always collapsed. That sound made me afraid.'

'Charlie's an East End boy,' Sarah explained. 'Don't be fooled by the posh hair, cultured mind, and good looks. He's just a barrow boy.'

'Should Peter go back to school?' said Charlie.

Peter pulled a face. 'It's only three days.'

'Or pretend to go back. Peter, can we get someone to be you?' asked Sarah. 'It would fool the Organisation.'

Peter shrugged. 'Easy. Just use my ID card.'

'You get registered in every lesson?'

'Mostly, yes.'

'But you just have to say you're there.'

'We have to find someone to pretend to be you,' said Charlie.

Peter smiled. 'No need for that. Om can get into their systems. He's done it loads of times.'

Om blushed red. 'If I might explain, on the odd occasion, I convinced the school's computer system that Peter had been present when he was not.' There was stunned silence. 'Purely as a service to my master,' said Om, with a hint of irony.

'How very obliging of you, Om.' DS Raine smiled. 'What a friend you are. Peter will be shown present for his lessons until the end of term?'

'That will look suspicious,' said Om. 'He normally bunks off PE. I'll mark him absent for that!'

'Perfect!' Sarah said with a laugh. 'I wish I'd had a friend like Om when I was at school.'

Peter gazed at Sarah and Charlie. 'Thanks. I feel better now. I have some hope.' Peter's careworn features were now illuminated by the sun, his hair flicking across his face. Sarah resisted the urge to embrace him.

Peter reached into his jacket pocket once more. 'We could use this.' He loosened the drawstring on a tiny velvet purse and slipped the living crystal onto his palm. 'Put it on your hand.' He cupped both hands and stepped towards Sarah. She extended her right hand, her dark fingers long and slim, graced with a silver and sapphire ring, shaped like an asp.

'Place it just there.' Sarah pointed to two lines in her palm. 'Just there. Between the line of intuition and the line of the sun.' Peter did so. 'My mother studied chirology and healing.' She smiled at Peter. 'I feel it tingling.'

'It's reacting, looking for a home. Mum created it.'

'Is that Alpha?' said Charlie.

'Yes.' Peter nodded. 'And it's the reason my parents are missing and two people are dead.'

'The real reason is like you said. They wanted to kill an idea,' said Charlie. 'Fear. The oldest reason in the world. Can we use Alpha?'

'I can,' said Peter. He slipped Alpha back into the red purse. 'I want Alpha placed in my body, below the cerebellum.' He spoke solemnly and looked pleadingly at Charlie.

Charlie nodded. 'We could make that happen.' He walked with Sarah towards the curtain of oaks that fringed the garden. 'What do you think?'

'Too easy?' asked Sarah.

'Do you think we were meant to notice that? I don't know.' Charlie grimaced.

'The Organisation has suffered a big defeat here. They won't be pleased. And they won't stop. Rosencrantz is already planning the next step.'

'You mean they want us to find Peter's parents?'

Sarah shook her head. 'No. They want Peter to find them. Then they'll have him too.' They had arrived at the old brick wall at the end of Peter's garden. They looked up at the overhanging branch of the oak tree. 'It doesn't change anything. We still have to find them.'

'Somewhere between Lambeth North Station and Lambeth Bridge.' Charlie frowned. 'Needles. Haystacks.'

'What else did Esther say? Seven metal rings?'

'I've got an image of them in my mind ... from childhood.' Charlie scratched his head and looked back towards the graceful house. Peter was gazing at Harriet, who was carving spectacular lines through the azure sky. He turned towards Charlie and Sarah. 'We need Alpha,' said Charlie.

'Bet you can't climb over the wall!' Peter shouted. He headed towards them.

Sarah sighed. 'Alpha is Peter's choice. This is a boy who knows fear but doesn't feel fear. He looks it in the face.'

Charlie reached for the overhanging branch. He grasped it with one hand and swung briefly before dropping to the ground.

'Like this.' Peter placed one foot into the crevice on the brick wall and sprang up, clasping both arms over the bough. Then, expertly, he looped his legs over the branch before easing himself up, He leaned against the trunk, his legs dangling on each side of the bough. He smiled broadly down at them. 'I've made up my mind,' he said.

★   ★   ★

Tizzy stared into the green depths of the Plunketts' pond before raising his aged eyes to the line of ancient oaks that bordered the garden. Gideon stood by his side and looked down the valley towards the ruins of the stone shed.

'I'm gettin' on, Giddy. Don't like all this worlds collidin' and stuff.'

'Take it easy, old man.'

'I seen it all before. Don't want it happenin' no more.'

'This was an idea they could not destroy, Tizzy. A world they could not control.' They looked across the garden. A grey shape plunged from the sky, and Harriet's yellow talons gripped the top of a fencepost. Miss B pointed to the hawk, and Alison pushed Miss B's chair towards Harriet. Miss B drew out her sketchpad from the side pocket of her wheelchair while Harriet posed.

Tizzy grunted. 'Two more worlds they can't control, eh, Giddy?'

'C'mon, old man. Opening time.'

'Less of the 'old,'' said Tizzy.

The sea at Eastcombe crashed once more, its whisper and rattle born on the winds.

26

The Fear

'*I'll be off now then.*'

My long-suffering personal assistant, Yvonne, smiled sunnily. 'We said all that at the staff party last night. What Mr. Root said was right. They don't make them like you anymore.' I smiled at the memory of Mr. Root's speech — never knew the dusty old prof understood irony.

'Well, just as well, eh? I hope my successor is a lot more organised and doesn't wander around with his mind elsewhere.'

'It won't be the same. You made us all believe.' She stared earnestly. 'Don't forget the photos of your grandchildren.'

'I was leaving them 'til last. I'll put them in the box with the other presents.'

'Have you got your mobile phone?' Yvonne's eyes enquired.

'Erm, yes, it's in my pocket,' I lied.

'Well, you haven't got it, because I found it by the biscuit tin in the staffroom. Honestly you'd forget your head if —'

'Hmmm. Thanks, Yvonne.' I wondered

how many times I had apologised to her in the past. Probably as many times as there are fish in the sea.

'Here it is. It's switched on, and there are a couple of messages.' She placed the phone in my top pocket. I felt like a schoolboy, not for the first time. She looked at the presents in the box. 'You have some lovely things. Cards from the children. Who gave you the ginger wig?'

'Who else but the head of PE?'

Yvonne smiled. 'Who else indeed? Well, good-bye.'

'Good-bye, Yvonne.'

I kissed her soft cheek, and she turned quickly and left. I heard her high heels clicking on the stone steps down to the main entrance. I unpinned the photos and added them to the last cardboard box. It also contained a box file with all my teaching notes and another with all the favourite poems I had collected from the children over the years. I pictured myself with a glass of Côtes du Rhône, slowly leafing through them while watching the fat old sun setting over the sea.

'Time to go,' I muttered to myself. 'Time to give all this up.' I grasped the box, looping my hands beneath, and barged through the office door, which closed with a soft hiss, as if drawing a curtain. I was probably the last to leave. I reversed through the doors of the main entrance and went to the rear of my car and raised the tailgate. The other six boxes of junk that spoke of a life in teaching stared balefully at me like disgruntled children. 'Be grateful! You could have gone in the skip!' I slammed the door down.

Yes, I was the last to leave. The car park was empty; the evening sun was stretching the shadows of the trees across the tussocky soccer pitches and the grass athletics track, trampled by so many eager feet for . . . how many years? Before there was a school here, what dramas were being played out in the lea of the romantic moorland slopes that lay to the east? I looked back at the school — not a thing of beauty but a crucible for people to come and merge their energy and conjure the flowers of learning into bloom.

Just one more walk round the school. I pushed open the heavy front door and ascended the main staircase and looked down. Every day, streams of children flowed into these arteries and veins of the living, shifting entity that is a school. At the end of each day, they flowed out and left a small army of cleaners, like birds on a seashore, to pick at the detritus and restore the proper order of things. When the children and the teachers were all gone, I could still feel their energy shifting and moving as phantoms and poltergeists, suddenly slamming a door or rattling venetian blinds, a picture falling off the wall, the pages of a magazine flipping over, the soft buzz of computers left on. I drank in that energy, that sense of fate, happenstance, and serendipity that flowed in torrents down the corridors, mist flowing from the mouth of a river. Tonight it felt more intense. I shivered.

I stepped into the assembly hall, and my footsteps severed the silence. Late-evening sun through the deep casements cast long tombstones of light across the polished floor, and the cerulean stage curtains concealed the deserted scenery of The Forbidden Planet. All was silent and motionless. My phone buzzed and vibrated in my top pocket. My fingers fumbled for it, and it slid to the floor. I sat down on a bench and heard a voice — at least the phone wasn't broken.

'Hello. It's Yvonne here.'

'Oh, Yvonne. Sorry. I was just having one last walk round. Frightened the life out of me.'

'I forgot to mention those parents with their daughter who cancelled the other day rebooked to see you tonight. There was no other time I could arrange it. They will be outside your office now.'

'Oh, right.' It wasn't like Yvonne to forget

anything. 'No problem. I'll go up now.'

'One more thing.' Yvonne paused. 'We just wanted to say thank you. Thank you for everything.' She said this slowly.

'Thanks again, Yvonne. We've said all that.'

Maybe it was the phone, but Yvonne's voice didn't quite sound like the Yvonne I knew. She went on. 'We . . . we all wanted to give you a present. Something very special. You will receive it very soon.' The call ended.

I looked through the glazed hall door. The stone stairs up to my office were illuminated.

Fear was present — no question about that. The thrill of fear, running to the edge of a cliff, or standing on a platform's edge as you hear the growl of an approaching tube. It was good to feel that fear but also to know the moment to flip the switch to stop it, to turn back from the cliff, to stand back from the edge. That other kind of fear that paralyses you as you fall through the door into room 101, as the cliff edge disintegrates beneath your feet, or as you feel a push in the back that propels you off the platform's edge, was truly to be feared. I knew that was close. Right now. Turn back. Walk away. Now. Now.

I stood up and heard a door slam, and I felt my body rushing out of myself and running and running, and I felt a force on my back that sent me lurching through the heavy glazed hall door. I was back — on my knees in the entrance hall, with the main doors blown open, and the grinding wind's roar, rushing in and paper notices flapping crazily and the big ceiling lamps swinging. I breathed and I was back. A drop of blood slid from my head, splashed crimson on my white sleeve. Sure enough. The lamp in the hallway outside my office was casting a white hoop on the steps.

I ran to the doors, fastened them shut, and moved towards the white steps, ascending slowly into the aureole of light. I seemed to be moving upward silently, as in a dream. I heard voices. I turned the corner to see three faces staring — one of them young, familiar, with dark hair.

'Den and Jan Ferrett.' A square-shouldered, curly-haired man in a denim jacket extended his hand. 'Sorry, we're a bit late.'

I gulped down the fear that had gripped me. I was extraordinarily pleased to see them and shook their hands gratefully.

'This is Doris. Come on, Dor. Say hello,' said Jan.

Doris's green eyes stared calmly, and she smiled. 'Hello, sir.' Remarkably calm and composed, I thought.

'A warm welcome, Doris,' I said. 'How good to meet you and your family.' I shook her cool hand, and they sat down. I perched on a bench

'You're bleeding, sir,' said Doris, pointing at the blood on my sleeve.

'Yes. Oh, crikey, yes,' I spluttered, and found a handkerchief and dabbed at my forehead. 'Walked into a door! I don't expect you are as clumsy, Doris.'

'Our Dor is a clever little tick,' said Den. 'Much cleverer than me or Jan.'

'Much cleverer,' said Jan.

'We thought she 'ad special needs.'

'That was when she started talking about these friends.'

'Friends?' I said.

'We never met 'em,' said Jan.

'Invisible,' said Den.

'Invisible friends?' I said.

'Invisible. Thought she'd gone bonkers,' continued Den cheerfully.

'She said they was teaching her stuff.'

'We had to take 'er to that psycho-thingy bloke.'

'For an assessment,' said Jan.

'Teaching her what?' I enquired, and looked at Doris. She smiled and lowered her gaze to the table.

'Oh, drawin' and sums and spellin',' said Jan.

'And French.'

'Yeah, French. Least I think it's French.'

'Can't understand a bleedin' word of it.' Den looked at his daughter.

'Vous voyez, je les ai rencontré dans un rêve,' said Doris. She had a smooth and eloquent voice. 'You met them in a dream,' I said.

'Was that what she said? That's bloody clever, that is,' said Den.

'Dad,' said Doris, admonishingly, 'tu ne devrais pas dire des gros mots en public.'

'You must not swear in public, Mr. Ferrett,' I repeated.

'Oh, ah, bugger, er . . . oui . . . er . . . non . . . Oh, I dunno,' he sputtered.

'Mum and Dad just do not understand,' said Doris, rolling her eyes.

'My children said exactly the same about me, Doris. Parents never do understand everything. Don't be too hard on them,' I said gently.

Jan slid a manila folder across the table. 'Here's some of her work.'

'Oh, Mum. He doesn't want to read all that stuff.'

'I would like to read it very much. May I?' Doris smiled quietly. I opened the folder and fanned out the pages of Doris's art, poetry, and maths. 'Calculus?' I opened her sketch-book. There were drawings of a tumbledown shed by a stream with a storm lantern by the

315

door; a fine pencil drawing of a hawk; and a sketch of a young man and a young woman. 'Your teachers, I assume?' Doris smiled and nodded.

I pulled out a poem written in elegant script. It scanned perfectly. 'A Shakespearean sonnet by an eleven-year-old. You have had some fine teachers, Doris. What a daughter you have, Mr. and Mrs. Ferrett.'

'We are proud of her, honest. We love 'er so much.' Jan clasped Den's arm tightly. 'We're just scared.'

'Scared? Of what?'

'We're not very clever. She'll upsticks and leave 'ome first chance she gets.'

'That's not going to happen. Is it, Doris?'

'As I said, Mum and Dad just don't get it sometimes.' She slid her arm round Den's waist and rested her head on his shoulder.

'We've 'ad a good look round the school this afternoon. Doris just wanted to meet you,' said Jan.

'I'm pleased.' This was a serious under-statement of the truth. I was elated, alarmed, bewildered, stunned. 'I won't be here next term, but I will want to hear about Doris's progress. May I have a copy of your poem, Doris?'

'Yes, sir. Take that one. I have another copy.' Doris smiled again. That voice on the phone. This was my gift.

'We have to go, Den. Got the dog in the car.'

'Oh, you have a dog, Doris?'

She flashed a fierce look at her parents. 'I used to have a cat too. And I had a puppy.'

'Don't go over that again, Dor. A bad time was that.'

I was enjoying the Ferretts' company and wanted them to stay. I felt protected by them and was tempted to walk down the stairs with them and scuttle off to my car and depart with a cheery wave.

Den stood up. 'Come on then, Jan. Time to go.'

Doris held out her hand, and I shook it. Her beaming smile brought a lump to my throat. 'Good-bye, Doris. We may meet again. Who knows.'

I heard them descend the steps and exit the building. A few minutes' more silence.

Time to go.

Time to reconnect with the fear.

I flicked the light off and descended the stairs in near darkness, feeling for the wooden handrail. I marched quickly to the main door and barged through. It hissed shut. The moonlight dazzled as I strode to my car. Time to go. Give it all up.

I was looking forward to the drive home.

Soon I would be driving the narrow lanes that snaked a passage through the gullies and hillocks, across tumbling streams and over ancient stone arched bridges. There was my favourite river bridge at Caed-a-ford. It had narrow, tapering stone walls. I would deliberately drive slowly across it, then up the hill on the other side, to see the shining sea miles away, glittering as ancient man must have seen it, standing with his animals and children in the evening light. Would Savaric be there tonight, on the gentle slope down to the river by the bridge?

The headlights speared the darkness, and down this avenue of light I passed, swinging left, then right, away from the town, then rising, rising to the moor's edge. The rattle and vibration of the cattle grid. On, on, fingers of light swinging across the silent heath, spiny gorse and bracken, and drifting little bands of shaggy feral ponies, standing in the headlights, tilted hind hooves, patiently observing. On, on, and at last down to the ancient glittering river. There was Savaric, at the side of the road, broad shouldered, holding an axe. I always waved if I saw him. Should I speak to him tonight? I pulled over and got out of the car.

'Savaric!'

He waved and pointed down to the river. A

318

handsome car was lying on its back, silver water flowing like mercury through and around it. On the bank a stone crucifix lay flat, its head submerged in the river. I cannot tell you precisely what Savaric said. It reminds me of the old saying 'If a lion could speak, we could not understand him.' But we shook hands. Me, in my suit and raincoat; he, in his grey trousers and leggings, blue tunic, and cloak of fur, flapping from his wide shoulders. He has long greying hair and kind, if slightly ferocious-looking, eyes. We have known each other a long time.

'Did you see the car leave the road?'

Savaric shook his head and pointed to the hill on the other side of the river. I walked down the slope. It was a very fine car, lying on its back, roof concertinaed like a giant's toy.

I have long stopped asking what is real, and right now, on this hill, I was standing astride time. Savaric laid down his axe and joined me at my side. Had I really met Doris and her family? If I had, there would be something in my top pocket. I was almost afraid to reach inside my jacket but did so.

Neatly folded was her gift to me. Here it is. I read it aloud to Savaric. The words left my lips and fluttered away like starlings.

The Dream Factory

I label things; I want to make them mine.
I call, I name, I own, I take control.
Security and order by design
that lasts until the world starts to unroll.
First Tigger and then Buddy disappears,
not dead, but shifted somehow from this
   space
so far from me, but had I known, so
   near.
Their labelled absence always left a trace.
So when I first took refuge in closed
   eyes,
to learn that half the fight was to forgive
and letting anger rule me was unwise,
I found, in sleep, that I could start to
   live.
I'll find what's lost; a loving heart
   redeems
by searching in the factory of dreams.

Savaric nodded his approval.
Time to go.

Tizzy was right . . .
When worlds collide . . .

Until we meet again, enjoy the world in
   yourself.

320

The Author

John Simes served as principal in two of the UK's largest comprehensive schools after his career as a teacher of English Literature in state education. He founded a consultancy for school improvement, and he continues to support programs to set up new schools in the UK and Africa. In 2013, he established Collingwood Publishing & Media Limited to develop new interactive fiction, poetry and video for young adults. He now writes fiction for Collingwood and is establishing a collective of new writers. John lives with his family in south Devon, England, where he grapples with his addictions to cricket, poetry, and the stunning local landscape — and he is still fascinated by schools and teaching.

Find out more about the author at: http://johnsimes.co.uk/ or follow John on Twitter @johnthepoet2010. Go to www.visit-thedreamfactory.com — you can enjoy Mark Duffield's interpretations of the songs from 'The Masque' and Doris's poem, and much more.

We do hope that you have enjoyed reading this large print book.

Did you know that all of our titles are available for purchase?

We publish a wide range of high quality large print books including:
Romances, Mysteries, Classics
General Fiction
Non Fiction and Westerns

Special interest titles available in large print are:
The Little Oxford Dictionary
Music Book
Song Book
Hymn Book
Service Book

Also available from us courtesy of Oxford University Press:
Young Readers' Dictionary
(large print edition)
Young Readers' Thesaurus
(large print edition)

For further information or a free brochure, please contact us at:
Ulverscroft Large Print Books Ltd.,
The Green, Bradgate Road, Anstey,
Leicester, LE7 7FU, England.
Tel: (00 44) 0116 236 4325
Fax: (00 44) 0116 234 0205